what of

jesus in love

"A truly mind-blowing creation. The writing style is just perfect. The non-biblical sounding voice is one of the reasons I think the book succeeds. Kitt Cherry's presentation provides a very satisfying answer to the sexual (and homosexual) issues that to this day remain mysteries about the life of the real historical Jesus. It all fits into the traditional myth/story—and it is *always* interesting to see how she puts the words of Jesus into his mouth in the context of her drama. ...A wonderful, gay-sensitive, and delightfully 'shocking' reassessment of the stories of the old-time religion. I promise you, you'll be surprised by the book."

—Toby Johnson, author of *Gay Spirituality* and former editor of *White Crane: A Journal of Gay Spirit*

"People who want to understand how erotic love can be sacred, and divine love can be erotic, will delight in this novel. So will anyone who wants to be stimulated theologically, sensuously, and spiritually, all at the same time. And for those interested in moving beyond our society's rigid gendersexual norms, this book is a feast."

—Virginia Ramey Mollenkott, Ph.D., author of *Omnigender, Transgender Journeys* and *Sensuous Spirituality*

"I loved it. I understand why it rubs some conservative folk the wrong way, but I say rub 'em. For every person who's offended, there must be another that revels in it."

—John Fleck, gay performance artist of the "NEA Four"

"Breathtaking—well-characterized, well-written, emotionally and, dare I say it, theologically *mature.*"

—JoSelle Vanderhooft, editor of *Tiresias Revisited: Magical Tales for Transfolk*

OTHER BOOKS BY KITTREDGE CHERRY

Hide and Speak
A Coming Out Guide

Womansword
What Japanese Words Say About Women

Equal Rites
Lesbian and Gay Worship, Ceremonies, and Celebrations
(with Zalmon O. Sherwood)

COMING SOON

Art That Dares

Jesus in Love: At the Cross

jesus in love

a novel

BY

KITTREDGE CHERRY

Jim,
May christ
be with you.
Kittredge Cherry
Dec 2006

andro
GYNE
press

*andro***GYNE***press* | BERKELEY, CA

AndroGyne Press
1700 Shattuck Ave. #81
Berkeley, CA 94709
www.androgynepress.com

contents

For
LEONORA HELEN PUGH
1918-2006
with thanks for being
my Aunt Leo

acknowledgments

WRITING *JESUS IN LOVE* has been an exercise in learning to trust and depend on others. My writing process was so closely linked with my healing process that the two cannot be separated. I am grateful for the people who assisted me during and after my most severe period of chronic fatigue syndrome, the same years when I was writing *Jesus in Love*. They have been angels without being aware of it.

First I must thank those who enabled me to physically put words on paper. I couldn't have done it without Marci and Stina at ExacTrans Reporting Services, who transcribed many, many tapes when I was barely strong enough to read my handwritten scrawl into a tape recorder. Martha Paterson, an expert in ergonomics and occupational therapy, showed me how to make the most of what strength I had left, and taught me a precious truth, "There is no perfect." Dave "the Computer Guy" Levine and Jed Unrot each struggled valiantly to create a computer station where I could type despite my disability. I regained the energy to write under the enlightened guidance of Dr. Keith DeOrio and his staff of holistic healers.

My family banded together and bought a speech-recognition program so I could write by speaking to my computer. The Dragon NaturallySpeaking program was a godsend, even though it made many mistakes such as changing, "He will order his angels to guard you" into "He will order his angels to argue." For that and much more, I thank my mother, Kit Humphries; my late step-father, Les Humphries; and my brother, Craig Cherry.

No task was too big or too small to merit the best efforts of the multi-talented Linda Drake, who kept me supplied with easy-to-use Dr. Grip pens, drove me and my wheelchair cheerfully through horrendous traffic jams, and generally became my knight in shining armor. When all else failed, I could count on Gary Frederick and his pack of happy Chihuahuas.

Judith Finlay and Lissa Dirrim each gave me her friendship and the careful, brilliant commentary that makes a manuscript into literature. Judith and I did theological reflection by exchanging tape-recorded messages that illuminated my darkest hours and her longest commutes. Lissa used her unique alchemy to transform my hardest problems into golden opportunities, including the introduction that led me to Andro-Gyne Press.

Many more supporters emerged during my quest for a publisher. Leading the way was Jim Curtan, the archetypal spiritual director. Toby Johnson took a chance on me and became my ex-monk mentor, offering a steady dose of wisdom mixed with the right amount of heresy and humor. Artist Becki Jayne Harrelson, the lesbian Leonardo Da Vinci, shared my literary-artistic quest. Priest-turned-professor Daniel Helminiak blessed me by being my toughest critic. Oversight Design's Franklin Odel provided an elegant new way for me to minister to the world when he built JesusInLove.org. Bill Phillips at Business Partner of

Beverly Hills took the sting out of manuscript submission by doing the grunt work for me.

AndroGyne Press came out of nowhere to give *Jesus in Love* the launch it deserved. Its founder was so moved by *Jesus in Love* that he established AndroGyne Press to ensure the novel's publication. His vision, courage, faith, sensitivity, and exquisite skills made me a better writer and a better person.

Encouragement from the following writers also brought out the best in my manuscript: Jim Bailey, Chris Berardo, Malcolm Boyd, John Dart, Sally Gearhart, Chris Glaser, Mary Hunt, Theodore Jennings, John McNeill, Virginia Mollenkott, Michalea Moore, Dennis O'Neill, Will Roscoe, and Kazue Suzuki.

Other kindred spirits who urged me onward include Peggy Alter, Doug Blanchard, Mark Bowman, Louie Crew, Alex Donis, John Fleck, Sue Gottscalk, Jan Griesinger, Janetta and Richard Haxton, Tiffany Held, Beth Keck, Bob and Hedy Lodwick, John O'Brien, Pamela Pasti, Sylvia Perez, Jodi Simmons, Janie Spahr, Matt Walker, Frank Wulf, and those known collectively as the Sillies (Audrey "A-Plus" Lockwood, Ron Steen, Raymond Urgo, and Dean Asbury). I was also nurtured by the Arroyo Arts Collective, which honored my poetry, and United University Church, where music director Tom Griep set my words to song.

Audrey Lockwood, my life partner, stayed with me from start to finish. There's never a dull moment in life with Audrey. She has been a fountain of brilliant ideas, always up for an intellectual adventure—but also willing to slow down and push my wheelchair or surf the Net with me in search of the "mother lode" of potential book buyers. Audrey, I particularly dedicate the scenes with Old Snake to you, my mythic beast.

I salute all of the above, who did much more than I can record here. I appreciate them and those whose aid was less direct, sometimes as simple as a smile from a stranger. Together they inspired me to be my best. Those who helped with this book have been Christ for me. I, in my turn, hope that Christ will move through my words to show them the impact of their generosity:

> May your kindnesses
> return to you ten-fold, a hundred-fold, more.
> Someday, beyond Beyond,
> may you know
> the stretch and strength
> of all that your kindness has set in motion.

introduction

PEOPLE ASK WHY I WROTE *JESUS IN LOVE*. The reason is that I love Jesus and writing about him healed me. I met the queer Christ in the depths of my own heart and the book flowed through me—and I myself wonder why that happened.

What people usually mean is: Why did you make Jesus queer? Simply put, I wrote about a sexual Jesus because human beings are sexual, and he is bisexual-transgender because I did not want to limit Christ's sexuality to a single approach. I don't feel that I "made" Jesus queer when I wrote *Jesus in Love*. During the writing process, Christ seemed to reveal this aspect of his all-encompassing self to me, not as a historical fact, but as a spiritual truth. From my perspective, the book resulted from surrendering the most receptive, vulnerable part of my heart to Jesus Christ as God, and the fact that he is queer is almost incidental.

The Jesus who narrates this novel is too queer for most churches, but too Christian for most queers. The readers who can handle Jesus' sexuality are often appalled by his suffering. Why, they want to know, did you make the crucifixion part of God's plan? This question has a similar answer. I wrote about a Jesus who must suffer and die because human beings must suffer and die.

Through *Jesus in Love* I hope to keep alive what

could be called the "myth" of Christ's life, the archetypal story that rings true to the human spirit. His miraculous tale has inspired and healed people for two thousand years. I want to introduce readers to the Jesus I know, someone who is fully human and fully divine—not in a bland, statement-of-faith kind of way, but with all the raw, messy, passionate intensity that is humanly possible.

"We shouldn't look under Jesus' robes," a gay seminarian warned during a class discussion back when I was a young lesbian studying for the ministry twenty years ago. His view is still the consensus, even among lesbian, gay, bisexual, and transgender (LGBT) Christians. I didn't see why it was disrespectful to know Jesus intimately, or to imagine that he might share my queer sexuality. After all, the Bible says that he is the divine bridegroom who became human out of love. It says we are created in God's image, sexuality included.

However, for most of my life I kept a polite distance from Jesus, mainly because he didn't interest me. A disabling illness changed all that and brought me closer to Christ than I had ever dreamed possible. I wrote the bulk of *Jesus in Love* slowly, with enormous effort and heroic help during a four-year period when I was often barely strong enough to press pen to paper.

It's important to state up front two factors that were definitely *not* among my motivations in writing this book: First, I did *not* write *Jesus in Love* as a strategy to gain LGBT rights in the church. Nothing was further from my mind. My health had collapsed after seven years of ministry in the LGBT community, much of it spent promoting dialogue on homosexuality at the

National Council of Churches (USA) and the World Council of Churches. I was sick to death of persuading people that homosexuality wasn't a sin, and I had retreated to a place where it wasn't an issue. In my home and in my heart, Christ's unconditional acceptance of queer people was a given.

Second, I was *not* trying to prove that the historical Jesus was gay. Nobody knows whether the historical Jesus was attracted to other men, although some contemporary scholars do think so. Jesus of Nazareth, the first-century historical figure known through scientific and academic disciplines, was probably nothing like the Jesus in this book, and that's okay, even liberating. At the time when he walked the earth, the concepts of sexual orientation and gender identity didn't exist. *Jesus in Love* grows out of my belief that Christ, being divinely omniscient, would have had access to twenty-first century ideas about sexuality as he lived out his legendary life on earth. I relied on scientific research to learn about Biblical Palestine, but I used another method entirely to know Jesus: prayer informed by scripture. I trusted Jesus' promise, "I will be with you always."

When the manuscript was almost done, I discovered that my vision was part of a larger trend: Queer Christ images are emerging now all over the world. *Jesus in Love* is the first novel published about a queer Christ, but the theme is appearing in theology books, at art galleries, on stage, and across the World Wide Web. The queer Christ comes at a time when Christian rhetoric is used as an anti-gay political weapon. He is a beacon of hope in a world where Christians and gays seem to be at war. He mends the split between body and spirit that has led to violence, poverty, and ecological destruction. Like the Jesus of first-century Palestine, the queer Christ images have come to teach, heal, and free anyone who accepts the challenge.

I tried to include something for everyone—gay, lesbian, straight, bi, or trans—but my preconception was that the novel would matter most to queer people. Surprise! When I started circulating the manuscript, I found out that heterosexuals loved it, too. The queer Christ is not just for queers, but has a broad appeal, calling to mind the hit television series *Queer Eye for the Straight Guy.* Some people are offended by *Jesus in Love,* but those who like it include women and men of every sexual orientation and from all walks of life. It doesn't seem to matter whether they identify as "Christian" or not. Nonbelievers like it as much as believers. Many told me that they enjoyed reading it out loud to a boyfriend, girlfriend, or significant other.

An editor at a mainstream Protestant press was the first of many publishers to reject *Jesus in Love.* I had always known her to be cool and composed, but her voice quavered as she dismissed the book as too "flat-out shocking" to ever be published anywhere. She was shocked, shocked, *shocked* by the frank eroticism. Then for a moment she sounded wistful: "It's quite beautiful...." Suddenly she switched to an angry, judgmental accusation. "You couldn't have honestly expected us to publish this! Why did you write this? To shock people?"

"I don't know if it's shocking," I began, and I truly didn't. During my years of spiritual introspection, I had grown so close to Jesus, and so far removed from the politics of religion, that I did believe a church press would print *Jesus in Love*. I wasn't trying to shock anybody. If anything, my hope was that the book would console others, as Jesus consoled me during years of disability.

My last editor, the one who finally said yes to *Jesus in Love,* had a different reaction. A priest with a Ph.D., he told me he wept tears of healing over the manuscript. Then he added, "There is nothing doctrinally that they can condemn. There is nothing unorthodox about this book. I read it very carefully for that." *Jesus in Love* follows standard Christianity except in one respect: It explores Christ's human sexuality in a way that has been avoided until now. Here Jesus is openly, erotically alive as a bisexual and transgendered person. It's natural to wonder, once again, why I wrote such a book. A fuller answer may be found by exploring the circumstances that led me to write *Jesus in Love* and the value it has for society today.

Growing up without Jesus

Perhaps I was able to write *Jesus in Love* because to me Christ's biography still feels fresh and virtually free of childhood memories. Many people assume that every American knows Christ's life story, but I had only a vague impression of it while I was growing up. When I'm asked why I bothered to retell such a familiar story, I think back to myself as a girl in a secular Iowa family, and I know for sure that there are people who haven't heard it, despite all the Christian references that surround them.

Born in 1957, I was an un-baptized kid whose knowledge of Jesus was pretty much limited to the Nativity scene that we set up at Christmas. Easter was all about bunnies and Easter eggs. My mother taught me the Lord's Prayer, which is still the basis of my prayer life. She occasionally took me to various Protestant churches, where the adults didn't seem to believe in the God that they described to me as a powerful invisible man. I didn't believe it, either. They told Bible stories in odd little snippets that made no sense to me, especially because they had no connection to anything that I learned in my public school. Men ran the churches and starred in the Bible stories, and I felt left out as a girl, even before I knew I was a lesbian. Whenever a Biblical movie came on television, I would change the channel immediately.

At the cusp of puberty, I was attracted to God and I was attracted to girls, not necessarily in that order. I also loved to write and I had a gift for describing emotions in all their lush subtlety. I did feel what I now know were mystical longings, but the churches that I visited were much more about social control than spirituality. Sexual attraction was considered normal, but religious sentiments were an embarrassment. Church leaders countered my interest in God with advice to engage in heterosexual dating rituals. They denounced the rock opera *Jesus Christ Superstar,* the basis of my first connection with Jesus.

Thwarted by the church, I learned the Gospel by gleaning what I could from *Jesus Christ Superstar* and its musical cousin *Godspell.* I watched *Godspell* over and over when I was sixteen as a volunteer usher on the

Showboat Rhododendron in Clinton, Iowa. Looking back, I smile at my own naivete because I had a totally mixed-up idea of who was singing what, and yet the words themselves had power for me.

I tried to find my own answers during high school by reading the Bible from cover to cover. After wading through the entire Hebrew scriptures, I was sorely disappointed when I finally got to the scenes between Jesus, Judas, and Mary Magdalene. They were so short and dry! I was outraged. It wasn't fair that a book could be so long, and still say nothing about the emotional life of Jesus. That adolescent longing, the desire to read between the lines of scripture, never completely left me. It became one of the motivations behind *Jesus in Love*.

I majored in journalism and art history at the University of Iowa, where I met Audrey Lockwood, my college sweetheart and my life partner to this day. One of her pet names for me was "Little Infidel" because I scoffed at religion. She, on the other hand, attended Mass every Sunday while the rest of our dorm slept, and that intrigued me. Audrey and I stayed in the closet not because homosexuality was a sin, but because it was socially unacceptable.

After graduation I worked as a newspaper reporter for three years, then went on a journalism scholarship to Japan—where my life was turned upside down by my father's unexpected death. I did not believe in life after death, and yet I could feel Daddy's spirit as an ongoing presence. In shock, I resorted to church, specifically Kobe Union Church. It was an interdenominational English-speaking congregation with members from all over the world. There I felt God reach out to me, just as I am, lesbian and all.

As soon as I knew there was a God, I knew that God accepted homosexuality because otherwise God would not have bothered with me. I met other Christian lesbians and my faith empowered me to come out as a lesbian, first to my family and then to others. I knew that God loved me and valued truth, so I was no longer enslaved to social approval.

I did object to Christianity's oppression of women, but my eyes were opened by Japanese feminists, many of whom are Christian. They said that conversion to Christianity set them free from sexism. Raised Buddhist, they saw Christianity as a fresh, egalitarian religion that established schools for women and ended legal prostitution. They and others pointed out the Bible's female images for God. I learned that Jesus consistently defied the norms of his culture to empower women. Living in Japan, where only two percent of the population is Christian, afforded me a clearer view of Christianity's value. The lack of social pressure to join a church freed me to make my own decision. I was baptized at Kobe Union Church in 1984.

Full of passion for God, I moved to San Francisco, studied at seminary, and was ordained by Metropolitan Community Churches, a denomination that ministers primarily in the LGBT community. My spiritual mentors taught me that sexuality and spirituality were one, but they didn't apply it to Jesus, presenting him as a bloodless "historical Jesus" who said almost nothing. We spoke of God only in genderless "inclusive" language. I thought that serving the church was identical to serving God, and church leaders did little to rid me of that misconception. I worked as clergy on staff at Metropolitan Community Church of San Francisco in the late 1980s at the height of the AIDS epidemic. In the 1990s, I served as ecumenical and public relations director for the whole denomination, advocating for LGBT rights at the national and international levels in every branch of Christianity.

One day I caught mononucleosis, and my life came to a crashing halt overnight. "Some people never recover," the doctors admitted when the crippling pain and fatigue continued month after month. Everything they tried made my condition worse. Eventually they changed my diagnosis to chronic fatigue syndrome. As months became years I lost much of what had made life worth living: job, clergy role, church, friends, the ability to drive. The liberal Christians I knew didn't value suffering, and they didn't seem to value *me* now that I was suffering. Audrey, my hero, stuck with me.

I found an incredible doctor who began healing me with homeopathy and holistic medicine while honoring God as the true source of all healing. The treatment demanded physical and emotional detoxification that I was barely strong enough to endure. I was often home alone, too weak to do much more than meditate while lying in bed. I was living out one of my favorite quotations from St. Teresa of Avila, "God alone suffices." Those words, which once comforted me, now made me sad and angry. Sometimes I felt like I had nothing left but God, and it wasn't enough! And yet, with no other hope on the horizon, I clung to God with a desperation that I had not felt before. I prayed for healing. I surrendered my will to God.

Writing *Jesus in Love*

Western medicine had failed me, and so had the kind of progressive Christianity that I had believed in at the time I fell sick. I began exploring ideas that had been forbidden to me as a good liberal Christian: humility as a virtue, demons as a reality, a male God, and the saving power of Jesus' blood and death on the cross. I had to pull out all stops and experiment with every theological concept and form of prayer in order to heal. One of the many methods I tried was visualizing myself in "safe places" from childhood and inviting Christ to be there with me. I first learned that meditation technique during seminary, when a traditional-looking Jesus would walk silently beside me. My closest Christian colleagues were embarrassed by Jesus, with his vulgar display of blood and his scientifically indefensible miracles. But they were all gone, and in my illness I was left alone with Jesus, unmediated.

Now, in my imagination, a queer Christ sat down right beside me and invited me to walk with him through his "heart-memories." We began what seemed like a guided tour through the Gospels. Divine omniscience enabled my guide to re-experience his long-ago life with today's psychological and sexual sophistication. "I lived my life as a love letter to people in the future," he declared, "And you can help me deliver it." His offer was irresistible.

Jesus in Love was not channeled from Jesus, but felt like a kind of collaboration. I consciously chose the scenes and the personal details for each character, while Jesus seemed to filter his words, his thoughts, and his loving attitude through my soul. The erotic charge appeared to come from Jesus as he opened his heart to me. The stories would play in my imagination and I would try to write down everything at once, but my muscles quickly gave out. I had to let the scenes play over and over in my mind, savoring each sentence as it distilled over time.

I wasn't sure whether I was writing fiction or nonfiction. The Gospels unfolded in my mind and I simply tried to record the "good news" with the same accuracy that I applied to the local news when I was newspaper reporter. Jesus' contemporary voice, which some readers find distracting, is the voice I heard in my imagination. I like its sense of intimacy and immediacy, a reminder that Jesus was a human being who spoke his immortal truths in real conversations. Using the Gospels as my framework, I finally got to fill in the blanks between the lines of scripture that had haunted me since high school.

During the four years it took to write *Jesus in Love*, I read the Gospels of Matthew, Mark, Luke, and John over and over—but avoided any book of the Bible that was written later. I wanted to dig deep and get in touch with the original Jesus, undiluted by even the earliest interpretations. I also consulted a variety of other resources, especially *The Land and People Jesus Knew* by J. Robert Teringo, Neil Douglas-Klotz's works on the Aramaic Jesus, and the writings and music of medieval Christian mystics such as Julian of Norwich and Hildegard of Bingen. I reached beyond Christianity and found support for my writing and my healing in the Hindu chants of Krishna Das and the Buddhist teachings of Sharon Salzberg.

Jesus in Love grows out of my own biggest 'why' question: Why does God allow suffering? For me the book is as much about suffering as about sexuality. I searched for answers by exploring related questions: What if the miracle-working Jesus of the Bible really embodied both sexuality and spirituality? What would motivate such a Jesus to endure the cross?

Jesus doesn't address homosexuality directly in the Bible, but he talked a lot about love and sacrifice. I didn't try to put pro-gay rhetoric into the mouth of Jesus. It's natural to assume my Jesus might say things that I used to say, but he wasn't like that. I was surprised by what he said, or how he applied scriptures to new situations. The Christ of *Jesus in Love* assumes that queer sexuality is okay and he sees no need to justify it even as he experiences it. He stays present to his body, whether he feels pleasure or pain. He showed me that honoring suffering does not deny the body, but is a way of valuing it, listening to it regardless, despite aversion—instead of blocking its truth. Those who refuse to abandon their own experience, even in the midst of pain, are whole.

I wasn't trying to shock my readers, but I did want to wake people up by challenging some common preconceptions. I made John older than Jesus, defying the prejudice that equates youth and sexiness. I figured that Jesus would have been attracted to someone with maturity, and that John the Beloved Disciple was not necessarily the same person who lived long enough to write the Book of Revelation. I made Mary Magdalene a prostitute as well as an apostle, even though the current trend is to assign those roles to two different women.

I wanted to emphasize Jesus' ease with sexual outcasts of all kinds, and I saw no reason why a reformed prostitute couldn't become a smart, competent spiritual leader. I wrote about the rather taboo topic of blood sacrifice because I was trying to understand the purpose of suffering from a guide who had lived as a Jew in first-century Palestine, when animal sacrifice was a respected path to God. Tired of inclusive language, I gave God gender.

My close encounters with Jesus did not cause the quick physical healing that I had sought in prayer. My health actually got much worse and stayed that way for years before I started getting better. Typing was impossible. The slightest pressure injured my hands. My muscles became so weak that I could no longer drive and I had to use a wheelchair to go beyond our yard. Depressed by my inability to travel, I reminded myself that I had equal access to first-century Palestine through the power of my imagination. On my worst days I could only scrawl a few lines of *Jesus in Love*. I extended my capacity by learning how to write with both hands. Then I would read my messy manuscript into a tape recorder and mail it to a transcription service for typing.

I struggled with a voice-activated computer dictation program that made several errors per sentence. Some were funny: "No sex with other people" became "Knows excellent other people." Still, it was hard to remember what I intended to say when I had to stop and spell out every correction. Then the dog would bark and the computer would translate his barking sound into sentences such as, "Look for low world war." Through every distraction, I kept returning my attention to Jesus' story. In the end, I produced a manuscript long enough to be split into two volumes. The second volume, *Jesus in Love: At the Cross,* will be published soon.

I wanted to contribute my remaining energy to a higher purpose, passing on the legacy of Christ's life to a new generation. Jesus' bloody, sexy story helped me endure the dark night of the soul. It gave my life a focus and a purpose when I felt as if I was dying. It empowered me to see God's image in my disabled body instead of turning away in horror and disowning myself. At one point my doctor told me he finally understood why Jesus came to me like this: "Because you wouldn't have made it otherwise."

Sharing *Jesus in Love* with the world

Like the original disciples, I felt that Jesus wanted me to tell others what I witnessed. My strength slowly began to return during what turned out to be a two-year journey of rejection by many literary agents and publishers. The first friend who looked at my book proposal advised, "Just ask Jesus to get you a publisher." But working with Jesus was nothing like that. Yes, I put Jesus in charge—and he was in no hurry to see the book in print. I could only watch in frustration mixed with awe as God gradually touched people through the manuscript. *Jesus in Love* seemed to have a life of its own, and purposes of its own beyond my comprehension. Perhaps it affected me most of all.

I was amazed to discover that while I was writing *Jesus in Love* in isolation, men and women all over the world were also portraying the queer Christ. I was part of a global revelation! No novels had been published about the queer Christ yet, but there were paintings, sculptures, photos, a play, and books of anthropology and theology. Seminary professors such as Theodore Jennings seriously proposed that the historical Jesus had a homosexual relationship. I eagerly began contacting these kindred spirits, most of whom did not know each other. They became a network of support for me. I also found out that *Jesus in Love* is one of the only Jesus novels ever written by a woman.

While editors mulled over my manuscript, I decided to build an author's website. Web designer Franklin Odel helped me create JesusInLove.org. It quickly evolved from a publicity vehicle into a modest ministry featuring not only my books, but also a wide variety of other gay-Jesus and woman-Christ books, art, and links. News of JesusInLove.org spread like wildfire across the Internet. Hundreds of gay news sites covered it and bloggers battled over whether it was "sick and disgusting" or "a rather heavenly idea." The response convinced me of the need for an art book as well as a novel. I began to compile the visionary images into *Art That Dares: Gay Jesus, Woman Christ, and More.* Even before *Jesus in Love* was published, it had already inspired another book and sparked a series of new friendships.

When I put my search for a publisher into Jesus' hands, I expected to find the right one out of the hundreds of existing publishers. Instead Christ made a way where there was no way. I met a man who believed in *Jesus in Love* so much that he created AndroGyne Press for the sole purpose of publishing *Jesus in Love* and other books like it. My novel, a misfit to the publishing industry, helped build a new press where other queer voices could be heard.

As publication approached, I got a better understanding of the role that *Jesus in Love* might play in today's world. The novel is useful because it can free people to imagine God in new ways, and thus to recognize the divine image in oneself and others. A vicious battle is raging now between conservatives who use Christianity to justify anti-gay hate and queer activists who reject religion. Cynical powerbrokers use religion as a tool to make people go to war. The queer Christ can open people's minds and thereby change their behavior and heal their souls. Conservatives shouldn't be the only ones who get to interpret the central figure of Christianity. It's time to take back Jesus—not just for gays, but for the good of all.

Jesus in Love can be an antidote to the right-wing monopoly on Jesus, and also to the secular monopoly on sex. Today's hypersexual society is reducing sex to an addiction or a sales tool. It is crucial to find models for reconciling body and spirit. Sexual ecstasy symbolizes divine union in almost all spiritual traditions, but in Christianity the concept has been buried. *Jesus in Love* dares to reclaim this lost treasure. Erotic interludes and the Biblical metaphor of marriage effectively convey the intensity of God's love for humankind. With Jesus as guide to the sacred sexual, the human body and the human spirit are reunited and revitalized to face whatever comes.

Some consider *Jesus in Love* to be blasphemy, the denial of a religion's core values. Jesus himself was accused of blasphemy, and it was one of the charges that led to his crucifixion. I believe that *Jesus in Love* is not blasphemy, but a blessing that enhances Christian faith and builds upon it. Christians are called to explore Jesus' same-sex attractions and female side because, according to Christian faith, he represents everyone, including the sexually marginalized. He was human, so Jesus must have experienced sexual desires. He was also divine, so he must have loved everyone he met. Living every human experience, he surely tasted a wide range of emotions, gender identities, and sexual orientations. Traditional doctrine says he was born free from sin, so he had no need to be ashamed of his body. By engaging the queer Christ, Christians can begin to compensate for the institutional church's often disgraceful past omissions and biases.

Jesus in Love may also hold special value for LGBT people. Over the centuries, queer people learned to hate themselves in order to stay in church, or else they turned away from spirituality in the false belief that God hated them. The queer Christ can cleanse people of internalized homophobia and thereby heal the soul. The Gospels are a great literary achievement, but they only come alive when people can see themselves in the stories. For queer people, that may mean taking liberties to imagine that Biblical characters were attracted to people of the same sex or didn't fit into standard gender roles.

I count myself in the queer vanguard as we move from reaction to empowerment. The conventional Jesus is no longer adequate, but we're not going to waste all our energy battling conservative Christians. We're claiming our power. With courage and faithful imagination, we dare to create our own queer Christ images out of our own life experiences. Everyone deserves to hear about God in their own language. Finally the good news is available with an LGBT accent.

I have summarized my best understanding of why *Jesus in Love* came into being. I look forward to seeing how it fulfills its purposes after publication. Some reasons behind the book may remain a mystery. In the end, I rely on what Jesus tells his disciples in *Jesus in Love: At the Cross:* "The answer to all of your 'why' questions is love."

jesus in love

prologue

SEEING AS GOD SEES got me into trouble from the start. I simply didn't notice what other people found both obvious and important, such as whether someone was male or female. I was able to focus on these details, but part of me didn't care.

In some ways I came across as a dreamy, absent-minded kind of person. At other times, people thought I was deliberately trying to rile the authorities by breaking taboos, but usually I wasn't. I was just being me.

Most people see from the inside out. They begin by observing another person's body. Then gradually they perceive the inner qualities of mind and heart, and eventually perhaps a glimmer of the soul, the energy field that generates and outlives the body. With me, it was the opposite. My first and overwhelming impression was of the soul, and only later did I sense the more superficial particularities of emotion, thought, and finally the physical body.

I also lost track of time, so that I didn't notice if the day I was living was a sabbath or not. I didn't experience time as a line or a series of fragments like people tend to do. Part of me occupied all moments simultaneously. My memory is only loosely connected to human notions of time and space, but I do know that I taught the same ideas in every context.

chapter one:
proposal

"LET'S MAKE LOVE," the Holy Spirit whispered while I was praying.

Each of us was both Lover and Beloved as everything in me found in the Holy Spirit its complement, its reflection, its twin. We took turns switching roles and switching genders. The momentum of reversing polarities stretched me further and further until I was almost overcome by the force that we had generated.

"Marry me, Jesus," the Holy Spirit sighed.

Unprecedented pleasure accompanied this most unexpected proposal. When the Holy Spirit kissed my mind and heart, I also felt a tangible touch run down the inner spine of my physical body. Enjoyable arrows of energy shot toward my crotch, concentrating power in my genitals.

I had gotten into this situation by praying over and over, "Your will be done." Now I stopped and became silent. I was stunned that my prayer life had aroused my body sexually, and I was worried about what might happen next.

I pulled away from God, including my own divinity, and tried to remember where I was in time and space. As the heat between my legs began to cool, I could feel my back pressed against grassy earth. I opened my eyes and my divine senses showed me the stars in three dimensions, some far more distant than others. I perceived each star's unique movements as well as the spinning of the planet on which I rode. I felt the tiny tug of every star's gravitational pull.

Suppressing my divine vision, I switched to my human eyes and waited for the night sky to appear flat and motionless. Then I sat up and looked around. I recognized the rolling hills near Nazareth, my hometown. Crickets were singing and I was breathing the warm, dry air of a late summer night. This isolated hilltop was one of my favorite places for private prayer and meditation. I was thirty years old.

My pelvis still tingled from the all the energies that had been assembled there. I felt I had to confide in someone about my increasingly erotic visions of the Holy Spirit. The only person who might understand was the one who had first taught me how to reach mystical states of oneness with God. The two of us had the gift of being able to move easily in and out of religious reveries and raptures. I stood up and began to walk home.

It took me a few days to work up the nerve to talk to my mentor about the latest development in my spiritual life. One morning, well before sunrise, I accompanied her to the hillside grotto where she liked to go for pre-dawn prayers when the weather was nice. Here we could meditate uninterrupted and unobserved. She wasn't surprised when I joined her because we had prayed together almost every day for as long as I could remember. We sat down as usual, side by side, both of us facing east as the Temple in Jerusalem faced east. It was so early that the skyline was still completely dark.

Our practice was to pray and meditate before discussing the revelations that we had received, but I would be embarrassed if I got sexually excited by a vision right in front of her. She was about to start chanting a psalm when I broke the pattern.

"Mom, there's something I want to discuss with you, but a son shouldn't talk about it with his mother."

"That never stopped us!" she laughed. "Go ahead."

I smiled as I remembered how Mom had broken taboos to let me help her care for my younger sisters and brothers as if I was her daughter instead of her son. In my childhood, I had a reputation among the neighborhood boys as a good ball player and an even better story teller, but I also loved helping Mom with childcare and being beside her when she was breastfeeding one of the little ones. While nursing them, Mom taught me holy mysteries. She said that I was conceived when she let God "overshadow" her before she married the man we called Papa-Joe. She knew better than anyone else what intimacy with God was like.

I began to explain. "I've been meditating a lot about this prophecy from Isaiah: 'As a bridegroom rejoices over a bride, so will your God exult over you.'"

I waited nervously while Mom considered this. I wondered if she was going to bring up the fights we used to have when she and Papa-Joe tried to force me to get married. I had insisted that I would never marry, without telling them about the strange feelings that blocked me whenever I tried to pursue my sexual attractions, whether with a woman or a man.

Mom seemed to be lost in thought. To my divine senses, her soul looked like a clear crystal that magnified any light that God chose to beam through it. I could have used my divine senses to find out what she was thinking, but I respected people's privacy and rarely read their specific thoughts during my earthly life.

I tried to calm myself by taking a close look at Mom while she reflected on the prophecy. She was not the type of person who dries up and becomes brittle with age. Instead she looked more solid but softer and, I thought, more beautiful as she got older. The moonlight brought out the silver of her hair, which she wore in a simple braid. All I could really see of her was the outline of her motherly figure draped in her robes. Her silhouette reminded me of the rounded hump of Mount Tabor, whose rough places had all been worn away by time and weather, leaving only the essential form. People said that I resembled my mother and I think that we did have the same round face, wide-open eyes, and disarming smile.

"Go on," she said at last.

"You know that I started calling God 'Father' when I was a little boy. I still experience God in the familiar way as my Father, but since Papa-Joe died, God has also begun coming to me in a new way, as the Holy Spirit."

"You've been keeping this inside since Papa-Joe died?" she asked in surprise. "That was almost a year ago."

"It was?"

She chuckled, for she was all too familiar with my difficulties in keeping track of time. "Yes, it was. So tell me about the Holy Spirit."

I had to strip the Holy Spirit down to a single gender in order to even begin describing my omni-gendered Beloved. "At first She—You and I know that God is both male and female, but I'll say 'She' to balance out my Father's masculinity. At first She just comforted me in my grief over Papa-Joe's death, but now she comes to me as a potential lover...who wants to *marry* me. Every time She comes to me, it's more intense and more...sexy...."

I felt awkward talking about God this way and paused to see if Mom would say anything. I expected the image of God as lover to shock Mom as it had shocked me. When she spoke, there was astonishment in her voice, but not for the reason I had predicted.

"You're afraid to say yes to God!" she exclaimed.

I bowed my head, feeling ashamed. "Well, if you put it that way, the path I should take seems clear."

She put a reassuring hand on my arm. "You can always trust God."

Mom's sensible, matter-of-fact approach caught me off-guard. She saw that I was still troubled, so she asked, "Didn't the men at the local synagogue teach you that this might happen? Or the men at the Temple? We sent you to study at the Temple in Jerusalem when you were a teenager so you could learn all about God. You were there for more than a year before you decided that you had had enough. Surely the men who run the Temple told you about making love with God."

"The priests, elders, scribes, and Pharisees?! No!

They never discuss anything like this! I mean, they taught me that prophecy from Isaiah, but they said the divine marriage was a symbol of God's relationship to the nation of Israel, not that God could actually marry an individual person. Of course, they didn't believe God could be the Father of an individual person, either."

"Hmmmpf." She dismissed all the religious instruction I had ever received with a grunt of contempt. "I know what I experienced."

Everything fell into place for me then and I laughed with joy. "I'm going to say yes to the Holy Spirit."

"Congratulations!" Mom hugged me and gave me a kiss on each cheek. The eastern horizon was beginning to glow outside the mouth of our grotto.

Some uncomfortable questions still nagged at me. I had to ask. "But how do I make love with the Holy Spirit? I mean, what do I do with my body?"

"You can trust God to lead you and to love you."

"Yes, but..." I stammered. Now came the topic that was hardest for me to raise. "Maybe you could tell me what it was like when God 'overshadowed' you and you conceived me. I know it's personal, but it would help me."

"I never even discussed that with Papa-Joe," she replied rather primly.

The first glimmer of dawn must have highlighted the inner turmoil on my face, because she relented. "Well, Papa-Joe didn't need to know, but you do. I want you to be ready when the Holy Spirit makes love to you."

A wave of sensual longing passed through me. It was like a hot wind that left my heart racing and my whole body tingling with anticipation. We were crossing into a level of intimacy that was unknown in my culture.

"When your Father overshadowed me, it felt good in every way—spiritual, mental, emotional...*physical,* too," Mom explained. "You said the Holy Spirit felt 'sexy.' Yes. I was a virgin, so I didn't know how it would feel to make love, but sex is no secret to a farm girl like me, who grew up in a one-room house full of people. I did know that it was possible to form a sacred sexual bond with God because I had learned about such mysteries from the elderly matriarchs."

I looked at the ground, feeling bashful. Normally if I felt unsteady in some way, I reached right out in spirit and braced myself against my Father's being. But what if God decided to appear to me as the Holy Spirit? I wasn't ready to have this conversation with *Her* present.

Mom continued. "It didn't happen suddenly or all at once. Your Father paused at every stage as He made love to me to make sure that I wasn't just saying yes out of duty or fear. He whispered marvelous promises to me over and over. Most concerned His relationship with me, but some were about you."

She smiled at me with a mother's pride in her offspring, then resumed her story. "They were the same promises from the scriptures that they recite in the synagogue, but while He was making love to me, they seemed incredibly intimate, as if they were just for me. I was very eager. Jesus, it was so real! I had faith before, but this was nothing like that. This was feeling God caress my heart, my breasts, my private parts...."

Mom gazed into the sunrise, letting the bliss on her

face tell me the rest of the story. Wind ruffled through the wildflowers growing outside the grotto. Mom looked in my eyes and patted my hand. "You will be bonded with God permanently."

I hugged my own knees like a security blanket as I remembered the other side of the Holy Spirit's proposal: a cup of blood that my Father kept wanting me to drink.

Mom paused before adding, "Of course, the purpose is not just for you and God, but to bring new life into the world."

"What do you mean?"

"Well, I gave birth to you. I expect the Holy Spirit has something similar in mind for you to do."

The tingling sensation in my belly curdled into a knot of resistance. My divine side was not limited by gender and in some ways, neither was my human self. I was comfortable with my male anatomy and the sensations that went with it. Sometimes I felt intensely male, which made me want to direct my strength and bravery outward to make things happen and protect and provide for others. At other times I felt all female, so accessible and nurturing that I even felt like I had breasts and a womb. Still, I had never gone so far as to believe that I would carry a real, live baby in my phantom womb. And yet, with God anything was possible. "You think I am to bear a child?!"

Mom laughed. "I doubt that you will bear a baby since your Father chose to give you a male body. It's more like you'll...*fertilize*...the Holy Spirit. I can't say what kind of new life will spring from that union."

Mom's vision of my life purpose stunned me. I

couldn't even form a thought in response. I tried to focus my eyes on the landscape being illuminated before us by the rising sun. The grain fields on the valley floor below were still in shadow. Apricot, almond, and olive trees shone brilliant green on the terraced hillsides. Purple grapes were ripening on vines trained around some of the tree trunks. I regained my equilibrium by gazing at the horizon where heaven and earth meet.

I felt ready to tell Mom more, without telling all. "God does want me to bring life to the world, but it involves pain, suffering, and terrible sacrifice."

Mom dismissed my fears with a cackle. "That's what giving birth is, Jesus! You've heard women screaming during labor—myself included. You have to be ready for that if you're going to get married."

I spent the next few days walking south from Galilee, the lush agricultural region where I grew up, into the dry, bleak land of Judea. I prayed a lot, telling the Holy Spirit that I accepted Her proposal. When She didn't wed me immediately, I felt equal measures of disappointment and relief. Mom had prepared me for my wedding, but I wanted someone to help me face the ominous cup that went with it. I decided to visit my favorite cousin at his camp in the wilderness beside the Jordan River. He had baptized so many people there that everyone called him the Baptist. I walked into a mountain landscape that grew increasingly harsh, with deep ravines and bone-colored limestone outcroppings. The dry season was almost over, so the weeds that grew in the crevices between rocks were all dead and parched.

In this landscape, it was easy to sense the Baptist's soul, which was strongly bonded to God, like a branch growing from a tree trunk. I heard the Baptist yelling before I could see him. "Repent, because God's kingdom is near!"

I scrambled down and around a bend in the last ravine to see a crowd of men, women, and children. They had gathered at a place where the river ran slow and wide. On the riverbank, the weeds grew green and trees found enough water to survive. All of us had dusky skin that echoed the brown colors of the earth.

While I walked toward the crowd in the late afternoon heat, I surveyed the souls of the people gathered there. As soon as I encountered anyone in the physical world, I liked to almost breathe in that person's soul, or sniff that soul, to examine traits such as its clarity, turbulence, ripeness—its readiness for each of the infinite dimensions of contact and intimacy with me. I felt an undercurrent of love for each individual and I longed for them to love me back. Today I was struck by the beauty of one particular soul that looked like a cascade of vibrant jewels, colored sky-blue and wine-red.

I used my human eyes to match the soul with a body. I saw a well-built man at the edge of the crowd. He was taller and older than me with smoldering good looks. He stood next to an acquaintance of mine, a man whose soul reminded me of the wind. I approached them and greeted the one I knew.

"Hi, Andrew."

"Oh, hi, Jesus," Andrew replied with casual hospitality. He was young, just old enough to marry, with straight, black hair and a direct gaze from his soulful eyes. "Hey, I want you to meet my buddy John. He's visiting for a few days to check out the Baptist."

"I'm just open to wherever God leads me," the intriguing stranger corrected him in a booming bass voice.

His many wrinkles emphasized the deep-set eyes that brooded beneath his tightly curled, salt-and-pepper hair. He had olive skin, a large nose, and full lips, giving him a look that I found appealing.

Our eyes met. God's light glimmered in his fiery eyes and his colorful, bejeweled soul. I imagined how his soul would dazzle if I could find a way to shine more divine light through it. He smiled back at me, pleased by what he was seeing.

Andrew introduced me. "This is Jesus of Nazareth. He's been coming here even longer than I have, and he was here for my baptism, but he still hasn't taken the plunge."

"Not yet. But I'm going to ask to be baptized tomorrow. I'm ready to take the plunge." I smiled into John's dark eyes. I liked that his name was John. That was also the Baptist's name, although nobody used it anymore.

"John and his brother are fishing partners with me and my brother," Andrew explained. "We left them back on the Sea of Galilee to do all the work."

They looked at each other and laughed like mischievous boys.

I joined in the fun. "My brother Jim is mad at me, too, for leaving the family carpentry business to come here. He told me I should get married instead."

We all shared a laugh over my brother's mundane solution to God's call.

"What makes him think a wife is the answer?" Andrew chuckled.

"He found out that I've been seeing prostitutes," I explained. "He didn't believe me when I said that we don't have sex. They're teaching me their strategies for facing rejection and suffering. It's not just prostitutes, either. I've started hanging out with the blind, the lame, beggars, eunuchs, and slaves. I like being with outcasts who live on the edge in some way. They're helping me figure out what to do when people reject me."

While I was speaking, Andrew's mouth dropped open in astonishment. "Reject you? But...everybody likes you."

"Nobody even knows who I am!" I retorted. "And I won't deny myself anymore."

John shot me a sly smile.

Suddenly the Baptist's impassioned voice interrupted us. "The Lord will punish sinners!" he shouted. "Report that to the hypocrites at the Temple who collaborate with the Roman oppressors. And I have a message for King Herod, too. It is not lawful for him to marry Herodias, his brother's wife!"

The Baptist wore a crude garment of camel's hair with a leather belt around the waist. It had to be uncomfortable, but it served to dramatize his obedience to God above everything, even personal comfort. He let his hair and beard grow untamed, too.

His rage was directed at a group of men wearing distinctive long-tasseled robes. I couldn't see their faces, but I recognized the uniform worn by members of a strictly observant branch of Judaism. As Jews, we all wore blue tassels at the corners of our clothing to remind ourselves to follow God's Law, but these men made their tassels ostentatiously long.

"What are all those Pharisees doing here?" I asked.

"The Temple sent them to investigate," Andrew answered. "We're afraid that they're going to arrest the Baptist, and maybe even kill him."

The Pharisees were bunched together near the river, badgering the Baptist with questions. "Who do you think you are? Are you the Messiah?"

The Baptist seemed pleased that he had maneuvered them to this point. Without intending it, they had set the stage for him to expound on one of his favorite topics:

"We Jews are always talking about the Messiah—or maybe you think it's more fashionable to use the Greek word and call him the Christ. Either way, it means 'anointed one.' God anointed him like a king or a priest is anointed when he takes office. The prophet Daniel saw him come out of the heavenly clouds to rule the world, and he looked like 'a son of man.' You know that that phrase means a regular human being. He's somebody, anybody. He could be standing here today."

"Does that mean you are the Messiah?" the Pharisees persisted.

"I just use water to baptize you. He's going to baptize you with the Holy Spirit and with fire—hot, hot fire that burns away all your impurities!"

The Baptist liked to talk big while others enjoyed the spectacle of his righteous indignation. As he ranted on with fierce rhetoric, I savored the knowledge that I was going to reveal myself to him as the Messiah as soon as he baptized me. Meanwhile, he didn't have a clue that his long-awaited Messiah was his cousin and protégé. I indulged in happy fantasies of how pleased he would be to see my full majesty.

I became distracted by the not unwelcome presence of somebody standing close behind me, closer than necessary in the loosely packed crowd. I sensed that it was John, and spun around to see him planted there like a tall cedar tree. He leaned against me, eyes flashing. "I can't wait for the Messiah to come. I've seen him in visions."

"Really? Tell me what you remember." It was exciting to find someone who was aware of God's efforts to communicate.

"The Messiah is like a gentle lamb who sits on a throne with a rainbow around it. And yet his eyes flame with fire, and a sharp sword comes out of his mouth to strike down evildoers."

"The truth is large," I said.

"Are you saying my vision isn't true?" he challenged.

"No, I'm not saying that. I expect that you will see more."

When John smiled, his faced crinkled into a fascinating landscape of wrinkles. His eyes felt black and mysterious like the midnight sky as they roamed over me. "Do you want a prayer partner tonight?" he asked.

If anyone else had asked, I would have said no, but I looked again at John's handsome, bejeweled soul and his long, sinewy body.

"Sure," I agreed impulsively.

Only then did I notice that the Baptist had finished preaching. John steered me toward the caves where the Baptist and his inner circle of disciples lived. Lower-ranking disciples were ready with water vessels and towels to assist everyone with ritual purification before we ate a spartan meal of locusts and wild honey. One of them approached me.

"Wash up, and we'll get together after supper," John said as we parted.

The person who came to wash me had a soul that was fluid, flowing, and a bit muddy like the water that she poured. Her dark, intelligent eyes met mine as she poured river water over my hands with flair and care. She made the mundane task into a dance by lifting her pitcher high as she poured. I don't know how she managed to do it without splashing a drop onto my clothes. She obviously wanted attention, so I gave her mine in full. I noticed then that her face was pretty and her body was well-proportioned, in a plump sort of way. She was past the prime age for marriage, but still younger than me. She had half-succeeded in taming her glossy black hair by weaving it into a long, loose braid. Her skin was golden.

"Thank you," I said as she finished. "I haven't seen you here before."

"I'm new. Would you like me to wash your feet, too?" she offered.

Footwashing was a common way to show hospitality in our culture. If there were no women or slaves around, the youngest male performed the footwashing, as I occasionally had done for Papa-Joe or the Baptist. Sometimes it was a formality, but my feet were dirty, hot, and tired from days of walking cross-country.

"Go ahead," I agreed. I sat down, leaned against a boulder and thrust my feet out. I kept my sandals on to let her know that she could touch me.

Under our Law and tradition, touch was carefully regulated, and in many circumstances women's touch left men ritually unclean. These were the kind of rules I always had trouble remembering, but some people at the Baptist's camp were rigorously scrupulous about following them. I usually didn't know that I had broken some rule until other people got upset about it.

Kneeling in front of me, the bright-eyed woman untied the leather thongs on my sandals and eased them off. She wet my weary feet with cool, refreshing water. As soon as she touched the soles of my bare feet, I knew that this would be no ordinary footwashing. She ran her fingertips slowly and carefully over my feet, then massaged them by applying the perfect amount of pressure in exactly the right places. Her every move was tailored to address my nuanced needs.

I sighed aloud so that she could hear my contentment.

The corners of her mouth turned up slightly as she continued massaging. Her ability to read my feet reminded me of the way that I could read souls, and that comparison pleased me, too. I gazed deep into her eyes with unguarded admiration. I had never found a way to touch other souls with my own divinity. I felt a pang of intense longing to be able to respond to the souls around me as directly as this gifted woman was touching my feet. People almost always averted their eyes when I looked at them from my divinity, but she took it all in, fascinated. She sent her energy into me through her hands and I let it circle back to her through my gaze. I lost all track of time in our endless loop of love, and I think that she did, too.

I snapped out of it when someone yelled at her. "Hurry up, Mary! The Baptist is waiting for his cousin."

Now I knew her name.

"The scriptures say patience is a virtue," Mary retorted while she hurried to dry my feet.

"You know the scriptures," I observed.

Mary didn't notice that I was pleased because she was caught up in her own reaction. "Women have freedom to learn here," she replied defensively.

"And are you free to teach? I'd like to learn from you."

She was too startled to say another word. She tied my sandals more quickly than I had ever done it. Then the two of us started walking toward the main cave where the Baptist lived. She set a fast pace, then turned and looked at me in surprise when I didn't keep up. I was trying to show her how important she was to me by strolling with her in slow silence.

When we reached the Baptist's cave, we sealed our budding friendship by exchanging small, hopeful smiles. Only a select group of men were allowed inside when the Baptist was eating or teaching there. Everyone else stayed outside to listen and eat. The Baptist called me into the cave to join tonight's chosen few. All the other women of Mary's age had several children and were using this interlude to nurse their babies, but Mary seemed to be unattached. She sat down right at the mouth of the cave, where she wouldn't miss a word of the teaching.

chapter two:
baptism

THAT NIGHT JOHN AND I climbed high in the cliffs to the small, out-of-the-way cave where I usually stayed. We sat down together on some sandy soil in front of my cave. The earth itself seemed to relax in gratitude for the darkness that covered it after the sun-baked day. I spoke first. "You said that you receive visions from God. What's your favorite way to make them come?"

"It happens sometimes after I chant a prayer, if I really clear my mind and open to whatever God wants to give me." A moth flittered onto John's grayish curls and he brushed it away.

"Let's pray together that way," I suggested. "After you've had your vision, just start singing a line from a psalm and I'll join in. Then we can discuss what God revealed to each of us."

"You have visions, too?"

"All the time."

John smiled broadly. "So I'm not the only one!"

I lay down. "I like to look at the sky while I meditate."

"Really? You don't face east?"

"I face east for prayer, but when I want to receive a divine vision, I look up to heaven," I said.

John's eyes twinkled in the starlight, as if I had proposed a great adventure. "I'll try it your way," he said. He took off his cloak and spread it over the ground, rolling one end of it into a long pillow. "Here, lie on this. I don't want you to get cold lying on the ground."

I did feel goose bumps, even though the air was still warm and my tunic had dried quickly in the desert night. I rolled onto his cloak and looked up at him in his sleeveless tunic, his muscular arms exposed. Then he lay beside me.

I felt warm and cozy as I prayed aloud, "Your kingdom come. Come, come, come...."

There was no need to teach John how to pray with me. "Come, come, come," he repeated automatically. His voice was deep and soft like distant thunder, except this thunderstorm was right next to me. We took turns praying the phrase a few times, then lapsed into silent meditation.

I decided to begin by supporting John's soul in its quest to receive illumination. His soul was complex, with many layers of brightly colored segments that sparked as they bumped against one another, constructing and deconstructing multidimensional patterns that inspired me to caress them with rays of light. I discovered that his soul could not absorb my light unless I dimmed it way down. Then his soul unwrapped itself and worshipped me by dancing in my dusky light.

The rumble of John's voice stirred me from my meditations. "Love and devotion will meet. Peace and justice will kiss each other," he sang.

We chanted the line together a few times before I asked, "Did you have a vision?"

"Yes, but it was different from the ones I've had

before." He slipped his arm under my neck and drew me into his story. "Usually I see complicated images, but this one was very simple. An unbelievably gorgeous, pure white light came and shined on me until I felt utterly loved."

"You saw that?!" I propped myself up on my elbow and looked down at him in astonishment. I had given up hope that anyone would ever be able to perceive this side of me.

"Yes, I saw it. What does it mean?" John asked.

"You saw me! You saw me as I am!"

The phrase "I am" was one of the names for God in our Aramaic language, so I had made a play on words. John smiled up at me, bemused.

My heart was racing and I'm sure that my excitement showed on my face. I didn't know if I had changed or if there was something unique about my relationship with John, but either way, I felt overjoyed to finally have someone who could share this part of my life with me.

"Would you like to know what else makes me feel close to God?" John asked.

"Yes."

"Doing this." He wrapped his arms around me, cradling the back of my head with one hand, and gently drew me on top of him. Then he kissed me—first on the cheek and then, when I didn't protest, full on the mouth. Wonderful! His taste and scent excited me. His kisses were like him, searching, fiery, flavorful, artistic, mature. I yielded, then kissed him back. I sensed my Bride, the Holy Spirit, watching without jealousy or judgment.

I loved that John had walked the earth much longer

than I had. I stroked the wrinkles on his face and his grizzled beard. Those long, slightly gnarled fingers of his slipped under the collar of my tunic and fondled my neck. Then he gripped me tightly and I realized that he was physically stronger than I was. He could over-power me if he tried. He found the slits in our tunics and laid his bare leg against mine, up to the thigh, as our lips and tongues explored and affirmed each other. I wanted to welcome him into me and let him extend and expend himself in hot pursuit of all that I had to offer. Desire surged in me and I told myself that this time it would be different.

But then his soul opened to me in the way it should open only to God, *worshipping* me with kisses and sub-mitting completely. I couldn't ignore it. I wasn't half-human and half-God—I was fully both, so I had to respond as God, too, and when I did, when I accepted his soul's adoration, my sexual desire began draining away. I had reached this point before with people. I could be a divine lover at the soul level, but not a human lover in time and space. The power imbalance was just too great.

John sensed the change immediately. "What's wrong?" he asked tenderly. "It's not your first time with a man, is it? I mean, the way that you were looking at me today, I thought…"

Our bodies were still pressed together, and I was still enjoying our closeness. I had never found an easy explanation for myself once I got into these sexually charged situations, so I just answered his question truthfully. "I've kissed men before, but I've never gone all the way."

"Oh, that's okay. I'm experienced. I'll show you some of the things that men can do together."

I was curious to find out what he had in mind. A fresh wave of desire swelled in my body. I squeezed my eyes shut for a moment to let it pass. "I don't want to take advantage of you," I said.

"I think I'm the one who is taking advantage of you, young man," he chuckled.

"That may be true, so far." I laughed a little, too, and raised myself up on my elbow again, so I could gaze straight into his eyes. "Beloved, you've seen me as I really am. I *am* the light you saw, only much, much more powerful than what I let you see. If we made love, I would be taking advantage of you. I refuse to do that."

All John understood was that I had said no. He sighed in frustration and sat up. "Well, if you don't want to, then you don't want to. It's because we're both men, isn't it?"

"No. That doesn't make any difference to me. I usually don't even notice whether people are male or female, especially when we are kissing."

John laughed. The good humor and maturity with which he faced my rejection made me feel attracted to him on yet another level.

"Give me back my cloak and I'll be going," John said as he stood up. "I'd better get back soon or else Andrew will think that we had sex. He knows how I am."

"I don't care what others think."

"Really?" John looked down at me in surprise.

I was still lying on his cloak, and I made no effort to move. "I don't want you to go yet."

He paused, pondering whether to walk away or whether I was worth the effort.

"You really are quite the flirt," he teased. We laughed together until he added, "Okay, maybe we can do this again tomorrow night."

"Sounds good," I smiled. I rolled off his cloak and handed it to him.

After he was gone, I poured my suppressed energies into prayer. My divine senses always offered me the option of sensing the subtle natural dramas that cycled around me as a backdrop to every human action. Now I tuned in to what was happening at the mouth of the cave: the flirting of crickets, the sigh of a seed waiting for water, the satisfaction of a spider spinning her web by starlight. To be with these life forms in the physical world in my physical body, perceiving them with my physical senses, joining them in praising God, and at the same time to *be* God receiving our praises created an incredible sense of peace and oneness.

I held that sacred unity for one ecstatic moment. Then something or Someone—wavering light in human form—sat down beside me. The head was turned downward, with hair falling over the cheek and hiding the face so I couldn't even see if my visitor was male or female.

"Hello, Father," I said.

He raised His head. When He faced me, He looked like my own reflection when I saw it shimmering on the sunny surface of the Sea of Galilee. During my childhood, I thought He looked much older and wiser than me. He hadn't changed, but now I realized that I was almost as old as He was.

My Father did something that He had done several times before, starting on the day that Papa-Joe died. He held out a cup and offered it to me. It was solid gold, unadorned but lovely for the balance of its proportions. I knew what was inside, and it scared me.

"This is my blood, given for many," He said.

"Your blood?!" I protested. "That's *my* blood."

"True. We are one." He looked at me kindly.

This was the other side of God's marriage proposal.

My Father would never say much about the enigmatic cup. He had first offered it to me when Papa-Joe was deathly ill. Papa-Joe and my Father were both ready to move on to the next stage of their relationship, but my human side wanted Papa-Joe to live longer with me on earth. Nobody expected me to prolong his life. I tried anyway, digging deep into myself to find the ability that could heal him. I discovered that I could make healing available to some people, but only by becoming one with God and letting God decide the outcome.

I had overcome many kinds of temptations before Papa-Joe's illness, but none was as strong as my desire to find a way to use my own personal powers to prevent Papa-Joe's death in defiance of God's will. By offering me the cup, my Father conveyed to me that there was a way for me to defeat death much more decisively. As soon as I let my humanity rest quiet in God's will, Papa-Joe died peacefully.

The image of the cup had haunted me ever since his death. I became aware not of my divinity—I'd always sensed that—but of its purpose, *my* purpose, why my Father sent someone like me into the world. I reviewed the prophecies in scripture and tried to comprehend how they applied to me. I came to understand that my Father meant for me to show God's infinite love for people by overcoming death itself. That would mean teaching and healing, yes, but my Father required more of me. Slowly, in fits and starts, I sensed, both through meditation and through observing human behavior, that being a teacher, healer, and role model would not be enough. My blood was required. I was to die as some kind of sacrificial lamb. The thought of it made me restless.

My Father was still holding the cup out to me, offering, not insisting. I hesitated.

That is how the cup meditation had always ended, with me and my Father at a stalemate. Now I looked in His eyes and saw love that was different from what the Holy Spirit gave me, but just as intense.

"Dare to obey me!" His words were not a command of the sort that I was used to hearing from other people. His affectionate tone both invited and challenged me to obedience.

"All right, I'll drink it if I have to. Your will, not mine," I declared. For the first time, I reached so He could give me the cup.

Just then I felt a pinching pain inside my lip and tasted blood in my mouth. The stressful prayer had made me bite myself! I became aware again that I was sitting outside a cave in rocky Judea. My Father turned into a shaft of light that danced through the stars and disappeared into other dimensions, carrying the cup with Him.

I lay down and explored the little wound with my tongue. It was so small that it had already stopped bleeding. While I watched the stars, the Holy Spirit came to me and communicated by touching the part of my mind that listens in faith. "Dare to submit to my will. Hold my life in your heart," She coaxed.

Her speaking style was to repeat a phrase over and over, letting its echoes sink deep into me before moving on to the next thought. The holy invitation condensed into its essence as it echoed in my mind: "Dare to submit...Dare...."

I said yes, yes, *yes* and yes again, giving my life to God.

"You are mine. *Mine,*" She seemed to whisper by strumming over and over against invisible energy cords that I never knew lay inside me. "My Beloved...."

"Yes, Beloved, yes." My reply became Her voice, a single reverberation of divine love filling the cosmos.

I let go of my sense of self and succumbed to the Holy Spirit's majesties and mysteries. In this emptying of self, I became more myself than I had ever been before. Deliciously more. It was more vivid and all-encompassing than any interaction I had had with other humans, because finally I was with Someone who understood all of me and could love me as my equal. She connected with the parts of me that I considered female as well as all my male parts. Every psalm and prayer that I had ever memorized took on fresh significance as a source of endearments with which to please and honor Her. She reflected them back as Her vows to me.

In the Holy Spirit's presence, my human concept of gender came unglued and disintegrated into its most basic components, which we jumbled and reallocated between ourselves again and again in a kaleidoscope of continuously flowing patterns. We alternated roles and applauded each other for dreaming up divine new anatomies with which to enact them. She shuffled me through as many different genders as I could take, then I shuffled Her...Him...Whomever, for there were no words in my native Aramaic or any human language for the ways that we mixed masculinity and femininity.

Our prayers caused waves of potent pleasure to roll through me, so intense that I released my entire being into the rapture of oneness with God. The Holy Spirit seeped into the core of my human heart and soul, into virgin places intended only for God, and there She awoke potentialities that even I had never dreamed of. I let Her magnify Her love through me to bless all beings. She soaked Herself into me and I into Her, so that we were wed. The boundaries between us effaced themselves and I was whole, One. Total synthesis. I had never felt so helpless—nor so virile.

"Heart of My own heart...One Heart...." We breathed together, Her through me and I through Her, throughout timeless time.

We experienced the sweep of eternity and infinity as states in which our love was endless because it continued to grow and evolve in unlimited variations, giving rise to life that begat life and love that begat love in world after world. In our creation we allowed hate and horror, too, all for a purpose. Peace welled up in us and we rested.

At sunrise when I awoke, I knew that I had participated in a shift within God's own being. We had forged a new relationship among manifestations of the divine that defied definition, but could be named as Father, Son and Holy Spirit. Our forces had fused into what I now called my divine heart, a core of love designed for giving and receiving.

"Beloved," I whispered in my new divine heart, and She was there.

"I'm right here. Always."

I clung to Her some, and She promised, "We'll make love often."

She was letting me feel human again, grounded and separate, but it was not the same as my experience of humanity before our wedding night. In the past, I had been like a passive, lonesome spectator in life compared to the way I felt now. I had a new readiness to *be* love, whatever that would mean. I was awed by the sequence of changes that We had set in motion in my life. I could only glimpse how my transformation was going to affect my relationships with other people. The change within me was so profound and indelible that I could not hide it, nor did I know how to display it.

I was still in the same dreamy, honeymoon mood the next afternoon when I was standing on the bank of the Jordan River with a group of people waiting to be baptized. The other initiates whispered to me. "Go on, Jesus."

The Baptist had finished his preaching and prayers and was waist-deep in the river, gesturing impatiently for the day's first initiate to come and receive his blessing and baptism. Everyone assumed that we were going to go in order based on our connection to the Baptist and our social standing in Jewish culture. "Jesus, you should go first," they urged.

"No. I want to go last," I replied.

"Last! You mean after the other men."

"No. *Last.*"

It disrupted their sense of order, but they couldn't *make* me go, so they all went ahead of me in turn. I enjoyed watching each person wade into the river and be rinsed clean in the ritual. We had all removed our cloaks and sandals and were dressed only in short-sleeved linen tunics for the occasion.

The afternoon sun was hot and the river looked deliciously cool. Sunlight danced on the ripples in the semi-opaque green water. I sensed tadpoles and other small swimming creatures among the smooth stones at the bottom of the river. The shore was crowded with people who had been baptized on previous days or who were considering it for the future. They sang a psalm softly, "Put a fresh, new heart in me, O God."

When the first woman presented herself for baptism, the Baptist glanced over at me in surprise, assuming that I had decided not to be baptized that day. Then he resumed his work.

Eventually he had baptized everyone except me and Mary, the extraordinary woman who had helped me wash the night before. She hesitated, debating in her mind which was more rude: to go ahead of a man or to speak to a man without being spoken to by him first. She decided to speak. "I don't mind going last."

"Neither do I." We smiled at each other, pleased to find such similarity of mind. I wasn't sure why she was put in last place. She was certainly not the youngest there.

She sashayed into the water with style, raising her arms high above her head in the pose of a dancer. The others had all kept their pre-baptism conversations with the Baptist inaudible, but she yelled out loud enough for everyone to hear: "Give me a clean heart!" She quoted the psalm with such passion that I knew that she thought her past sins were deadly.

After a few quiet words, the Baptist dunked her underwater. She didn't just stand back up as the others had done. She jumped for joy as she emerged wet and glistening. She seemed to bounce all the way back to the shore.

Thinking he had finished the day's baptisms, the Baptist started wading back, too. He looked surprised when I began wading out to meet him. "Jesus! Come here, kid!"

Mud squished between my toes and the cool water invigorated me as I walked to where the water reached my waist. "Hi, cousin," I smiled.

We hugged each other. His camel's hair tunic was rough against my arms and he smelled of the river. My touching pushed the limit of what was acceptable in my culture, but, like most people, the Baptist couldn't help enjoying how it felt when I showered him with love.

During our hug, I heard John and some other newcomers whispering, "Are they really cousins?" I sensed John studying us in search of a family resemblance. The Baptist and I were both of average height and build and we were often mistaken for each other, but my hair was more silky and my movements were more graceful.

We released each other and stood face to face in the middle of the river. The slow currents swirled around us. His passionate eyes were at the same height as my compassionate ones.

He waited to hear if I was going to say anything more. When I didn't, he spoke. "Baptism means you are ready for the Messiah to appear. It means letting your old self die so you can become God's new creation. You understand?"

"Oh, yes!"

"You've let go." The Baptist gave me one of his rare grins. He looked so happy that I realized he must have dreamed of baptizing me.

I took a deep breath and let the Holy Spirit blow away a kind of intangible veil that had hidden my divinity from the Baptist and everyone else. I let him see me, all of me. Anyone else who was ready could see me, too.

Disbelief crossed the Baptist's face, followed by an expression of deference that he had never shown me before. "You want me to baptize you?! It should be the other way around."

"Let's do it this way for now," I assured him.

He placed his hands on my shoulder and said, "I baptize you in the name of God." Then he pushed me underwater and held me there longer than I wanted to stay. He was strong and I realized I would have to fight if I was going to come up for air before he allowed it. As my need for air became critical, I understood with a shock that the baptism was not merely symbolic. He actually intended for me to confront my fear of death. With my lungs aching to breathe, my divine heart also gulped for air. I sensed the Holy Spirit breathe into me in a new way. I knew She was guiding the Baptist's hands. Panic gave way to trust.

As soon as I trusted, the Baptist released me. I stood and sucked in breath upon breath of air as fast as I could. I was in too much physical distress to pay attention to my surroundings or other people's reactions at first. Then I noticed a bright light shining on the Baptist and the water around us. I turned around to find out what could be so bright. There was nothing. The light was coming from *me*.

A voice from heaven declared, "You are my Son, my Beloved. You make Me happy."

I was still panting some, but otherwise I felt pretty ordinary. *Other* people experienced it as a once-in-a-lifetime event. I just let all my energy spill freely from me and allowed them to join me in the kind of vision that I experienced frequently. I was startled by how clearly I could perceive every soul laid bare as if a dense fog had cleared away. In revealing myself to them, I had also removed a barrier that had prevented me from seeing them as they were. Their beauty and their pain both seemed much more acute than before. It brought tears to my eyes.

The Baptist's reaction was to spread his arms wide and shout to the crowd. "Here is the Lamb of God who takes away all our sins!" He meant me!

Most people looked mystified. The others cheered—they were the ones whose souls were awake. These souls began to dance around my divine heart. Mary's soul spun in whirlpool fashion, while Andrew's twisted like a happy cyclone. I felt a jolt of all-too-human joy when I picked out the soul of the man I hadn't been able to forget. John's soul was firing off glad bursts of colored light in the swirling ring of souls.

I was eager to be with the people who were cheering for me. I waded back and stepped on solid ground again. John helped me dry off, rubbing my legs vigorously with a towel, and Mary tied my sandals onto my feet.

"What makes you think Jesus is the one?" some of the others asked the Baptist.

"I saw the Holy Spirit land on him like a dove. That can only mean that he is the son of God," he replied.

Everyone backed away from me when they heard those last three words: "son of God." Most of them had heard me refer to God as my Father, but they just thought I meant we were all children of God.

"I saw the spirit-dove fly to him, too," Andrew exulted.

"Me, too!" added several others. All whose souls were dancing spoke up, except Mary. I looked at her and in a lovely flash of recognition, she knew that I knew that she knew.

"Okay, so he's the Messiah," one of the Baptist's disciples said. "Now what?"

The Baptist was quick to answer. "He is claiming his power, but I must step aside. I'm just a friend of the bridegroom, fortunate to be a guest at his wedding."

I was amazed that the Baptist had been able to see that I was a bridegroom. Before I could speak for myself, the Baptist dismissed the crowd and ordered me to walk upstream with him. We found a forested bend in the river where we could talk alone.

chapter three:
aftershocks

AS SOON AS WE WERE OUT OF EARSHOT, the Baptist launched into a long-winded explanation of what had just happened. He didn't give me a chance to say one word before he began trying to define my life for me. "You are the Messiah! You will judge the nations! You get to send all the goddamned idiots in the world to burn forever in the outer darkness!" He was thrilled and elated by what he was imagining.

"Stop!" I cried out. "I came to save people, not to judge them."

The Baptist stared at me, too surprised to speak.

"The Son of Man is going to be betrayed and killed, but three days later he will rise again," I explained.

"Son of Man? You mean that they will kill...you?" He really was a great prophet, for he understood exactly what I meant.

I gazed at him steadily while he wrestled with the implications.

"I myself am going to take the punishment," I confirmed.

Then he shouted in agony, terror, and love. "You think that God wants you to die?!"

I used my divine power to peer all the way into his mind for the first time, hoping to find a way to reach him. He was not the type to utter a compliment, but it became plain that he felt I deserved God's blessing.

I touched his shoulder to try to convey the tenderness I felt for him. "I know it's hard to allow someone you love to suffer and die, but it will be a blessing in the end for me, too. Didn't you hear me say I would rise again?"

"Rise again? Ridiculous!" He pushed me away so roughly that I slipped down the steep, muddy riverbank and fell in, right on my butt. I was immersed up to my chin, but he just kept yelling at me. He wouldn't even reach out to help me as I tried to climb out of the water. "You're talking crazy! God doesn't require *human* sacrifice!"

"God will no longer require *any* of the blood sacrifices we make at the Temple," I answered from the riverbed. "People shouldn't have to have a pigeon massacre in order to talk to my Father. I want everyone to be able to just talk to God: no intermediaries, no priests, just direct communication. People in the future won't even know how hard it was for us."

The Baptist kept arguing. "If God is your Father as you say, he wouldn't—"

"Child abuse is monstrous, I know. I have to endure whatever is most disgusting and repulsive in the world."

"But the sacrifice God requires is to do justice."

I struggled up the riverbank and faced him as water dripped from my now-muddy tunic. "Your idea of God's justice is actually very limited. I thought you would help me prepare to drink the cup that my Father has for me."

He started shouting again. "No! I don't want to have any part in you inviting such a fate on yourself!"

I doubled over as a sudden, sharp pain ripped through my being and stung me simultaneously to the core of my humanity and my newly forged divine heart. I had never before felt that kind of pain. Switching back and forth between my dual identities had been a sort of refuge for me until then.

"Oww!" I exclaimed. It hurt when he refused to obey God.

The Baptist's soul recoiled from me. Then one part of his soul splintered apart from God with a sickening sound like a bone breaking. I suddenly saw why I had to die. Part of me did die right then and there. This moment was the final stage of my baptism. It killed my faith that people could save themselves. My human self had believed the Baptist when he said he gave his will completely to God. If even he couldn't submit to God, then I knew that nobody could. The cup leading to death and resurrection was indeed necessary and inevitable.

I drew in a short breath and managed to stand straight even though the pain remained. Our eyes locked in shock at what had just passed between us. The Baptist loved me too much to let me die. I could see it in his eyes, as well as sensing it in every possible way available to me. How terrible that his love for me as a human being is what blocked his love for me as God!

He couldn't order me to obey God now that I had come up with this new line of reasoning, so he questioned me. "If what you say is true, why would God ask you to do that?"

Quietly, I answered through the pain. "Because God is *merciful!*"

My belief in God's mercy had never stopped the Baptist before, but today was different. He turned and stalked away. It was the first time that he ever let me have the last word.

"I'll be dying for your sins, too!" I called after him. I meant it as a gift, but he didn't take it that way. He just kept going.

I slumped down on the ground and leaned my back against a boulder. I was soaking wet and dirty, and I was getting chilly as sunset approached. All I knew was that I couldn't stand to go back and spend a month with the Baptist and his disciples as I had planned to do. Even another night with them was too much. I was married to the Holy Spirit, and nobody else. The Baptist had indeed prepared me for my future—but by rejecting me, not by giving me the friendly advice and encouragement that I craved. I would have to rely on God more than ever. I stared into space, unable to think.

I listened dully as God's words played over and over, this time like two voices: "You are my Son," my Father boomed, while the Holy Spirit crooned, "You are my Beloved. You make Me happy."

The voices from the distant heavens didn't make me feel any better.

I felt the glimmer of the Holy Spirit come and sit beside me, close enough to warm my skin. "Feel what you feel," She urged.

I curled my knees up, wrapped my arms around

them and lay my head against my forearm. I swallowed my own salty tears as I wept.

"Our honeymoon is over," She said. "Let me eliminate everything in you that doesn't serve love. Go to the wilderness fast alone."

The wilderness sounded like a good idea to me. It would soon be too dark for me to travel, so I decided to wait until the next morning. The river frogs were beginning to croak their night-time serenades. I went back to the gently sloped riverbank where I had been baptized and washed my muddy clothes there as best I could in the gloomy twilight.

As I walked toward the group gathered outside the Baptist's cave, I heard the sound of a solitary flute. The music suited my mood with an intricate melody full of longing and grief, but not without hope. Eventually I got close enough to identify the flute player: John. I should have guessed. I hoped that he remembered our vague plan to get together that night. I had to admit to myself that I was feeling awfully lonely after my rift with the Baptist, but I tried not to get my hopes up about John.

I approached the edge of the crowd where he and Andrew were sitting. I noticed that John's long fingers were gnarled and stiff as they played over the flute and this seemed to make the music he created all the more poignant.

"You are a musician," I stated, letting the look in my eyes communicate how much that charmed me. He played a trill.

I tore my eyes away from him and told Andrew what I had come to say. "Tell everyone to leave me alone tonight. I'm going to pray in my own cave tonight and leave at sunrise to fast in the wilderness."

"Okay," Andrew agreed, without paying much attention. Fasting and asceticism were the norm at the Baptist's camp.

I turned to go, but John stopped me with a question. "What about me? Do you still want me to join you later tonight?" His eyes, like his music, disclosed a soul aching to be loved.

"Come with me now," I urged.

There was tension between us as we climbed up to my cave and began chanting psalms together, sitting side by side. After a while I stopped and looked in his eyes seriously. "Beloved, it's going to take time for you to understand me, and for us to prepare for all the intimacies that we really can experience together."

He reached out and stroked my hair, feeling its silkiness between his thumb and index finger. "What are you talking about?"

"I'm talking about intimacies like when your soul danced in my light last night."

His eyes flew wide open, then narrowed as he struggled with my insight into him. "I never told you about the dancing part! How did you know that?"

"I was there. I *am* the light."

John stared at me. "I recognized that light. That light was God."

I kept my eyes on him during a pause that stretched to become uncomfortably long.

"I know the Baptist said you were the Messiah and I saw the holy dove land on you, but...." John's voice trailed away into another silence.

I became annoyed as John's thoughts about me began to draw his attention away from his actual experience of me in that moment. "Don't you see *any* resemblance between me and that light? Any continuity? You saw me. Can't you see me now?"

"Let me take a good look." Gently he put his hand on my shoulder and drew me closer. He was going to indulge me by pretending to take me seriously. His eyes now felt darker than the sky above us as they searched mine. He examined my face, then my body. Love shone from his eyes the whole time.

Inspired, I tried hard to calibrate the light from my new divine heart to the exact same brightness that he had been able to see during our meditation. Then I let it flood through my humanity. It was difficult to gaze at him in such a steady, unguarded way because my human self was like a prism that separated the divine light into a spectrum of differing kinds of love. As a human being, I felt embarrassed to let him see all at once the many ways that I loved him, and how intense it was for me. His soul stirred.

John must have perceived at least a glimmer of what I was trying to show him because suddenly he pulled his hand away from my shoulder as if he had touched a hot loaf of bread.

"Don't be afraid," I assured him. "You weren't afraid when you danced naked in my light."

"I never told you about the naked part," he stammered in alarm.

"I *saw* you. And Beloved, if you really experienced me in your vision, then you *know* that you have nothing to fear. Trust me, like you did in your vision."

John scrutinized me again, relaxing more with each breath. I sat still until his attentiveness grew to meet and almost match mine. Based on his new understanding of me, he kissed me on the mouth once more. This time our kiss was superlatively soft and smooth.

Then his soul kissed my divine heart. My first direct contact with another soul felt so shockingly new that I kissed him back hard. We lay on the earth, locked in each other's embrace. John kissed me with his mouth in exactly the same way that he was kissing me with his soul—and he was aware of both levels while he was doing it. When we kissed simultaneously in the flesh and in the spirit, we created a resonance that I had never experienced before. Our tongues were like silk sliding on silk. I almost swooned for bliss.

I sensed the Holy Spirit celebrating in the space between me and John, even though there was no space between us during that kiss. I thanked Her for bringing someone into my life who could see all of me.

His soul kissed my divine heart more passionately, and I discharged all my desires for John there, lighting up even buried crystals that had never seen light before. Like seeds, these soul-crystals germinated and began to produce their own rainbows of light. I was awed by the spectacle.

John couldn't sustain a holy kiss like that for very long. He needed more air and he pulled away a little so he could breathe through his mouth. I held him close to my chest as we both panted. Groping my way out of the kiss, I felt vulnerable and uncertain about where our relationship was going. I knew that such a kiss had to be even more intense for John than it was for me. I rubbed my beard over his neck so that each of us could feel our humanity and reattach ourselves to our position in time and space.

"I have to get out of here," John blurted and abruptly left me.

I spent a restless night reflecting on everything that had happened since I arrived at the Baptist's camp. I wrestled with the contradictory messages of empowerment and rejection. At sunrise the next morning, I laid out my few belonging on the floor of the cave: a leather bag, an extra tunic, a water vessel made from a gourd, a leather bucket for drawing water, a wooden staff as tall as I was to help me climb, a few copper coins, a favorite rock from Nazareth that I used for cutting and scraping, and a tiny oil lamp made of pottery. I checked the level of olive oil in a small oil flask that I used for personal grooming, first aid, and lamp fuel. I reached in my bag and made sure that I had my phylacteries, two little leather cases containing scriptures that, like all Jewish men, I tied onto my forehead and left arm for my morning prayers.

Mary and Andrew came to the mouth of my cave and stood there, blocking the light. Mary seemed much more at ease with me than Andrew, for she spoke right up. "Please accept these gifts for your wilderness fast." Each of them handed me a large gourd vessel.

Mary looked at me boldly as she gave me her present. "Will you be our rabbi?"

She used the word "rabbi," which means teacher and, more than that, master. If I was their rabbi, they would not only learn from me, but also, in a sense, belong to me. I wasn't ready to risk such a relationship after the Baptist denounced me and John fled from my kisses. I needed time away from people with their predictions and preconceptions. "You don't know what you're asking," I warned.

"You're right. We're ignorant," Andrew lamented. "That's why we need you to teach us."

"Look, I didn't come to bring peace on earth. I'm a sword that will chop families apart. Your relatives will become your enemies. Nobody can be my disciple unless they hate their parents, their spouse, their children, their siblings—and even their own life."

They were still just as eager.

"Besides, I can't do it now," I added. "I have to go further into the wilderness to be alone with God. I might be gone for a month."

I could see shock on their faces. They thought it foolish to go alone into the desert wilderness for so long, but they didn't dare to object. I noticed that a cut on Andrew's wrist was healing faster than usual, although he wasn't aware of it. I put on my cloak and began stuffing items into my bag.

I sensed the pressure of unasked questions building up inside them. "Go ahead," I relented. "Ask me about my trip to the wilderness. I'm the kind of person that you can ask anything. *Anything.*"

"If you stayed here, you could get all the Baptist's disciples to follow you. He said you were the Messiah. Why don't you do that?" Andrew asked.

"I seek God first. Nothing else."

Mary had been paying close attention to what I was and wasn't packing. "You don't have any food at all. Do you want me to bring you some bread for when you end your fast?"

"No. I won't need it. Here, I won't need these, either." I shoved the lamp into her hand and the extra tunic into his, and made each of them take half of my money.

"Are you testing God then?" she asked. "Do you want to see if God will save you when you are starving alone in the wilderness?"

"No. I would never do that. I'm going to fast in the wilderness because the Holy Spirit is driving me there."

"We will go with you," Mary proclaimed.

"Yes, we'll go, too," Andrew echoed.

Their words broke through the resistance I was feeling. With my new divine heart, I took a long, hard look at their souls for the first time since my baptism had sharpened my divine senses. Andrew's soul was light and airy, with a few dust-clouds of fear and sin blowing through it. Mary's soul had an exquisite fluidity and depth, but her soul-waters were badly troubled. She was imprinted with the disturbances of many other people, as if they had trampled in clay at the bottom of a stream and forced the water to flow around their foot-prints. Even worse, I glimpsed a number of demons lurking like sea slugs in her churning depths. I also noticed a change from the previous day. Now each of their souls was marked with the other one's unique energy pattern.

Both souls nuzzled up against my divine heart, sucking hungrily. I still wasn't used to being touched at that level. I cried out in surprise. "Whoa! Did you feel that?"

"Feel what?" Andy asked.

"I didn't feel anything," Mary added.

Pleasant sensations squiggled through me as their souls continued to root against my divine heart. I drew them toward places where the good feelings were centered. I instinctively sensed that I could feed them. The barrier that used to separate me from people was gone.

The Holy Spirit interrupted, speaking silently in my mind. "Not yet," She instructed. I forced myself not to get attached to their souls.

With the sweet vision still in my mind, I picked up my staff and my bag and stepped out of the cave. I smiled at Mary and Andrew in the light of the new day. "You can't come with me now," I said. "While I'm gone, you can pray about whether you really want to follow me. Then when I come back, I will find you, and we can talk about me becoming your teacher, your master, your guru, your friend, or whatever you want to call it."

Their faces lit up. "If I'm not here with the Baptist, I'll be fishing on the Sea of Galilee near Capernaum with my brother," Andrew said.

Mary sidled up close to him. "Andy will know where I am, Rabbi."

I chuckled. "I'm not your rabbi yet. And don't worry, I can find you wherever you are. I will search for you until I find you like a shepherd looking for a lost lamb." I had trouble with locations, but I could always find another person by tuning into their soul's energy signature. With my divine senses, I breathed in their soul-scents one last time so I would be sure to remember.

chapter four:
temptation

I HAD VISITED THE EDGES of the Judean wilderness before, but now I pushed farther into the wilderness and just *stayed* there, without trying to leave it or change it. I hiked for hours through steep, desolate canyons and gorges without seeing another person. Thorns and dead thistles poked out of cracks in the parched soil, rattling in the hot wind and scratching at my legs.

I found a small cave in a mountainside where I rested during the heat of the day. Staring out at the hard, blue sky and the stark mountains, I reminded myself that God alone was enough for me. The Holy Spirit was there, but Her presence seemed to expose me to harsh reality rather than shielding me from it. Perhaps I pushed Her away with my fears of the raw sexual powers that She had released in me. Sometimes I got to see a hawk or a vulture hovering high above the earth. At dawn and dusk, I ventured out, along with the creatures who became my companions: ants, beetles, grasshoppers, locusts. These small friends kept me company. I enjoyed the chance to get to know them and their ways more fully.

I was a few days into my fast—lonely and hungry—when I heard a new voice speak right to my divine heart.

"If you're the son of God, then make this stone into bread."

My belly froze. The disembodied voice was penetrating, impossible to ignore, with a raspy edge of cruelty. I looked around the cave where I was hiding from the afternoon heat. I couldn't see the speaker, but I noticed a stone at the mouth of the cave. That stone was the same shape and size as a loaf of bread. The words both seduced and challenged me. Maybe I could use my divinity to create food out of stone if I tried. Now I was curious as well as hungry, but I was determined to obey the Holy Spirit's command to fast.

"It is written, 'We do not live on bread alone,'" I replied, overcoming the first layer of the challenge.

"Of course you don't live by bread alone," the voice agreed. It had an absence of gender because it came from someone who couldn't create and wouldn't love. In my native language the word for "enemy" was "satan," and that is what I decided to call this force that opposed me.

Satan continued speaking. "You are nourished by your relationship with your cousin the Baptist and the rest of your human family." The voice twanged as Satan tuned it along the spectrum from male to female and back again in search of the mix to which I was most vulnerable: just slightly male.

"Your family doesn't understand or approve of what you're doing. Don't let their hearts turn to stone against you," he urged.

I fought back tears. The Baptist's rejection still hurt—and I still wished that he would support me as I had imagined. I replayed my last visit to him over and over in my mind, wondering what would have happened if I had said or done something differently. I was tempted to go back to him now and try to win his approval. My human side wanted to change *my* behavior, while my divinity felt an even more dangerous urge: To actually change what the Baptist thought and felt about me. I could easily overpower human will if I wanted to do so.

I was clinging to the special relationship with my cousin and my mother. God wanted to break open my whole definition of family, so anyone could join it and be that close to me. I resisted. Being human, it was hard for me to open my heart that wide. My experience with the Baptist proved to me that it was an illusion to think that my family could fully support me. Satan tempted me to chase that illusion, to turn my relationship with my family into "bread" when it was really "stone" in the world that God created, where human will was precious and inviolable. If I violated human will, would I still be God and would the coerced devotion still be love? No, my true bread lay elsewhere.

With so many thoughts and emotions spinning through my head, I had to concentrate hard to remember the end of the scripture that I had quoted before. "It is written, 'We do not live on bread alone, but God's word keeps us alive.'"

Satan seemed to retreat and my thoughts turned to John and the unfinished way that we had left things between us. My sexual entanglements always lead to trouble. Every time I fell in love with a person, the relationship ended badly when it became clear that I wouldn't perform sexually, but then again none of them had ever been able to see my divinity as John did. Maybe he would ask me to be his rabbi as Mary and Andrew did. I began imagining where our kisses would lead.

I became so lost in the fantasy that I almost didn't notice Satan's voice urging me onward. "That's right. You can feed on your new disciples. Make them into your bread and eat them alive."

"No! I live on God's word."

And so it went, with Satan's temptations rippling through my divinity in ways far beyond human comprehension. He had devious ways of wrapping one temptation inside of another, and then another, so what seemed hard to resist at first was actually much harder, and then harder still—perfectly crafted to exploit my vulnerabilities and disarm me. My own responses also echoed to the depths of infinity, as did my victories. I triumphed every time, only to face a more wrenching battle.

As Satan dug deeper into me, tempting me in ways that I could not consciously perceive, I discovered that my human self could support my divine heart by praying. I began honing my prayers to their bare bones, simple phrases that I could remember and pray through gritted teeth in times of distress. "Give us this day our daily bread," I prayed.

After I had been in the desert wilderness for a few days, larger beings began to trust and approach me. First came mice and hares, then gazelles and jackals.

They invited me to follow them and showed me their secret places where I could find enough water to survive. I expected the rainy season to come at any time to replenish the watering holes. The days were hot, but the nights were surprisingly chilly. Every night I wrapped myself tight in my woolen cloak and found a crevice in the warm earth where I could watch the heavens as I fell asleep. The hooting of owls and the howling of wolves mirrored my mood as they sang me to sleep.

The creatures who made the biggest impression on me during this period were the snakes, because people had taught me that they were my enemy. Some of the snakes in the desert were deadly: adders and asps, cobras and vipers. When they started coming to me, my human self wanted to kill them or run away as I had been taught, but there was nowhere to run if I wanted to stay in the wilderness, and I had chosen to fast from killing as well as from eating. I considered throwing rocks at them to scare them away, but I thought that might provoke them to strike. I ended up spending a lot of time watching them. I became fascinated by the way they slithered on their bellies through the dust and by their inquisitive, darting tongues. Occasionally their beady eyes glanced at me.

I remembered the story that I had been taught in synagogue about how a serpent had tempted the first humans to disobey my Father by eating fruit from the tree of knowledge of good and evil. They said He had responded by cursing the serpent to crawl on its belly and become an enemy. I searched my divine memory for my own recollection of such a curse. Ages ago, before I had my own separate life, I had created snakes, knowing that they would cause trouble. I had forgotten why.

My human self alternated between worshipping God and staring at snakes. I tried to keep track of the passing days by watching the phases of the moon. My wilderness fast had gone on for at least a month, and still the rains did not come. Satan, however, returned to speak to me again. There was indeed something snake-like about his invisible presence.

"You can have it all," he hissed, and in an instant he transported me to the top of the mountain where my cave was located. He coaxed me into using my divine senses to take in the glory of the world's kingdoms in every time and place, all compressed into one moment in time. Every soul lay open to me. Satan had a way of heightening my senses, or perhaps just whetting my appetite, so that I was mesmerized by the earth's potential. "I'll give it all to you, if you bow down and worship me."

I would never worship Satan! I hated his lies and the damage they did. "Get out of here! For it is written, 'Worship God, and don't serve anyone else.'"

"Don't be so hasty. Think about it. I'll let you run things your way. You can transform it into the kingdom your Father wants. What will you do first, create peace on earth? Will you do it by eliminating all their weapons? Or will you erase the ability to hate from their souls?"

He got me thinking. I could do all those things now! I didn't have to bow down to Satan in order to impose that kind of peace.

Or did I? I doubted that I could achieve the results my Father wanted by using methods that He forbid. If people weren't free to hate, they couldn't really love, either.

As Satan measured my responses, I experienced a pleasant emotion that I had only felt before in the presence of God: another being's appreciation of my true power. No human could understand my omnipotence and the self-restraint required in order to grant free will to human beings. They underestimated the value and cost of my greatest gift to them.

Shyly, I glanced at Satan for the first time. He had no visual appearance. We were opposites, but he was also a lot like my divine heart—a powerful supernatural being created by my Father and the Holy Spirit...created by *me*. I was still struggling to fathom why I had created my own enemy. The reason defied words, but it was there, lurking in the depths of my divine memory.

"It is written, 'Worship God, and don't serve anyone else.'" My words were the same, but Satan knew I meant them differently. I was reminding him to worship *me!*

He retreated, without surrendering. It would take more than turning the tables to resolve our relationship. Again he delved into my divinity and we struggled with more subtle variations on the theme of who would worship whom while my human awareness stayed in the wilderness. It was hot on the mountaintop and I was thirsty, so I hiked back down to my cave.

I had already used up the last of the water in my vessels. I waited until the cool of dusk, and then I went with the animals to the nearest watering hole where I hoped to refill my vessels as usual. The water hole had dried up. It was long past the time when the rainy season should have started. Discouraged, I watched the animals sniff and paw at the mud. I stared up into the sky. A few clouds, looking as dry as wads of wool, straggled across the heavens. The trip back to my cave seemed longer and more rugged than ever.

When I got there, I prayed over and over, "Your kingdom come," the same prayer that John and I had chanted before we kissed.

What came at dawn were more snakes. This time I was not alarmed. Here in the wilderness, I had learned how to tune into the thoughts of snakes. Now I picked the most open-minded snake and tried to send a thought to her. She was an elderly snake with a thick body and dull brown scales that matched the dust that coated them. Her venom was poisonous and I had seen her needle-sharp fangs once when she ate a mouse. She lay coiled up a few feet away from me.

I used my human mind like a buffer, slowing and simplifying a divine thought for her. "I love you," I thought down into reptilian thought-vibrations.

"Love? What is that? I only know what I can touch and smell." She flicked her tongue toward me, as if she might be able to taste this interesting mystery called "love" in the air.

We stayed like that a long time. I kept trying to communicate love to her all through the heat of the day and another thirsty night. The sun rose again, but still the rains did not come. Another day without water would kill me. I realized that there was only one way to make the snake understand. I was no longer controlled by the fear of death. I held out my hand to the snake.

"Come to me and let me love you," I invited. She might kill me, but she would learn what love was. Maybe this was where God wanted me to die.

Satan's voice interrupted my thoughts. "If you are the son of God…" he began. Suddenly he transported me far out of reach of the snakes, all the way to the pinnacle at the southeast corner of the Temple complex in Jerusalem. I was really there in the flesh, poised at the edge of a sheer drop from the highest point in Jerusalem down to boulders and thorn bushes on the floor of the Kidron Valley far, far below. My stomach flip-flopped as I looked down. It made me so dizzy that I almost lost my balance.

"You like to prop yourself up with what is written? Try these scriptures: 'He will order the angels to guard you' and 'The angels will carry you, so you won't hurt your foot on a stone.' If you believe that, go ahead and jump."

He was using my own weapon against me: scripture. Yes, I could have the angels catch me, but neither my Father nor the Holy Spirit wanted me to use my powers like that. In this way, Satan tempted me to defy God in order to do God's will.

I challenged Satan back. "Don't you know my Father would send me a million angels if I asked? But God has other plans for me."

"Go on, take a flying leap," he taunted.

I knew that I would have to die someday to fulfill my

destiny. I considered jumping without asking the angels to save me. For a moment, I thought dying sooner would be a shortcut to salvation for me and for the world. I could save myself a lot of suffering and do the world a favor by dying now, before my time, and yet I wasn't sure whether two aspects of God could stand in opposition to each other and still be God.

Turning to look over at the Temple, I drew energy from all the prayers being lifted to God there. I, too, prayed. It felt like breathing in fresh air. I found the strength to wait. I would neither hasten nor control the circumstances of my death. I trusted the plan that my Father and the Holy Spirit had chosen—that We had chosen, for I remembered Our oneness. I could feel encouragement radiating from my future self, the one that John had described sitting on a throne in heaven wrapped in a rainbow. It was exciting and also humbling to think that I would be exalted so.

I steadied myself, then glared at Satan and commanded, "It is written, 'Don't test God.'"

Instantly, I was back in the cave with my hand stretching out to the snake. The cool of dawn still hung in the air, as if no time had passed at all. "Your will be done," I prayed. I could sense that this was my most powerful prayer, the one that was tipping the balance so that my divine heart could overcome the cascade of temptations that continued outside my human consciousness.

To the snake, I sent a thought: "Let me love you." I tried to speak the words aloud, too, but my throat was so dry I could only whisper.

The old snake slid over to me, slow and silent. I

allowed her to flick her tongue over my hand. I made myself stay motionless as I felt her feathery inspection. Then she touched me! I didn't even flinch. My stability reassured her. She gently placed her head atop my hand and began to move up my arm. Her dark skin was surprisingly soft. She felt leathery and cool, the same temperature as the rocks in the cave, but I could sense her warming through contact with my skin. She stopped when her head was near my elbow.

I listened for her thoughts and tried to translate them, using my human mind to amplify them for my divine heart. "You are warm!" she was thinking. "I want warmth. Your arm is like a snake, but different: stiff inside, with strange skin."

"What is your name?" I asked.

"Name? I only know what I can touch and smell."

"Name is what other snakes call you. What do other snakes think when they think of you?"

She had rarely considered the thoughts of other snakes. It took her a long time to find the answer. "Old snake."

Fondness for her welled up in me. "Your name is Old Snake."

"Your name is Enemy," she hissed.

I felt insulted and stifled the impulse to push her off me. Instead, I began sending love to myself as well as to Old Snake. "No. My name is not Enemy," I told her firmly.

"When other snakes think of you, they think enemy."

I smiled. "Yes, I understand. But that is not what other *people* think when they think of me."

"What is people?" Living in the most remote part of the wilderness, she may never have met a human being before. If she did, she had made no distinction between people and other predators.

I squeezed my thoughts into her language. "That is not what other…enemies…think when they think of me."

"What enemies think?!" She had assumed that enemies lacked the ability to think. Old Snake struggled for a while to understand what I was trying to communicate, then gave up and basked in my warmth.

I concentrated and searched her whole energy system for what else would please her. Only love could enable me to look this deep into the mind of a snake. I discovered a subtle vibration within Old Snake that could be brought into harmony with me. I hummed my love to her in that tone, striking a chord of unity. "Will you let me touch you?" I hummed.

She gave a long, drawn-out hiss. "Yesss." Her eyes gleamed at me, still wary.

I could feel exactly where and how she would like to be caressed, almost as if she were a part of my own body. With slow deliberation, I moved my other hand to the top of her spine just behind her head, and let my fingertips make contact with energy centers embedded there, well beyond the range of ordinary perception. To me, they felt chilly and dense. It was much easier for me to hum my love songs into her with my fingers in this position. She lay still, soaking my melodies into herself along with my warmth. I felt myself relax and trust Old Snake more, too. I began to let my fingers dance in a slow, serpentine pattern, as if I were playing a flute.

I lost all track of time as we both enjoyed being synchronized with each other. Then beneath my fingertips, I felt a faint new vibration stir. It originated way deep inside the snake, so far away that its genesis was not within Old Snake's particular being, but in the snake-energy field that gave rise to all snakes everywhere throughout all time. My fingertips quivered as I strained to hear what she was trying to tell me.

"I..." she stammered. "I...*love*...you."

I connected with the unified core of myself that was deeper than the separation of opposites. I felt a rush of well-being. Yes, from this place I could embrace all possibilities, including the parts of me that didn't seem to be me. My divine heart reached to embrace Satan with love—not to bow down and worship him, but to love him. I brushed against him, a feeling not unlike touching Old Snake. Satan fled. Love scared the hell out of him.

Something was different in the cave and it wasn't just Satan's absence. I heard many breaths breathing. Angels, I thought.

"Moo." That was no angel! I looked up.

The cave was filled with animals and angels. The angels were like snatches of melody or wisps of light, singing a prophecy from Isaiah that I had loved since childhood. As they sang, Isaiah's vision materialized right before my eyes and I was part of it: "The wolf shall live with the lamb. The leopard and the young goat shall lie down together while the lion cub makes friends with the calf, with a little child to guide them. The baby shall play near the cobra's hole. Nobody will be hurt or injured on my holy mountain, for the earth will be flooded with the knowledge of God as water fills the sea."

Overjoyed, I looped Old Snake around my shoulders and watched with her as the animal enemies sniffed each other and tried to figure out how to express friendship to another species. There were whole families of each kind of animal, plus many species that Isaiah didn't name. I especially enjoyed seeing a full-grown wolf crouch before a lamb, laying his chin on the ground to bring himself down to non-threatening lamb level and sweeping his tail his tail back and forth to show that he wanted to play. Then a leopard cub pounced on his tail and all three rolled together in a mock wrestling match. The wolf used his toothy mouth like a hand to massage his little buddies.

Each of the animals also greeted me. I received their kisses, petted their fur, smelled their scents, and admired the beauty of each face close-up. They liked my whiskers because they reminded the animals of their own furred faces, and they liked my hands because none of them had anything like hands. They instinctively understood that human beings explore the world through their hands. They knew what I meant when I offered them my open palm in greeting or stroked them. I listened to their various yowls, growls, and other sounds. I also heard what was in their hearts and we had conversations similar to the one between me and Old Snake. Nobody was surprised anymore that enemies could think.

The scene reminded me of a story that Mom and Papa-Joe told me about my birth, so I tried to share it with the animals. "I was born in a stable, a place kind of like this cave," I began. It was tricky translating my thoughts into the vibrations of so many different species at once. Some understood more than others. "Animals were with me when I was born. There were some like you...and you...and you." I pointed at the sheep, the goats, the donkeys, and the oxen. "After I was born, I slept in a manger, a place where animals ate their food."

"Food!" Everyone was interested in this part of my story. We talked about food for a long time, until the sun began to set.

"You are like food. You make me feel good," Old Snake said to me, and the others sounded their agreement. She was coiled in my lap now, with her head on my knee. She spent a lot of time and effort forming her next thought for me. "What is your...*name*?"

"Jesus." They could hear me make the sound, but the meaning, which is something like "God saves," would not translate into their languages.

"Hiss-sus," Old Snake said, as she tried to pronounce my name. We all laughed together as the different animals attempted to say "Jesus."

I was no better at imitating their sounds. I laughed at myself even harder than I had laughed at their efforts. I had never noticed how funny human beings really are, just because we are human. At last we fell silent. I noticed that the animals were much better than humans at being together without conversation.

Old Snake cocked her head sideways and looked at me. "Try again. What is your name? What do other...*people*...think when they think of you?" We had all taught each other what we were: person, wolf, whatever.

I pondered her question for a while, remembering what the Baptist had said about me. "Son of Man. It means Someone, human one, an ordinary person."

"Your name is Sssson of Man!" she hissed with satisfaction and kissed my foot. The other animals murmured the name to each other. The last rays of light faded and the day eased into night. I was tired, cold, and incredibly thirsty.

The leopard cub's mother studied me with tawny, piercing eyes, keeping her head aristocratically high. At last she made me an offer. "I'll warm you. Curl up and sleep with me and my cubs."

Grateful, I lay down beside her, my belly curved against her sleek, speckled back. All day I had lived completely in the moment, thinking neither of the past nor of the future, but now agonizing thirst drove me to consider both. I realized that I would die the next day if I didn't get something to drink. My mind raced through various plans: Kill one of the animals to drink its blood? No, that was out of the question on this holy mountain. Ride an ox back to the Jordan River? I was probably too weak to survive the journey. Use my power to make it rain? That was like the temptations that I had just overcome. I really had believed that it would rain by now. I didn't understand why God would send me a peaceable animal kingdom, but not water. Not knowing what more God could want from me, I figured that I must be facing the death that God intended.

I began placing the loose ends of my life into God's care, beginning with my family. I wondered how they would fare when I was dead. I felt a lump rising in my throat. I made myself relax and snuggle against God in the same way that I was embracing the mother leopard. Then I remembered that the best way—the only way—to protect my relatives was to entrust them to God, who was already caring for them. I pictured them one by one, then released each of them to God's custody, ending with my brother Jim, then the Baptist, and finally Mom. I was only able to let go of her by trusting that God's strength and wisdom were greater than my own. I sensed how happy she felt in that moment as my Father's love enfolded her.

One promise remained that I had been unable to keep. I had told Mary and Andrew that I would return to talk with them about being their rabbi. Then there was John and the unspoken promises implicit in our kisses. I didn't know any of them well, so I was shocked to find myself hanging on to these three people more than I had clung to my blood family. I couldn't forget how good it felt when Mary and Andrew's souls cuddled directly against my divine heart. With John, all that held us together was a soul dance and a few kisses, but that was more than enough. All of them hungered for divine truths that I didn't think anybody else could teach them. I grieved for them as individuals and for what might have been between us. I kissed John one last time in my imagination and in my divine heart. With a sigh that was like a groan, I surrendered all three of them to God. Last of all, I relinquished my own life to God. I lapsed into a primal state and fell asleep, with my body still curled against the leopard.

✤ ✤ ✤

A faint light awakened me. I'm not sure if it was the predawn glow or the glimmer of angels, for angels were definitely there ministering to me and the mother leopard who purred beside me. Her cubs began to nurse. Guided by the angels, the mother leopard licked my face with her sand-paper tongue, then nudged me toward one of her nipples as if I were her own cub. The angels urged me to drink, too.

I was ready to end my fast, but not like that. An ingrained taboo seemed to scream in my blood: "No, adults don't to that! Humans don't do that!"

Then I felt the presence of the Holy Spirit, as if a fire had been kindled suddenly in my chest, radiating light and warmth. She spoke with such authority and love for me that I was willing to try whatever she asked. "Beloved Jesus, go ahead. Live."

I was overwhelmed, but my rational mind was still active, too. I wondered how I would know when it was my time to die.

I didn't address the question to the Holy Spirit, but She overheard and answered emphatically, "You'll know."

I took a few deep breaths, then heaved myself into the position designated by the angels. It was hard because I was shaky from dehydration and malnutrition. I placed my lips on the leopard's nipple, smelled her wild, earthy scent and sucked. I shivered when my first luscious mouthful of her warm milk hit my tongue and trickled into my stomach. My need for nourishment and its fulfillment melted into one automatic action as I drank my fill, cushioned by God's will and the leopard's willing body. I don't even remember falling asleep, for my mind had already been lulled into a zone beyond thought, beyond dreams.

Later a hushed, whispering sound persuaded me to begin waking up. Half asleep, I listened with my eyes closed, enjoying the blandness of the new sound without wondering what it was. I felt myself nestled, safe and secure, in the heart of the Holy Spirit. Gradually I noticed, then identified, the aroma of moist soil. I sat bolt upright and my eyes flew open to see if what I hoped was true: Yes, it was raining!

I stood and scrambled to the mouth of the cave, moving much better after my meal of leopard's milk. Rain was pouring down in sheets. Runoff from the mountaintop above formed rivulets that spilled down over the cave entrance in clear, cool streams. I cupped my hands under one of these mini-waterfalls. Soon my hands filled to overflowing and I drank. Water had never tasted so refreshing. My first words after wetting my throat were a song of praise to God.

I quickly gathered all my water vessels and began filling them while the animals lapped water from the puddles at my feet. When I was done, I filled my hands again, this time drinking slowly to savor the rainwater's fresh flavor and texture as I quenched my thirst. I began making plans to leave the wilderness when there was a lull in the rains. Between sips, I smiled down at my animal friends and saw that I was standing near the loaf-shaped stone that Satan had used to tempt me.

The Holy Spirit spoke to me. We were so united that Her voice in my mind came as no surprise. "I am the bread of life. Be the bread with me."

Overcome, I knelt down to pray. Old Snake came

and rested beside me without comment. She just wanted to be near me.

Then the Holy Spirit poured out an astonishing map of my future in terms I had never deemed or dreamed possible. With awe, I drank in the divine imagery that flowed into me as She kissed me. Together We cherished the vision of Our wedded future. It was so intense that even after We separated, I could still see myself as She saw me. I let the words play in my mind: "I am the living bread of heaven. Whoever eats my bread will live forever, and my life-giving bread is my very own flesh."

chapter five:
fishing

AS SOON AS I LEFT THE WILDERNESS, I tried to find Mary and Andrew. They were no longer at the Baptist's camp, so I walked back north to the Sea of Galilee where Andrew said he would be fishing. Since he and John were fishing partners, I expected I would run into John there, too. For better or worse, I was going to have to face the man who had run away from my kisses. I was afraid that I was too much for him. I wondered what, if anything, he had been thinking of me. I tried to keep my expectations low about John.

I arrived at the seashore near the town of Capernaum before dawn so that I would be there when the fishers rowed ashore from their night's work. After such a long period in the desert, my body delighted in Galilee's greenery and the freshwater sea with its autumn scent and the soothing lap of waves on the shore. I stripped off all my clothes and bathed naked in the sea, washing away the grime from my fast, drinking my fill, letting every pore soak in the water. I danced and praised God with the carp and eels, the sardines and the lampreys. I splashed in the cool, moonlit waves until the dawn turned them pearly gray.

When the small wooden fishing boats began coming in, I went ashore and turned away from them to dry off. I sensed someone's eyes on my back. I couldn't help smiling as I recognized the flow of fiery gems in the soul behind those eyes.

I put on my loincloth and turned around to see John jogging up to me. "Andy said you'd be here. I've been watching for you." The exertion of rowing and running made his skin glow while sweat sparkled in his silvery curls.

I tried to sound casual. "Hi, Beloved."

When he heard me use my special nickname for him, he wrapped his arms loosely around me and clasped me to his chest. We held each other for a while, enjoying the sensation of his flesh against mine and mine against his. It had been a long time since anyone had hugged me.

As our embrace continued, I whispered, "I thought about you during my fast."

When John heard that, he clutched me much more tightly, so I could feel the full length and strength of his lean, muscular body with my bare skin. His warm, moist breath sounded loud as it blew into my ear, which was at the same height as his mouth. He ran his large hands over my ribs and then released me.

"You're much thinner! Have you been fasting in the desert all this time? It's been more than forty days."

"Have you been counting?" I teased.

He laughed off my question, but concern clouded his deep-set eyes. "We have to get you something to eat."

"How about some fish," I suggested. I began putting on my tunic and cloak.

"We didn't catch any last night. We have some bread and dried fish, though. Come have breakfast with us. Andy is eager to see you again."

John pointed me toward their boats and we set off together. Andrew jumped from his boat and ran to me, yelling, "Rabbi! You're here! Welcome!" Happiness lit up his breezy soul and kind face, which still had a trace of baby fat.

After a quick hug, he announced, "I want you to meet my brother." He led me and John over to a boat where someone with a solid, earthy soul was still tending the nets.

"Simon, leave everything and get over here! This is the one we were telling you about!" Andrew called.

The brother climbed out of the boat and faced me.

"This is the Messiah," Andrew announced. The simplicity of his introduction caught me off-guard. Then I realized that nothing more needed to be said.

I tuned into my human senses to study Andrew's brother. He was conventionally handsome, with craggy features, a prominent brow, a full head of wavy hair and an impressively profuse beard. The strength of his soul kept my attention.

"You're like a rock!" I exclaimed. "I'll call you Peter." Sometimes I liked giving people nicknames, so we could be on familiar terms right away. The name I gave him meant "rock" in our language. We all spoke Aramaic with the same Galilean accent.

Peter crossed his arms. While Andrew was eager to impress his big brother, Peter saw himself as his little brother's guardian. "My name is Simon," he retorted. "And you're not the first Messiah that Andrew has run off to meet when he should be home fishing. The last one was the Baptist and before him there were a couple more. Israel is full of Messiahs who want to free our people from the Roman oppressors."

Embarrassed by Peter's hostility, Andrew tried to make excuses. "One of my brother's best traits is that he says what he means and means what he says. He always keeps his word."

"Always?" I asked. "Is that how it is for you?"

"Andy tends to exaggerate—in case you hadn't noticed," he replied pointedly.

I laughed and he began to relax. I looked in Peter's brown eyes. His soul opened to me. All the future possibilities of what could happen between us—and because of us—washed through my divine awareness in one breath-taking whole. I also sensed the certainties that would be shattered by contact with me. I ached when I felt the strength in Peter that would have to be broken in order to make him even stronger. The sorrow of it made me hesitate for a moment.

"Well, you *are* the first Messiah to visit us here at the seaside," Peter conceded. "Let's talk together over breakfast."

"I'll get the food from the boat," Andrew said.

I stopped him. "Would you take me out to sea in your boat and we could talk there? I love boats and it would feel so good to be out on the water after weeks in the desert. Plus we could have some private time there."

Other fishers and their families were already gathering around us to listen. Mary was nowhere to be seen. "Good idea," Andrew said. "I don't know why all these people are crowding around us."

"It's been happening to me ever since I left the wilderness. People like my stories and they say I heal them."

"Do you mean—"

Before Andrew could finish his question, we were joined by a man whose soul was similar to John's, but more subdued. "Hey, I want you to meet my brother James," John announced.

"Hello," he said simply. James looked a lot like his brother, except older and less striking. "Let's get away from this crowd."

They all climbed onto Andrew and Peter's boat and sat on the seats in rowing positions. The boat rocked when I stepped aboard. I chose to sit in the middle on the boat's floor. The wood itself welcomed me, creaking as it told me about its exploits as a boat.

"Nice boat," I said. "Built from at least a dozen different kinds of wood. These cedar boards must have been expensive."

All their eyes lit up. "You know boats!"

"I used to be a carpenter." It was the first time that I had tried out "used to be" regarding my old identity. They accepted it as completely natural and started rowing.

The crowd on shore cried out to us. "Can we come, too?" they begged.

"They're so hungry for the word of God," I said. "Keep the boat near the shore at first so they can listen, too."

Peter obliged by dropping a stone anchor there. John looked at me with care. "Eat something before you teach."

Andrew passed bread and dried fish to everyone on the boat. I said a quick blessing and began to eat. The meal tasted delicious to me, even though the bread was stale and the fish was tough with a strong fishy flavor. I felt gratitude and wholeness as I allowed the food to become one with my body. John watched me eat with a bemused sparkle in his eyes.

While we were eating, I considered how to present my ideas to the people who were with me that morning. Others had been calling me the Messiah, but this was going to be my first public self-declaration.

John noticed when I swallowed my last bite. "Wash it down with some of my wine," he offered. He held out his own personal wine skin to me so that I could drink from it directly instead of using a cup.

I scooted over in order to reach it, then leaned against his legs while I threw my head back and guzzled some of his watery wine. He placed his hand tenderly on my shoulder and let it linger there while I drank.

The others studied our interaction with benign interest, then exchanged knowing glances. I remembered that John had warned me of his reputation for sexual conquests. His friends were drawing their own conclusions about what type of intimacy we had shared. Meanwhile we continued to touch each other without shame. Their speculations didn't hold their attention for long.

"Tell us, Rabbi, what you have to teach," Peter asked.

I felt a sense of adventure as I began to speak, following the format used in the synagogue: Quote a prophet, then comment on the quotation. "The prophet Isaiah said, 'The Holy Spirit has anointed me to preach good news to the poor. God has sent me to announce freedom to the captives and sight to the blind, to liberate those in bondage and to proclaim the year of God's blessings.' You have just heard this scripture fulfilled."

I saw resistance on every face. I began to bounce ideas back and forth with the group of fisherfolk.

"Andrew, I told you before that you could ask me anything, and I make the same invitation to the rest of you. You can ask me anything. *Anything.*"

"Well," Andrew began, "why didn't you read the whole prophecy? You stopped in the middle of a sentence. Isaiah said he came to proclaim the year of God's blessings—*and* the day of God's vengeance."

"Yes. We love that part," John chimed while his brother nodded his zealous agreement.

"You're like sons of thunder, rumbling threats against sinners," I chuckled. "My purpose is forgiveness, not vengeance. You know what the psalm says about my Father: 'God is kind and generous, slow to anger and full of intense love.'"

"Your father?!" Peter exclaimed. "What's he got to do with it?"

"When I say 'Father,' I mean God."

"How dare you call him Father!" Peter protested. "He is the king of glory, *far* above us."

"You can call him Father, too. Start your prayers by saying, 'Our Father in heaven, holy is your name.'"

The idea of being so close to God had an obvious appeal to everyone listening. Since he couldn't deny it would be nice to have God as his parent, Peter changed the subject back to forgiveness. "How often should I keep forgiving someone who sins against me? As many as seven times?"

"Not seven times. I say seventy times seven times."

"That's not fair!" John protested.

"You're right," I replied. "I'm talking about something well beyond justice, and it's okay to be angry about it. I myself couldn't preach forgiveness until I was blessed by someone with the spiritual gift of rage: my cousin, the Baptist. God invites us to enter a process of forgiveness so deep that it is a kind of death."

Many people looked upset, but even those who disagreed with me did not turn away. Someone on shore cried out, "You said you came with good news. Where is it?"

I felt frustrated. Obviously they missed the point that forgiveness benefits those who forgive as well as those who are forgiven. I was ready to draw this part to a close and give them time to reflect. "Here is the good news: Repent, because God's kingdom is near!"

"That's exactly what the Baptist preached," Andrew said.

"Yes, but I take it much deeper. God's kingdom—the place where God lives and holds power—is right here with us, close enough to touch." I put my hand on Andrew's shoulder. "And also here inside each one of us." I touched my own heart. "You can enter the kingdom of heaven right now."

"How?" Andrew asked.

"What does the Law say?" I shot back.

"You shall love God with your whole heart, and with your whole soul, and with your whole strength, and with your whole mind—and love your neighbor as yourself," he replied.

"Exactly," I concluded.

I looked around at each of the fishers in the boat with me and added, "Take us out to the deep now."

✛ ✛ ✛

They seemed to enjoy the physical labor of getting the boat moving. I used my human eyes to observe them as they rowed. We all looked a lot alike with our dark eyes, bronze skin, and black hair and beards. I could tell they were showing off for me as they maneuvered the boat over the placid waters and through sea-places they knew well. I let myself be refreshed by the sea breezes, the newly risen sun, and the wide open space around us. When the shore became a lovely blue-green strip on the distant horizon, they let the boat drift and gathered around me.

"I told you the kingdom of heaven is in the midst of you. What would you say to God if He was *right here* in this boat *right now*?"

They said nothing.

"Come on, I really want to know. I want to listen."

They began by repeating the standard prayers that we had all memorized in the synagogue. Then we took turns choosing a favorite psalm to sing together. Compared to the others, my voice was on pitch and emotive, compensating for their deficiencies. John pulled his flute out of his bag and accompanied us as we sang. The force of his soul came through in his artistry and struck me again with its beauty. I listened in delight as I sang along. I watched John's knotty fingers as he moved them over the flute, appreciating how the act of playing through the painful stiffness actually heightened the evocative power of his music. John felt my gaze and thought I was looking at his flute, which was carved from a reed.

"Do you play the flute too?" he asked.

"Well, yes, actually," I replied. "I used to carve flutes and other musical instruments. I had to learn how to play them well enough to test their sound quality."

John handed me his flute. "I'd love to hear you play."

"Yes, yes," they all chimed.

I took some time to tune into his instrument as I ran my fingers over the smooth reed and the holes roughly gashed into it. It was much cruder than any of the flutes I had carved. It reminded me of Old Snake and a serpent song that she had taught me. "This song came to me while I was fasting in the wilderness," I said, and began to play.

They listened politely, shifting uncomfortably in their seats as if they felt a tingling at the base of the spine. The snake lullaby seemed monotonous to them. I chuckled, played a quick refrain from a Galilean folk song and handed the flute back to John.

"What else would you like to tell God?" I asked.

"I would tell God of my longing for the Messiah who will bring us the just, peaceful world that is promised in scripture," John said.

James, who rarely spoke, piped up now. "Tell him about the thunder and lightning."

"After the Messiah comes, fire will come down from heaven and consume all the people who are deceived by Satan," John said.

He and his brother both looked so enthusiastic at

this gruesome prospect that I laughed dryly. "You like that part? You truly are sons of thunder."

"We all long for God's vengeance," Peter said. "The money-grubbing Roman oppressors are ruining our nation. They're stealing our wealth with their outrageous taxes. Our people are starving so Roman pigs can get fat and rich while they corrupt our morals with their filthy, heathen ways. Our so-called leaders, like the high priest and King Herod, are all pawns, collaborators, and sell-outs. This is our land, but if we object to their policies, they murder us!" He almost capsized the boat with violent gestures as he shouted his rage.

John escalated the emotional pitch even higher. "Here's what I would tell God: 'I want those cruel bastards to feel every bit of the pain they inflicted on us!' Remember when Governor Pilate took money from our Temple and used it to build an aqueduct? My friend Samuel was involved in that big protest against it and the governor had him killed for it."

John began to weep, but the passion behind his story drove him to keep talking. "I should have been with Sam when he died, but I didn't understand what was happening until it was too late. We never got to say goodbye."

James hugged his sobbing brother. "I thought you got over this years ago," he said.

"Me, too," Peter and Andrew both added in dismay.

I wanted to console John with my embrace, too, but he was already growing calmer in James' arms. This was my time to listen and keep my distance. I did not offer them any explanation, absolution, or words of wisdom. All I gave them was my attention.

When John spoke again, his voice was clear, but despondent. "I didn't get over it. I just stopped talking about it. I *loved* Sam! So much of my life is dead now. I could walk away from my life in Galilee tomorrow and I wouldn't miss it at all."

Peter's brow furrowed with sympathy. "At least you have a good reason," he said in a low tone. "I feel the same way, and nothing bad has happened to me. Everyone thinks I'm a big success as a fisherman and a family man, but it feels empty to me. There must be more to life than catching fish, raising kids, and traipsing up to Jerusalem once a year to celebrate Passover. I have the potential to do something more, but I don't know what that something is."

Andrew stared at his brother in disbelief. "I didn't know you felt that way."

"Just because I fulfill my responsibilities here instead of chasing after every Messiah who comes along doesn't mean that I don't share your dreams," Peter snapped at his brother.

I intervened. "What else would you say to God if He was right here?" I asked Peter.

"I have nothing left to say," he sighed. "If God was here, I'd say, 'Lord, you say something. I'm listening.'"

"Let's try that," I said. "Let's sit together in silence and listen for God's voice."

I listened, too, opening as fully as I could to my divine heart and stretching that part of me toward my Father until I could feel our oneness, as if His breath moved my breath, while the wind of the Holy Spirit blew over the water and right through me. The boat rocked gently beneath the cloudless sky as the late-morning sun warmed me. I sensed the souls of the four fishers draw near to me.

Broken places in their souls seemed to cry out to me, and the longer I listened, the more they sounded like hungry babies bawling to be fed. I began to have the strange but unmistakable impression that my divine heart had grown something like breasts and these four wailing souls made them feel full and achy. I longed to cuddle and nurse their souls, but I wasn't sure whether I should.

I heard the silent voice of the Holy Spirit in my mind. "Go ahead. Feed them."

In the physical world, we still floated in a boat on the sea, but in a realm outside of time and space I let them nuzzle my divine heart while I cradled them. The direct soul-contact thrilled me as it did before, but this time I was more prepared. I kept quiet, unlike on the previous occasion. The souls were adorable and irresistible to me, so I guided them to places like nipples on my divine heart.

Souls speak a language of light, and in that language, I asked them, "Do you want me to feed you?"

Their soul-mouths opened.

The Holy Spirit showed me how to help them latch onto me. They sucked hard and it hurt. I worried that they might be draining me of some kind of energy that I needed. Again the Holy Spirit helped, repositioning me so my milk could flow more easily and assuring me that I was doing what God had prepared for me to do. Feelings of tenderness caused my divine heart to open wider, and I let the hungry souls draw love-energy directly from me.

I relaxed into the new sensations and began to feel both proud and shy like a first-time mother. I found that I had the capacity to nurse all of them at once. There was no end to the love that flowed through me. I had never allowed myself to give to others so deeply. Throughout my lifetime, none of the people around me had ever been aware of what happened at the soul level, but this time I wondered if maybe they would sense the change because for me it was so profound.

Andrew broke the silence. "You said we should turn our lives around and follow the commandment to love, but I still don't know how to do that."

"Here's how: Follow me. I invite all of you," I answered. "None of my followers will ever walk in darkness, but will possess the light of life."

There, I said it! I had never said such a thing to anyone before. I glanced in each one's eyes to make sure they knew they were all included, then I looked away, releasing them to the bottoms of their souls, and waited to see if they would reject me. I was not used to the vulnerability of showing others how much I *longed* for them to help me live out my divinity on earth. It was the first time that I actively drew others into a plan that I knew would vastly increase their suffering as well as their joy, and the joy of all humanity. I would have been afraid in that moment if I hadn't found a way to rest against God's strength, like I did at the end of my fast.

The sun felt hot, and I reached into the sea and splashed water on my face. Below the surface I sensed a multitude of fish swimming near me, offering their life force to help me through a pivotal moment in my life.

I nestled further into God and tried to focus on the splendor of human will, free will, so precious. They could say no to me and it was okay, even *good*. To my divine senses, each human will looked like a cord of spun silver. But I didn't look at my companions with my human eyes because they might not be able to resist the longing they would see there. I refused to manipulate their decision and buy their loyalty by performing some miracle, either. I didn't know what I would say if they asked for more explanation. I was looking for faith, not agreement on a particular plan of action.

Their souls were nursing from me, but I knew that all souls draw on God's love for nourishment. It had no bearing on how they would choose to live their lives. God is all-knowing and yet there is one thing that God doesn't know: how a particular human being will decide to use his or her free will. I knew I would fulfill my purpose, but I didn't know if John, Andrew, Peter, or James would be a part of it. I waited to see if they would decide to love me back.

I thought if anyone would join me, it would be Andrew first, since he was so enthusiastic right after I was baptized. Instead, Peter spoke. "I will follow you."

"Peter! My rock!" I embraced him and he laughed.

"Yes, I'll even let you call me that if you like."

Almost in unison the others pledged to follow me and we all bonded in one long group hug.

"I want to give you a gift," I announced impulsively. "Lower your nets for a catch."

"Rabbi, I didn't think you'd be testing us so soon," Peter said. "We worked all night and caught nothing! But if you say so, I'll let down the nets."

"It's not a test," I protested. I didn't think they would be doubting me so soon.

They stood and skillfully cast overboard a large drag-net secured to a ring of buoys.

"Hey, we have a catch!" Peter cried. He and the others stripped off most of their clothes and began to haul in the net filled with fish. Their bulging muscles gleamed in the sunlight. They spilled dozens of perch, carp, and sea sardines onto the bottom of the boat, and still the catch was so large that their nets began to break. We had drifted much closer to shore by this time, so Peter signaled to their friends on land to row out another boat to help haul in the catch. The crowd had grown many times larger while we were gone.

The boat was filled knee deep in flipping, flapping, floundering fish. The fishers shouted back and forth to each other in exultation.

"I've never seen a catch this big!"

"I've never *heard of* a catch this big!"

I just smiled and with my divine heart greeted and thanked each fish individually as its life force merged back into my own.

They filled both of the boats with so many fish that we began to sink. Peter fell down at my knees and cried, "Get away from me, Lord. I'm a bad man."

I knelt down among the slippery fishes and held him in my arms as he sobbed huge wracking sobs. "Peter, you are not to judge yourself. God is your only judge."

"That's what I'm afraid of! Just take Andy with you—he has sought God all along while I—" He choked as tears prevented him from saying what was in his heart. He wasn't used to my bold way of touching or the intensity of emotion I could stir in him.

Since he wanted to tell me his sins, I took a careful glance at them before I let forgiveness wash them from his soul into the bottomless oblivion of God's compassionate forgetfulness. A layer of his soul that had been like a rock relaxed and seemed to swallow divine forgiveness as it flowed through me. He wept on as I held him. "Peter, my beloved rock, your sins are forgiven," I repeated several times.

For me it was gratifying to have someone receive from me so deeply. I felt his soul move so that his heart, mind, body, and soul were all in alignment with God. I was sure that he could sense the shift on some level, so I whispered in his ear, "You are now in the right position between a soul and its God. A human soul is designed to be constantly asking for and accepting God's forgiveness."

Peter moaned softly. I detected a movement in a divine part of myself that was almost outside the range of my conscious mind. I sensed, just barely, a holy energy imprinting this position onto Peter's being, marking him as God's own in some new way and leaving a pattern that would make it easier for him to stay in and return to this position in the future. Peter's sobs grew shallower and less frequent as his breath gradually returned to normal. The others had rowed us almost to shore.

"Don't be afraid. From now on you'll be catching people instead of fish," I told him.

That made Peter laugh. I began to get up, but first he pulled my ear toward his lips and whispered, "Thank you."

Then I stood and addressed my new disciples.

"When we reach land, I'm going to be mobbed. I want to spend some time with the crowd, but then I want one of you to take me to a place where I can rest and spend the night. We'll all be leaving tomorrow."

They conferred and agreed that Peter would take me to the house in Capernaum where he and Andrew lived with their extended family.

"Be sure to bring along enough fish for yourselves and your families and friends," I added.

"What should we do with all the rest of this huge catch?" Andrew asked.

"They're my gift to you. You can do whatever you like with them."

"We could sell them and make a lot of money. There must be more than one hundred fifty large fish here," Peter said. "Rabbi, how much money will we need where we are going?"

"None."

There was an uncomfortable silence as they studied me in a new way, trying to figure out how much money I had, if any. My clothes were dirty and ragged from my stay in the wilderness. I had left behind even the bag and staff that Mary and Andrew had watched me pack. Instead of carrying my supplies, I preferred to establish a connection with the strangers I met on the road by allowing them to provide for my basic needs. My first disciples correctly guessed that I had nothing with me but the clothes on my back. "God will provide," I assured them.

They opened their mouths to protest, but each one stopped before any sound came out. How could they deny the truth of my words, when they were still struggling to haul in my gift to them, the biggest catch they had ever seen? It hit them then just how different their lives were going to be. Following me would be a total commitment. Even Andrew had only divided his time between fishing and hanging out with the Baptist. They would give up not just their livelihood, but the very idea of being self-sufficient as they placed all their trust in God. They stared at me, at the fish, at the crowd, and back at me again, speechless.

Then our boat hit the shore, and they busied themselves with the boat and the catch. John and I were the last ones on board.

He leaned close to me and spoke quickly under his breath. "Look, I'm really going to follow your lead as far as what can happen between us."

"Good."

He watched me expectantly, hoping I would give more details. When I didn't, he added, "You let me know when we can do more than just a little kissing."

"Okay."

Again he waited for me to impose some limits or give the go-ahead. We seemed to hang in uneasy equilibrium as we gazed in each other's eyes.

John looked away first. "Okay then," he said with a forced jolliness that hid more conflicted emotions.

I resolved to downplay the sexual side of my attraction to him so as not to overpower him. I wanted him to set the pace for our relationship. We stepped onto land.

✛ ✛ ✛

"Look at all those fish!" Lots of people were shouting in amazement as they gathered around.

Others pulled me away, hungry for the healing they found in my voice, my touch. I loved them all. When I let myself be drawn into the crowd like that, it was almost like entering a dream state, where I no longer chose to act but simply reacted with love to whomever came to me in need, one after another after another. I dove deep into my divinity, deeper than I had ever dared go when among strangers. I have no idea how much time passed before somebody wrapped a strong arm around my shoulders and began to pull me away.

"Come on, Rabbi. Let's go."

It felt like someone was waking me from a sound sleep. My spirits rose when I recognized Peter. "We're all ready," he said. "I'm taking you to my house."

I let him support me as I had supported him earlier. It felt good to take turns at looking after each other. I think it surprised him to find me so dependent on him, for he became gruff and protective as he pushed away people who were still clinging to me.

"Let go! Get back!" He was not aware that he was yelling at people who had just been healed. "Can't you see the Rabbi is tired?!"

"It's not that I'm tired, Peter."

"Are you okay?"

"Yes, but it's hard for me to let go of them, too. They're suffering and I *love* them. But I'm ready to go with you now."

He looked me in the eye and saw that I was returning to normal consciousness. "Lean on me, then."

"My rock."

I put my arm around Peter's waist, and he managed to disengage me from the crowd and pull me uphill away from the shore. When we had room to breathe, he asked me, "Is it always like this wherever you go?"

"Every time there are more people, and it gets more intense."

We both looked back at the crowd near the shore. Peter was estimating what kind of life lay ahead for him, while I was rebalancing my divinity and my humanity by feeling my body. I tried to listen again as a human being does, picking out individual voices and words. I could hear John, Andrew, and James still beside their boats, gleeful as they called out, "Come take a fish! Take two or three if you want!"

"We've got plenty!"

"Everyone can feast on fish today!"

A mean voice interrupted. "Not so fast—you owe some of those fish to Rome." Tax collectors had been waiting on shore with baskets of dried fish, which they exchanged for the more valuable fresh fish as a way to collect taxes for the Roman occupation.

Then I noticed people walking by us, carrying fish. Whole families passed by, with each one carrying a fish—a big carp in the arms of the parents, with smaller and smaller fish in the hands of younger and younger children. A few called out, "Thank you," as they passed me and Peter.

Joy burst in my heart and spread to saturate my whole being. "You gave away my gift! You're giving it to whoever wants it."

"We hoped that you wouldn't be angry," he stammered. "We set some aside for us, but after what you said...we thought...."

"Angry?!"

Peter was so afraid of my reaction that he couldn't see how pleased I was. I turned to stand face to face, holding both his calloused hands in mine, trying to open myself to him as much as possible so he could feel my pleasure directly. "You've doubled my joy by passing on my gift like this."

chapter six:
brothel

THE NEXT MORNING I was standing with my new disciples in front of the simple mud-brick home shared by Peter, Andrew, and their extended family. We had finished breakfast and said our goodbyes. They were drinking a last swig of water before we set out on our journey.

Peter voiced the question that was important to them. "Where are we going?"

"Andrew knows," I replied.

Andrew almost choked on the water he was swallowing. "No, I don't, Rabbi!"

"You don't?"

"No!"

"Don't you remember the discussion we had by the Jordan River, when you asked me to teach you?"

He reviewed his memory of that day. A look of misery crossed his face, showing that he did, indeed, recall what I meant. He was reluctant to speak again. We all waited in silence until he mumbled, "You mean...you want me...to take you to Mary."

"Exactly."

"Who's Mary?" his brother demanded.

"Yes, who is she?" John and James echoed.

"Where is she?" I asked.

He ignored their questions and answered mine. "In Magdala."

I struggled to pinpoint our location on earth's geography. "Is it far from here?"

Andrew seemed shocked by my ignorance. "Surely you know the town of Magdala! It's right near here, on the northwest shore of the Sea of Galilee."

"Good. Let's go." I was about to start walking when Andrew clutched my sleeve, holding me back.

"Rabbi, I must talk with you in private before we leave." His voice was urgent and trembling.

"As you wish," I agreed, then turned to the others. "We need some time."

They all looked frustrated at the unexpected delay. "Andy, tell me who this Mary person is!" Peter insisted.

"She's *nobody!* Forget about it," he retorted.

Turning quickly, he led me toward the morning sun. Soon we reached a secluded hillside spot with a sea view. The shoreline was almost deserted because the fishers had already finished tending their boats and paying their taxes on the previous night's catch.

I took the love that was flowing strongly between me and God at that moment and wrapped it around Andrew's soul as he sat down. His soul shivered. I knew then that he would be frightened if I wrapped my arms around him as I longed to do. I would have to comfort him more indirectly. "I've noticed that some people call you Andy," I commented.

"People who know me well do."

"Oh, I would like to be one of those!"

"Sure, call me Andy then."

"What's on your mind, Andy?"

He raised his voice, almost shouting. "We should not go to see Mary!"

"Why not?"

"She's possessed by a demon! Sometimes she's like a completely different person. And," an ugly, judgmental tone crept into his voice, "she's a whore."

"Good."

"Good!?"

"We can really help her. Anyway, I thought she was your friend."

"She's not my friend! She's just...." His voice trailed off.

"Just someone you had sex with?"

I felt a jolt in my divine heart as Andrew's anxiety level skyrocketed. I steadied myself by sensing my body against the earth, gazing at the sea, and tipping my face skyward so sunlight could fall on it as I let God's energy flow more deeply through me. I didn't want to do or say anything that would scare Andrew any further. I waited, embracing and encasing his shivering soul in love. I waited a long time.

"What makes you think we had sex?" he asked at last.

"I can see when two people have become one flesh. Their soul energies imprint each other for the rest of their lives."

He considered my words, then blurted in anger, "Yes, we did it! It's not really a sin since I'm not married yet and she belongs to no man, but I do regret getting involved with her. I've already repented. I sacrificed two pigeons at the Temple in Jerusalem on my way home. It's over."

"Then your sins are forgiven." His soul still shivered against me, refusing to drink even one drop of forgiveness. My divine heart began to ache as forgiveness built up inside me with nowhere to go, making me feel swollen and inflamed. "Maybe you'd like to talk about it," I offered.

"*Talk* about it?!"

"I don't mean talking about how hot she was in bed. I mean discussing what it means for you. Sometimes the Baptist's asceticism has the opposite effect. After you eat so many locusts in the desert, you start to long for some kind of sensual pleasure. And then when you and Mary both witnessed my baptism, you were united in supreme spiritual joy. Sometimes a human heart doesn't know how to hold all its happiness, so that night—"

"You even know when! How do you know? Did she tell you?"

"No."

"You didn't...*hear* us?" He was mortified, barely able to speak—but he had to know. "Or *see* us?!"

"No, Andrew. I just understand human nature. I don't know the particulars. All I saw was that your souls bore each other's imprint. You weren't like that before."

"All right, if you must know, I took her that night and several times after that out by the Jordan, but she wasn't who I thought she was." His words tumbled out fast and furious. "It was her fault. I had been staying with the Baptist and his disciples off and on for months, but she only arrived a few weeks before your baptism. At first she seemed virtuous with a pure heart.

She was enthusiastic about God and had a brilliant mind—I didn't know a woman could be like that. She almost tricked me into marrying her. When I found out she used to work as a whore, I left her and came back home to fish with the others. I was too ashamed to tell them anything about it."

The story didn't seem to be over, but Andrew stopped and stared at the ground as seabirds glided above us. "Nothing degrades you in my eyes," I said gently.

He looked at me like a trapped animal. "But that's not all. A few weeks later I heard that she was back at the brothel in Magdala where she used to work. I decided to go see her there. I thought I could talk her into going out to live with the Baptist in the desert again. I offered to give her some money for traveling, if that was the problem. Instead, she thought I wanted to buy her sexual services. I hadn't paid her before. She turned ugly: sometimes seductive, sometimes needy, sometimes cruel. Maybe she has more than one demon. She got me exactly where she wanted me sexually, and then she humiliated me. She ripped away every last shred of my dignity. I never want to see that slut again!"

I smiled into his outrage. "Mmm. That makes me *very* grateful that you're going to take me to her today. I understand that it will be hard for you. You don't have to go inside with me. Just lead me to the brothel."

Andrew was incredulous. "You *still* want to go to her after everything I told you?"

"Nothing degrades her in my eyes, either. You may not have noticed this yet, but my presence makes people heal and demons flee. Don't you want me to help someone you once cared about? Based on how much she upsets you, I'd say you still care for her."

"I *never* cared about her!"

"Well, that's your sin, then."

"What?"

"You failed to love Mary. That sin makes you susceptible to the power of the demons, too. Forgive her. Try this prayer: 'Forgive our wrongs, as we forgive those who wrong us.'"

All this time, Andrew's soul had kept shivering in the blanket of my divine love. At last, as he opened to the possibility of forgiveness, his soul became still and permeable, absorbing some of the warmth and protection I offered. Immediately Andrew began to shiver as the disturbance moved outward to his body.

"I'm so cold all of a sudden!" he exclaimed.

"Yes. Come to me and I'll wrap my cloak around you to warm you." It was an unusual solution, but Andrew came right to me. I hugged him to my chest and drew my heavy woolen cloak around us as he shivered more violently.

"What's wrong with me?" Fear tightened his voice and made him shake harder. "I've never felt like this. I must have a fever."

"Don't be afraid. It will pass soon. It's a deep form of healing. Just let yourself experience how it felt to be so close to someone possessed by a demon."

As his soul relaxed, I could see that it was injured. It let me explore the wound: a long, third-degree burn where a demon had swiped against it.

"My beloved Andy," I whispered. "It can be terrifying to come in close contact with a demon like you did, especially for someone like you who has devoted a lot of time and energy to seeking God." His teeth began to chatter and I felt his muscles clench in fear.

"How could I be attracted to someone who just wanted to use me?" he lamented. "She actually *enjoyed* hurting me."

With sighs too deep for words, my divine heart wept and I let the sacred tears water his soul. I cried for Mary, too, knowing how terribly she must be suffering if just being with her could do this much harm to another. With my divine heart I cradled her soul near us and assured it that I would be there in the flesh soon.

Andrew gradually stopped shivering and in the silence, he tentatively put his hand over mine. When his soul had healed, it flexed and luminesced. "Do you really think it would be good if I...*loved*...her?" he asked.

"Oh, yes. Always love God first, but yes. Love your enemies, help those who hate you, return curses with blessings, and pray for your abusers. If someone hits you on the cheek, offer the other to them also. When thieves steal your cloak, let them have your shirt, too."

Andrew considered this. "You don't need me to help you find her. I remember you said you would seek us out wherever we were like a shepherd finding a lost sheep."

"I could do it without you, but...." I let Andrew fill in the blank rather than telling him why I valued his participation. I snuggled against him even more closely, happy that he had remembered the shepherd image.

"You're going to ask her to follow you and join us, aren't you?" he asked.

"Yes. There will be many more after."

Together we looked out at the sea, blue like the sky that it reflected.

"Well, I asked you to teach me. I suppose I should at least try your way." He pulled out of my arms and searched my face for more reassurance.

I smiled.

"I'll take you to her now," he declared. We went to rejoin the others.

"This is it." Andrew and I stood in broad daylight in front of a cluster of ill-kept mud houses in the worst section of Magdala. Stray dogs, thin and scraggly, wandered past us on the narrow street. We could hear someone screaming inside one of the buildings. Andrew listened nervously when he recognized Mary's voice. "Maybe I should go inside with you after all."

"Thank you, Andy, but I want you to go back and wait for me with the others."

I turned and started toward the door of the main building, but still he stood there, hesitating. "Maybe if she saw me...."

"I'll bring her with me tonight if she wants to follow me. Otherwise, it's best you don't see her."

He left and I knocked on the door. I felt calm, completely centered in God, and eager to see Mary again, whatever her condition.

"How may I help you?" A young woman—still a girl really—came to the door. Her flirtatious manner was a mask that did nothing to hide her sweet soul from me.

"I'm here to see Mary."

"She's not seeing customers today. Maybe *I* could please you?"

She curtsied, arranging her robe in such a way as to reveal her calves and the rounded tops of her breasts.

"No. Mary asked me to come visit her. I'm her rabbi."

"You are the Baptist?" She looked doubtful. She had probably heard stories about him. He would *never* have visited a brothel. And my clothing was quite normal compared to the scratchy camel's hair that he always wore.

"No, I'm Jesus of Nazareth."

She dropped the mask completely and knelt to kiss my feet. "Rabbi!" She would stop to say a few words, then resume kissing. "You're the one who heals everybody! We heard about you."

I noted that she was more aware of my healings than my own disciples were.

"I'm so glad you came," she continued, peppering each sentence with more kisses. "Mary is desperately in need of healing. She's delirious. Demons have taken her over. She has a fever and she hasn't eaten for two weeks. We think she's dying."

"Take me to her."

"Let me wash your feet first and bring you something to eat."

She was obviously used to catering to men's whims, but her hospitality was sincere. She, too, longed to be with me.

"Thank you for the offer. Your name is?"

"Tamar."

"Thank you, Tamar, but I have to take care of Mary first. Just bring me a simple meal that I can share with her."

Tamar left and returned with a tray containing a pitcher, two cups, some unleavened bread, and a bowl of lentil stew that smelled of mustard. A bunch of tiny, round grapes sat on the side. "Mary used to love this kind of grape," she explained as she led me toward the unintelligible screaming.

The hut where the cries originated was the smallest and dirtiest in the complex. The shutters on the windows were closed. When we stood outside the door, I could finally make out Mary's words: "Don't make me die alone!"

"Is she alone?"

Tamar looked down in shame. "Yes, Rabbi, but it's not like it sounds. As soon as we go in there, she starts yelling for us to leave."

I took the tray from Tamar and opened the door.

"Get out! I don't want anyone to see me die!" Mary wailed.

I stepped inside and closed the door behind me. It was too dark to see Mary, but I could smell her, stinking of sweat, urine, and cheap perfume. The squalor didn't scare me. I tended to see such hardships as gifts that gave a soul some extra incentive to grow.

Her screams verged on hysteria. "What do you want with me, Jesus, son of almighty God? Please don't torture me."

Demons were speaking through her. To my divine senses most demons that inhabit people seemed rather like earthworms—cool, dark, and slimy, yet weak and simple to dislodge. More disgusting than the demons themselves was their corrosive effect on human souls and the cruelty with which they bound those souls in shackles and injected them with lies and other poisons.

I might have feared the demons in the past, but now that I had faced Satan directly in the wilderness, demons didn't upset me at all. They were part of my creation, too, and actually I loved them. My affection for them, not my power, frightened them and made six of them leave Mary in quick succession. One remained and coiled itself in a stranglehold on her soul. I decided to take my time with that one.

"Suddenly I feel completely better. Thank God!" Mary said. "My fever is gone. I'm not going to die."

I felt my way to a window and opened the shutters. I stood there for a while with my back to her and let the sunlight and a fresh breeze wash over my face and pour into the room.

I turned to her. My face was in shadow as the light streamed from behind me. Mary was lying on a mat on the dirt floor. I recognized my old oil lamp sitting near her, unlit. She was naked except for a light linen loincloth loosely draped around her hips. I could see that she was much thinner and her golden skin had turned sallow. Her long, thick hair was tangled around her neck in greasy snarls. Worst of all, the spark in her eyes had grown dull. She rolled onto her back slowly, as if it hurt to move.

"I called you Jesus, didn't I? I don't know why I said that, but I'm going to find him wherever he is and beg him to let me follow him. I can't wait any longer. Sir, do you know where Jesus of Nazareth has gone?"

"Mary." I sat down beside her and placed the tray of food and drink nearby.

The most glorious joy broke over her gaunt face as she recognized me. "Rabbi!" We embraced and she clung to me while I upheld her. I poured each of us a cup of watered-down wine from the pitcher. I blessed the meal and encouraged her to eat. She nibbled some grapes, then dipped her bread in the stew and ate it.

I took the opportunity to carefully assess and map out the demon within her, the damage it had done, and the healthy soul tissue that remained. The demon taunted me, exposing the most pristine parts of her soul and daring me to feed them, knowing that any energy I gave her would quickly strengthen the demon who sapped her life force. I didn't care. I was far, far stronger than any demon would ever be, so in compassion I let her thirsty soul nurse directly from my divine love. Even in this state, her soul flowed like a fountain that whetted my thirst for fulfilling my life purpose, whatever the cost. I was very glad I had come to her.

"So you're still calling me Rabbi," I said. "Did you pray about it like I asked?"

"Oh, yes, Rabbi."

"Then you may become **my** disciple today. I will call you Magdalene because **your** journey with me began here in Magdala."

"Oh." She pulled away **and** looked at me, dismayed. "I want to forget this place."

"Leave it behind and **don't** look back, yes, but don't deny your past or how **you** were wounded. When your deepest wound heals, it will become your greatest gift. You have to let that happen, Magdalene. That's what it means to follow me. You may think you can gain your life by pretending you were never a prostitute in Magdala, but you must lose your life in order to gain it."

"All right. You can call me Magdalene if I can call you Rabbi." We embraced again.

Her confidence in me evoked my tenderness as well as a grim determination to remove the last demon as soon as possible—and yet with the least amount of damage to Mary's own soul. The demon was wrapped so tightly around Mary's soul that any way I uprooted it was sure to cause more harm in the process. The injury would heal, but I wanted to leave her soul intact rather than damage and repair it, especially because she had so little untouched soul left. Ever so gently, I stopped nursing her soul and began moving it into the optimal position for extracting the last demon. I was going to make it as easy as possible for her to maintain her commitment to God.

"How did you find me here, anyway?" she asked.

"Andy brought me."

"Andy!" She spat out the name as her whole body tensed. "That pig! I had left this place behind and gone to be baptized. I thought Andy would help me start a new life. I thought he would marry me! Instead, he— oh, I was a fool. All men are alike."

Then she looked at me as a man for the first time. A change came over her entire being. She still seemed vulnerable and desperate for love as she sat next to me, but she channeled her insecurity into projecting an image of sexiness. She was an expert at it. We had embraced several times that day, but now I noticed her nudity and the way that her golden-white soul light glowed through her skin. Her illness had left her a little too thin, but she adjusted her position almost imperceptibly to accentuate the voluptuous perfection of her physical proportions. Her body looked younger than her soul, which bore a lifetime of damage. I saw she was at the height of sexual ripeness, or perhaps just past her prime. She tilted her head back so her profuse, black hair cascaded down to her waist. She simultaneously parted her lips, exposed her throat, and thrust her breasts upward. She let her eyelids close halfway over her dark eyes and purposely dimmed the raw intelligence that I had seen sparkling there.

She began to kiss me, slowly at first, on my beard, then on my mouth. She pushed me down and lay beside me, undulating her torso against mine. She knew exactly where and how to touch me to make my whole body feel good. She wasn't just using techniques that worked on men in general. Maybe her first move was like that, but her body could read my most subtle physical reactions to her and then respond in delicate ways that enhanced my pleasure.

She slipped a hand under my loincloth and rubbed my pelvis, delving a little farther below my bellybutton with each stroke. I felt the urge to plug into her female power. I wanted to penetrate, please, and fill her with me in every way possible. How exciting it would be to thrust and entrust myself into her deepest recesses! She caressed my hand, gently sensitizing it, then placed it on the softness of her naked breast.

The nub of her nipple barely stiffened against my palm, revealing that her own arousal was all fake. What made me want to have sex with people was when they wanted sex with me—and I could sense that Mary didn't, regardless of what she was doing. The sexual pressures inside me swirled backward, then dwindled further when her soul yielded to me.

Her soul was like water waiting to take the shape of any vessel into which it is poured. I let it flow into my divine heart. Her soul felt so pliable and helpless against the inner chambers of my divine heart that all my sexual desire was transformed into divine energy.

I pumped my love for her out of my body and into my divine heart, where I accepted the virgin part of her soul and made it mine. I fertilized it in mutually satisfying ways that would inspire growth and transformation. By pouring myself into her soul, I changed her energy signature permanently so that every demon would know she was loved by me and she herself would be able to feel love more easily.

At the moment, though, she was unaware of what had passed between us at the soul level. Slowly I moved my hand from her breast and turned my mouth away from her kisses. I wanted to be exceedingly gentle, because nobody who seeks God should be rejected, no matter how they express themselves. I still held her close enough for us to feel each other's heartbeat. "I don't do that," I whispered.

"Don't do what?"

"Sex."

Jumping to a seated position, she reared back and gawked at me. "What? Not at all? Or do you mean you like guys?"

I sat up again, too. "No. I mean yes, I do find men

as attractive as women. I mean, it's hard for me to tell the difference between male and female, but that's not why I don't have sex with people."

She giggled suggestively. "I'll be *happy* to teach you the difference between male and female."

Playfully, she reached for me. I stopped her, holding her by the wrist so she couldn't come any closer.

"I *know* the difference between male and female." She made me feel playful, too, so in a light-hearted way I gave her a peek at who I really was by quoting scripture. "God created me long ago at the beginning of the world. I was beside God like an expert worker when the earth was formed. I was God's daily delight, and together we rejoiced in the inhabited world and all humankind."

"What?" She laughed uncertainly. She couldn't tell if I was joking or not.

"You forget who is talking to you." I looked her right in the eye, waiting.

"If you're holding back because you're a rabbi, you don't have to worry about that. I've had plenty of rabbis—and priests, too."

I had to either laugh or cry at this news, which she announced cheerfully. I chose to laugh. "Oh, that *really* makes me want to make love to you," I teased.

"I had another Messiah, too." She was bragging.

I couldn't hide my anger at him. "Well, he certainly wasn't the real one!"

"You really are a virgin!" she exclaimed. "I can't believe it, a man of your age, so handsome and fun-loving and passionate! I might have believed it about the Baptist. He won't even eat regular food. But I found out that even he isn't celibate."

"You find it harder to believe I'm a virgin than that I'm the Messiah!" I marveled. "Sex is how you understand the world, isn't it?"

"Yes, that's what really motivates everyone."

I let go of her wrist and looked at her kindly. "Then let me tell you more about my sex life. My sexuality is directed toward God as the Holy Spirit. You've heard me call God my Father. But my relationship with God is multi-faceted. The night before I was baptized, I also bonded with God as my Beloved who satisfies my sexual longings as well as all my other needs."

"You experience God as your Father *and* your Lover?"

"Yes."

"That's gay incest!" Suddenly her tone switched to shocked prudery.

I chuckled. "You do have insight into human sexuality, our most secret desires and horrors."

A look of wonder came over her face. "You know that side of people, too," she marveled.

"Yes," I agreed. "Anyway, what happens with me isn't simply gay. I fell in love with and married a pangendered, omni-erotic Spirit. We'll have to limit the Holy Spirit to one gender just to be able to talk about Her—or Him. I'll let you pick the gender for our discussions. Do you prefer God to be male or female?"

Mary's eyebrows shot upward in surprise at my unusual question. She issued her answer as if it were a challenge: "Female!"

"My Bride didn't take away my sexual desires," I

continued casually. "Instead She fulfilled them in the most gratifying way. The mechanics of it are a mystery. I wouldn't try to describe it."

I gazed into Mary's eyes and decided to press further. "You can think of me as female, too, if you like. My nature can't be captured in the confines of human language, either. I switch between being gay, straight, lesbian, bisexual, trisexual.... If you want to get technical about my love life, it's masturbation as much as incest, since we're really all one Being. But none of the labels really fits."

"After a while, it becomes ridiculous," she admitted in bewilderment. She was impressed by my ease with the vocabulary of sex and comforted by my comfort with my own absurdities. She shifted into a more relaxed posture and asked, friend-to-friend, "So you don't know what sex with another person feels like?"

"Sometimes I kiss the people I love, like you and I did. I know how good that can feel. That's also how I learned that I can't have sex with other people. Because of who I am, there is a huge power imbalance between me and every possible sex partner. Nobody would be able to resist me if I tried to make love to them, so it isn't possible for me to have consensual sex. And coercive sex doesn't interest me at all. I don't mind using my divine power to heal people, but the thought of using it for my own sexual gratification is a total turn-off to me. And I can't *not* use it—I am fully divine as well as fully human."

"But you don't make me feel ashamed. If you were the real Messiah, then you'd make me feel ashamed."

"Why in the world would I want to do that?"

"To make me repent."

I let my love for her resonate in my voice. "Oh, there are much better ways to do that." I looked at her, waiting.

Her intelligence shone in her eyes as she thought over what I had said.

She didn't say anything, so I explained some more. "You already know that sex belongs in a lifetime commitment, but sex itself is no cause for shame. Sex is good. It can bond people in love and it can create life. Your body, including your sexual organs and feelings, are created in God's image to be a vessel for the Holy Spirit."

She watched me in silent thought. I liked how she had never made a move to cover her breasts and thighs. She allowed her flesh to be as naked before me as her soul was.

"Of course," I continued, "sex can be a weapon to control and hurt others, too. You must have experienced that."

"I use sex to control men all the time. I can *make* them desire me and do what I want."

"I was asking about when someone used sex against you as a weapon. It's almost unbearable to remember the time when you were way, *way* too young and some man forced his penis into your—"

"Stop!" This time she grabbed both of my wrists. She dropped her seductive act and looked at me with the wide, terrified eyes of a small child. Her soul shifted into the position for which I had been waiting.

"Okay." I let her keep restraining me, even though she was digging her fingernails into my skin. I could feel the sweat on her palms. I offered her soul its first sip of divine will. "Beloved Magdalene, there's one demon left that's choking your soul. I want to cast it out, but you'll still have to work hard to break the habits it instilled. It's sure to come back with a whole pack of even nastier demons. You'll be in even worse trouble unless you learn to trust God and stop controlling others through sex."

She tightened her grasp until I winced, but she was too lost in traumatic memories to notice. "How am I supposed to control others if I don't use sex?"

"You're not supposed to control people. Just let God protect you."

I almost lost her then. The initial bitterness of God's will caused her soul to pucker up and withdraw. At the same time, she released my wrists and shoved me away. The demon took this opportunity to jerk its grasp on her soul much tighter, until it almost cut off all circulation. Then it injected her soul with a large dose of poison.

"Where was God when I was raped as a little girl? *Where?!* I never told anyone about what happened to me, but you seem to know. Where was your Bride when I really needed Her?"

I answered quietly. "Right there...loving you through it."

"I can't trust a God like that!"

"It seems risky to trust God, but it's your greatest safety."

"I cannot trust that kind of God!" she repeated.

With every breath, I found it more difficult to allow this demon to continue eating away at Mary's priceless soul. I could cast it out easily enough, but worse ones would take its place as long as she had such doubt. I began to cry, and not just a few tears, but huge sobs as grief overwhelmed me.

"What's the matter?"

"You have found your ways to numb the agonies that your soul felt in the past and feels now, but I can feel *all* your pain intensely. I can hardly stand it."

She pulled me down on the mat and we lay side by side while she held me and tried to comfort me. Her touch was very different from before, although she was still just as intuitive in knowing exactly where and how I liked to be touched and what would feel good to me. Now her caress felt soothing and authentic. Still I couldn't stop crying.

"I trust your tears," she whispered. "I'll try to stop using sex as a weapon because I trust your tears."

Her promise stilled the sobs that convulsed me. She continued holding me while my breathing gradually smoothed out. She wiped the last tears from my cheeks with her own hair. Meanwhile, I grabbed that demon and sent it hurtling to the depths of the earth.

"You're free!" I kissed her once on the cheek and jumped to my feet in exultation.

"I am?" she asked as she stood up. "I feel the same."

Her soul was bleeding profusely and writhing in spasms of shock as it adjusted to the absence of the poisons and pressures to which it had grown accustomed. As extensive as the soul damage was, I had succeeded in leaving as much healthy tissue intact as possible. I wrapped it in layer upon healing layer of divine love and it immediately began to mend.

"I don't feel any different," she insisted.
"You will."

chapter seven:
night in magdala

MARY AND I FINISHED OUR MEAL and she got dressed. Night had come. As we entered the dark courtyard to leave, Mary pulled my sleeve to prevent me from heading back through the brothel's main entrance. "Let's sneak out the back way," she whispered. "I don't want Reuben to see me and talk me out of leaving."

"Who's Reuben?"

"He's my...." she searched for a euphemism, then just said it flat out: "He's my pimp. He thinks he owns me. He's talked me into staying before. And into coming back."

I stopped and looked straight into her eyes. "If you're afraid to say goodbye to him, then he *does* own you."

Her silence told me how frightened she really was.

"All right. I'll help you tell him goodbye." I started marching toward the entrance.

"No! Rabbi, *Rabbi*, stop!" She grabbed my arm and used her full weight to try to stop me, but she wasn't strong enough. "He has two big thugs who work for him. If you make him mad, he'll have them beat you up!"

"I'm willing to take a beating to win your freedom." As I neared the entrance, I started to yell. "Reuben! Get out here, Reuben!" Tamar and some other women were loitering near the entrance. They scrambled inside when they heard me shouting.

I surveyed the soul that responded to my call. It was in much worse condition than Mary's soul had been. By enslaving others in the physical world, it had automatically bound chains around itself on the spirit side. Demons had taken advantage of its weakness, feeding it lies and forcing it to work for Satan. They had fooled the soul into working harder and harder as the chains kept getting heavier.

The man with this miserable soul swaggered out the door in a deliberately casual style. His prostitutes peeked out of the building behind him. Reuben had once been handsome, but his looks had been eroded by age and a life of excess. He slid his heavy-lidded eyes over us. I noticed a spark of relief as he observed that Mary was back in her right mind. Then he studied me, calculating how he could profit from the situation. I sheltered Mary under my arm while she clung to me, so scared that I could feel her heart racing where her side pressed against mine.

"Mary has something to tell you," I announced. "And if you don't like it, you can answer to me."

She hid her fear behind a voice of defiance. "I'm going away and I'm never coming back. Goodbye!"

Reuben never even glanced at her. He kept his eyes fixed on me. "Naturally, you want her, and you can have her—for a price."

"Yes," I said grimly. "I'll pay the price—to God."

"To God!" he laughed. "She's a valuable piece of ass. A valuable *asset*, you might say. Look how beautiful she is: Her lips are like a scarlet thread. Her breasts are like pomegranates. And she's fantastic in bed, too: just the right mix of compliance and sassiness. You'll pay *me* or you won't take her."

"Okay," I countered. "Then you can have me, too. I'll stay here with her."

He appraised me coolly, considering how he could use me.

I gave the same treatment to his brothel buildings and courtyard. "This will be a good location for my preaching and healing," I continued as I looked it over. "Plenty of people can fit in here. Of course, I can't keep the lepers away. That may cut into your business." We both knew that lepers were considered ritually unclean and people would do almost anything to avoid being near them.

"Lepers?" For the first time, Reuben appeared uneasy as he wrinkled his brow. "Who are you? Are you that Messiah that Mary's been raving about? I think she called him...Jesus of Nazareth."

"He's the one," Mary affirmed.

"I heard the girls talking about how you healed some lepers near here." He looked at me long and hard, then at Mary. I knew he was thinking about how sick she had been before I arrived, and wondering if it could be more than a coincidence that she was better now. He gazed into space, weighing his options and counting the economic cost of each alternative. When he was done, he shot me the charming smile of a businessman who knows how to lose graciously. "Oh, all right. Take her and have your fun. She's great in bed, but she's crazy and she's more trouble than she's worth to me. You can have her."

I addressed the women who were gawking at us from the brothel doorway. "Tamar! You and the other prostitutes are welcome to come with us. Now is your chance!"

They all giggled and retreated further into the brothel, whispering to each other. Mary breathed a sigh of relief as we turned to go.

"Consider her my donation to God!" Reuben called out after us, then laughed heartily at his own joke.

Something about that last remark tugged at my divine heart. "We're not done here," I whispered to Mary. She resisted some as I wheeled around, but she was not about to let go of me.

Reuben's soul responded to my presence with a dim flicker of recognition, but it was too feeble to move inside its many chains. I reached over and placed divine truth against a link in one of the chains until it melted, just to show his soul what was possible.

"Reuben," I said aloud. "I helped Mary gain her freedom and I can set you free, too. You can come with me now, if you like." Mary pinched my arm to show me how intensely she hated that idea, but she didn't deter me.

He laughed. "I'm not in bondage! I own this place. I make lots of money from it and I can have as much sex as I want. *All kinds* of sex."

"Satan's most effective lie is to say that bondage is freedom," I informed him.

After a moment's reflection, he replied, "You are slick. You would be good at recruiting and breaking in new girls for me."

His idea was so ludicrous that I started laughing. I left him with one final thought before I started walking away with Mary. "Remember, you can have your freedom if you ever want it."

"Enjoy your 'donation!'" he sang out after us.

✝ ✝ ✝

Mary and I set off together down the unlit streets of Magdala toward the house where my disciples and I were spending the night. We were both giddy from our victory over the demons and the new bond forged between us. As we walked by the scant light of a crescent moon, we held hands and bantered back and forth, laughing so loudly that a man opened his door and shouted at us.

"Shut up and get out of here, you sinners! You woke up my whole family," he raged from his doorway.

This made me laugh louder. "Happy are the servants who are awake when their boss comes home," I yelled back.

"You have a demon!" he bellowed.

Mary tried to shush me. I let her loop her arm around my waist and pull me away, but I called out a parting thought: "Just remember: God's kingdom is near."

He stomped inside and slammed the door.

"You are wild!" Mary exclaimed. "I didn't think you would be wilder than I am. I thought the real Messiah would be dignified and serious."

I laughed some more, walking with her arm still

around my waist. "You don't really know me yet. I came to wake people up."

As we crossed into the well-to-do side of the village, the houses that we passed began to look tidier and have more space around them.

"Where are you taking me?" Mary asked.

"On the road to Magdala, my other disciples and I met a landlord who invited us to stay in one of his houses across town. The rest of my disciples are waiting for us there. That's where we'll all spend the night. When you meet them, remember you don't have to act the way you did in the past."

"Oh, Rabbi, I know that!" Mary squeezed my waist for emphasis.

"Satan likes to tempt people right after they make a breakthrough, so watch out."

"I feel so close to you now, I'm sure tonight won't be a problem." She tilted her head so it rested on my shoulder.

"You're already letting your guard down. Do you really think it's going to be so easy when you see Andy again?"

"Andy?" Her voice trembled. "Andy's going to be there?"

She let go of me. Her soul, which had been nursing steadily from my divine heart all this time, now retracted some, so I wrapped a thicker layer of divine love around it to guide it back. I started walking more slowly.

"Of course he'll be there. You both asked me to be your rabbi at the same time. And he led me to you today."

"I forgot about that. I'm sure he hates me." She sounded like a little lost girl.

"Do you think he would have led me to you if he truly hated you?"

We walked without speaking for a while as she considered my question.

Mary broke the silence. "You know that Andy and I had sex, but I haven't told you about all the sins I committed with Andy...I mean, against Andy."

We continued walking in silence for a long time as the locusts sang.

"Maybe I should tell you," she ventured.

"You can tell me anything."

"When Andy and I had sex for the first time, I felt something that I had never felt before, even though I had pretended to feel it with men hundreds of times. But that night the big thrill was *real* for me. I'm not sure why it happened with him. It certainly wasn't his looks or his technique. He's actually rather clumsy in bed, although I did like the way that he let me teach him."

I listened with compassion and without comment to Mary's side of the story that I had heard that morning from Andy.

"Maybe it was so different with Andy because we had been learning God's ways together for several weeks at John's camp," she continued. "Andy saw something in me that nobody else ever noticed. He spent a lot of time teaching me scriptures—you know, holy things that men never discuss with a woman in regular life, but it became possible out there in the desert. He was so kind and he knew a lot because he had studied with many different rabbis. The two of us were so excited when you got baptized and we saw the Holy Spirit land on you like a dove! That night we discovered that we each had the same dream: to be your disciple. One thing led to another and we ended up making love—*for real*. I've never felt so loved, before or since. Even you don't make me feel like he did."

I laughed a bit then. "The door of your awareness is still closed to the joys of your soul," I said and snuggled her soul tighter against my divine heart. "You don't yet know how it feels to be loved by God."

"But then I ruined it," Mary sighed. "I knew he wanted to marry me, but I couldn't just wait until he was ready to ask. I wanted a guarantee that I had him forever, so I tried to *make* him ask me. Sex became an act again. The harder I tried to recapture the magic, the worse it felt. My rule is never to let someone else dump me, so I dumped him first. He refused to let go of me, so I told him all about my past as a prostitute. It's strange that he never suspected. Most people figure it out right away, but Andy saw me differently. He went back to his fishing boat and I tried to keep living the locust-eating life in the desert while I waited for you to return, but I couldn't do it. I gave up and ended up back at the brothel where you found me."

She paused, waiting for me to say something.

"I'm still listening," I confirmed.

She looked at me for any sign of condemnation. Finding none, she resumed her story. "Then Andy came to see me at the brothel. I couldn't believe it! He said he wanted to help me, but I felt humiliated. Just seeing him reminded me of how much I had lost and, worst of all, he made me *feel* again. I had to stop the pain—it was almost like a reflex, like hitting a dog that's biting you. I had to be so cruel to him that he would never, ever come back again. A prostitute knows a lot of tricks for inflating a man's ego, and they can also be used in reverse to destroy him—that's what I did to Andy. The part that I regret the most is lying about that first night."

A tear slid down her cheek, her first one that day. "I got him hot for me and then I told him that I never liked him, that I was secretly contemptuous of his private parts and the way he made love the whole time. I didn't just make up an ordinary lie to hurt him—I denied myself, my own truest, best feelings. I thought I was attacking Andy, but I was destroying what was holy and good in me. Not long after he left, the fever came upon me."

We had reached the house where my disciples were staying. I stopped and held Mary in the middle of the street. "Your sins are forgiven," I whispered.

"But...."

"You are forgiven!" I assured her and adjusted the composition of the love that she was drinking from me so that it was pure divine forgiveness, thick and sweet. I felt profound peace as she accepted huge quantities of my love. I let myself become lost in the moment as I emptied myself. I wanted her soul to be filled to overflowing before she went inside, so to encourage her I whispered, "Take and eat, for this is my body."

"What?" Her soul didn't pull away, but her mind did. She looked at me, startled, and wiped the tear from her face.

"Oh," I said apologetically, sensing that I had spoken

too soon. It took me a moment to reconnect with my body and its exact location in time and space: Magdala, on an autumn night with the sliver of a moon overhead, outside the house where my first disciples would meet each other—*early* in my ministry. "Oh, I'll teach you about that later."

She adjusted her head scarf and stood tall, though she was still not as tall as I was. "I'm ready to meet them," she declared. I led her to the house and opened the door.

My disciples were sleeping by lamplight on floor mats in a hut very similar to the one where I found Mary, except it was much cleaner. The sound of the door woke them. When they saw Mary enter the hut with me, all of them sat up and stared. I switched my mind so I was relying primarily on my human senses and took a good, long look at her myself. She was dressed modestly in a plain woolen cloak with a scarf draped over her head and shoulders, but she had a naturally graceful way of draping herself that accentuated rather than hid her fine proportions and flowing movements. She looked ravishing as the lamplight made her golden skin glow lustrous. Tears had left her eyes glistening. The love I was still pouring into her soul gave a magnetic softness to her being. After a quick glance around the room, she cast her eyes down politely and did not look up.

"I've seen her before! She was at the Baptist's camp,"

John exclaimed, speaking as if she wasn't there. Then he looked hard at Andrew.

"This is Mary Magdalene," I said. "She's one of us. Andy and Mary came to me together at the Baptist's camp and asked me to be their rabbi. Today she was set free from some demons."

The others kept staring at her, except for Andrew, who looked away, his face tense.

Mary lay herself face-down on the floor in a gesture normally used to greet those far superior in rank. She aimed herself toward Andrew. "God has regarded the low estate of this hand-maiden," she said. "Blessed are they who take no offense."

It was obvious to everyone that this was not a happy reunion for Andrew and Mary. The others turned their attention to me, uncertain as to what I expected of them. I knelt down beside her.

"Get up, Mary," I said, touching her shoulder lightly. "Rise and sit beside me."

The others still did nothing to match or even respond to Mary's posture of extravagant greeting.

"Is this how you show hospitality to strangers and travelers when they arrive?" I asked them.

They sprang into action, fetching water for us to wash our feet and hands, digging through their bags to find us bread and cheese, and unrolling two more mats for us. All of them continued to ignore Mary. Their half-hearted hospitality displeased me.

I uttered the standard blessing as we washed our hands. Then I blessed the drink they had brought—water with a dash of wine—and offered Mary a cup. The others sat and watched. I poured a drink for each of them, too, while I explained, "All who glorify themselves will be humbled, but all who humble themselves will be glorified."

The uncomfortable silence returned, so I spoke again. "Any questions?"

Silence.

"They're not usually like this, Mary. They like debating my ideas," I told her, then turned to the others. "Take your time, then, and we'll talk tomorrow after we've all gotten some sleep. But before we say goodnight, at least introduce yourselves to Mary."

The silence continued one beat. Then I looked right in Peter's eyes and nodded emphatically. At last someone other than me spoke. "I'm called Peter."

Mary lifted her gaze for the first time and examined him, memorizing so she could match face and name. I tried to see them as she did. A shock of wavy hair fell casually across Peter's forehead and framed his chiseled features. He and the others all appeared rather similar: sleepy, bearded people in the prime of life with the muscular bodies and no-nonsense posture of those who made their living by fishing.

John's bass voice rumbled. "My name is John. My brother James and I are fishing partners with Andy and Peter. I mean, we were until yesterday when we decided to join the Rabbi." I feasted my eyes on his unusual, fleshy features and the dark eyes that blazed from deep sockets.

"I'm James," his brother said. Like John, his weatherbeaten face was framed by silver-tinged ringlets of hair. The brothers resembled each other, but somehow James looked more conventional.

Last was Andrew, the youngest, and the one with the most delicate features. He was plain with big, puppy-dog eyes and straight, black hair. Andrew tried to speak, but emotion choked off his words. He rolled his eyes at me in alarm and I felt his soul shiver against me. "You remember Andy," I said.

They both made such a point of looking away that the others couldn't help noticing and wondering why. Peter in particular studied his brother with surprise.

"Just as you all gave up your lives as fishermen, Mary has left her life as a prostitute," I concluded.

Mary flinched as if I had slapped her when I said "prostitute." She shot me a look of anguish before she hung her head. The word had an electrifying effect on the others, too. Their eyes burned as they stared at her, at me, back at her, at Andrew, and back again at *her*.

"I need to spend some time alone in prayer," I announced. "Good night." I went up to the roof. I intended to be alone, but Mary followed me immediately. I sat down and she sank next to me.

"How could you do that to me?" she demanded in a loud yet pathetic tone.

"Do what?" I touched her wrist lightly to calm her.

"You said I was a prostitute!"

"I told you: Your wound will become your greatest gift when it's healed. It's not something to hide."

"And you didn't warn me that I'd be the only woman here!"

"I don't *think* you are...." I paused, trying to remember who was there and what their genders were.

"Peter is a man and so are James, John, and Andy."

"Hmm. I guess you're right. But I'm here, too."

"*You're* a man!"

"I'm not just a man," I said gently, trying to fully expose to her my female side, which was substantial. I also lifted the edge of a kind of veil so that she could glimpse my divinity directly. She was too upset to notice, so I gave up and explained, "You're going to help me reach more women. I will have lots of followers, both female and male. We can find some more women tomorrow if you like."

"But what about tonight?" she wailed. "I'd love to do that tomorrow, but tonight you have to come back down there with me. You can't tell a bunch of men that I'm a prostitute and then leave me alone to sleep with them!"

"I do need some time alone with my Bride before I sleep."

"But they'll think you brought me here to service their sexual needs—and yours!"

I considered her point. "They *might* think that. Just tell them no."

She was dumbfounded. "I can't tell a man no. I've never told a man no. I mean, I said no, but I meant yes, if you pay me more or do what I want. I can't just say no and mean no."

"You're going to have to learn how to stand up to men sooner or later in order to take back your power. Only then can you give your will to God. Tonight is a good time to start."

"But they're stronger than I am and there are four of them. They could force me."

"Oh, I don't think they would do that. I know them and I know their state of mind right now."

Fear flashed in her eyes.

"I'll tell you what," I offered. "I'll come down and sit right outside the door to pray and if anyone approaches you, all you have to do is call out and I will be there and I *will* put a stop to it. And they *will* be sorry, believe me."

Frightening memories flickered through her mind and held her in their grip, making her replay and relive them. I knew how terrifying the memories must feel to Mary, since this was her first time to face them without a demon to numb her as it fed on her fear. I was moved that even her most potent fears did not make her withdraw from me. It would have been easy for her to go back across town to the familiar brothel where she had dulled her pain before, but she chose to stay with me.

I put my arm around her. "I don't mean to belittle your fears."

"Help me," she whimpered.

"Okay." Her request gave me permission to explore all her thoughts and memories, including the private places designed for God, but where God will not go uninvited. In Mary, the receptors in many of these regions had been desecrated by others. I decided to start the cleansing process by healing some specific memories. My divine memory kept a record of loving her through every rape and violation that she had ever experienced. I had relied on that memory earlier in the day to discern the vague outlines of her history.

Now I began reading her memories from her point of view. Human memory has a sharp quality, like bright sunlight in the noonday desert, illuminating and drying some surfaces while casting others into deep shadow.

Looking at memories in this kind of light can be painful because God's presence is obscured or blotted out entirely. Mary's memories—seemingly relentless experiences of brutality—were almost more than my humanity could bear.

I saw that I was going to have to dig deeper, not into Mary's memory, but into my own divinity. I breathed deeply and gazed up into the infinite reaches of the night sky as I searched the resources available to me, not just in that moment, but throughout the entire past—and the future. There, in my own personal future living on earth as Jesus, I found something that caught my attention. I stopped trying so hard to help her and simply spoke to her from my own need.

"I haven't experienced what you have experienced," I said. "I don't know—yet—what it's like to have others inflict great violence on my body. But I will experience it. I hope you will teach me how to endure it."

I revealed this to her without expectation that she would understand or be comforted, without any expectations at all. She surprised me by turning to me with her full being, body, soul, heart, and mind. Her mind began to clear as she softened the focus on her memories.

"I've only been your disciple for one day, and I can already see that people are going to want to kill you for the way you challenge the status quo. But God won't let them hurt you."

"Of course He will. He let people hurt and rape you. Why would he protect me and not you? You don't believe you deserve to be raped, do you?"

She was stunned speechless. Her soul began to blossom toward me in a way I had never seen before.

"I'll tell you the answer," I said. "No, you didn't deserve to be raped. I want you to teach me how to endure violence and still be able to love."

"But that's what I wanted you to teach me."

"Mmm." I lay my cheek on the top of her head. "Some things we'll have to teach each other."

Suddenly her soul, which had been nursing steadily from my divine heart all night, reversed the flow of love between us and began in a sense to nurse me. I had been nourished by people's love of God throughout my lifetime, but this felt different—more intense, given more personally to me as the Messiah. It flowed into a place at my navel where I had never received love before, except perhaps in the womb. Pleasant sensations flooded me. Receiving Mary's soul-love in this way was so unexpected and powerful that I must have cried out and jerked involuntarily because she raised her voice in alarm as she asked, "Are you all right?"

"Yes." I wasn't sure how to talk with her about what was happening between us. I doubted that she was even conscious of the soul-shift, but she could tell that I was dazed and almost unable to speak. I needed to pray by myself to make sense of what was happening. I felt the Holy Spirit billowing up around me like a rising tide.

"You need to be alone with your Bride."

I gasped in surprise. "How did you know?"

"Well, you told me so quite a while ago. I've been selfish, clinging to you when you needed time alone with God. I'll go now and spend the night with the other disciples as you asked."

She stood and I started to get up to go with her.

She stopped me with a new tone of confidence. "You don't have to come and sit right outside the door. I can say no to a few men." Laughing, she added, "And if I need to, I can definitely yell loud enough for you to hear me up here."

After she left, I lay down on the roof and looked up at the heavens. I let myself float into the outer layers of the Holy Spirit. She lifted me and guided me in understanding and proceeding into the new relationship between myself and humankind. She shaped my attention with Her soft touch and minimal use of language. "Relax...remember...."

She showed me how to let Mary's love flow through previously unknown channels in my energy system and pour into my divine heart. The Holy Spirit touched other places throughout my being and pointed out that I had many receptors like the one in my navel, ready to absorb any love that my death and resurrection could someday evoke in people.

As I began easing the receptors open, I discovered to my delight that Mary was only one of countless souls who would love me in this way. They spread into the future for hundreds, even thousands of years. The impressions were faint at first, so I tried to stretch my receptors wide open to intensify and clarify my perception. I could feel each individual soul, most of them yet unborn, as if they were right there with me in Magdala that night. It was like being alone with each one and at the same time feeling the whole multitude with me together.

I initiated a personal relationship with each individual in that moment, so that in a very real sense they all would accompany me throughout the rest of my earthly life. I was falling in love with every single one. They would help me endure what I had to endure. I let myself suck in more of the love that my sacrifice inspired. It addressed a loneliness in me that had been there so long and was so all-pervasive that I had never even noticed it, much less thought that it could be filled.

I began to crave their love then, hungering for it in a way that made me start to feel ashamed before God. I had never let human love touch me so deeply. I had reserved such intimacies for my Bride alone. But then She gently laughed away my embarrassment, urging me onward. "Relax, my clumsy new Bridegroom. Let yourself love and be loved. Let me love you, too."

The stars appeared to brighten as I tuned my perception to increasing levels of sensitivity. Now it looked like a skyful of suns might blind me. The stars were so dazzling that I had to close my human eyes. As I lay on my back, feeling completely exposed, the Holy Spirit began to uncover and excite me further. I was aroused by desire for God.

We tried to strip each other down to our naked gender, but always found a more remote and complex gender hidden under every layer. In excitement, we bared our extremes to each other. Together we sampled the endless spectrum of gender flavors available, creating more as we went. We tried on different gender possibilities, looking for new ways to tantalize and please each other. It was like our wedding night, only better because we could build on the foundation that we laid before. Delicately She...or He...peeled layers back from my heart, leaving each layer attached like the petal of a flower. I felt so sensitive and accessible that it was almost unbearable.

Just when I thought I couldn't stand it any more, the Holy Spirit washed over me with wave upon wave of divine love, Her response to the love I was expressing by giving my life. She flooded every sensitized receptor with a pleasure that was many orders of magnitude stronger than the human soul-love on which I had been feasting. Unlike a human lover, She could withstand and match the sheer, blinding force of the love I felt in return. I let go in automatic spasms of ecstasy.

Energy surged through and beyond Us in one strong flow. Then We breathed in and out together as One. In this rapture, I recalled my own role in preparing the deadly cup that was later offered to me by Father. I remembered choosing my ordeal because it would release love in human souls like nothing else ever would or could. Angel voices were singing so sweetly that I could taste them. Drifting in God as God, my consciousness expanded until I felt every star in the infinite heavens tingling within me.

chapter eight:
law of love

SUNSHINE ON MY FACE woke me in the morning. A rooster crowed. I looked around and saw that I was on some roof somewhere, but I couldn't recognize where I was in space and time. I felt disturbed because I could usually identify my location if I really tried as I was trying in this moment. I was used to moving in and out of ecstatic trances, but last night's vision was the most intense yet. Countless souls had loved me last night for my death and resurrection. I strained to remember which one had actually been with me in the physical world, too. All I could remember was the bliss of the previous night's prayer time and the new type of love I had learned to feel and could still feel now at my belly-button.

The Holy Spirit Herself kissed me good morning and showed me how to manage the new reservoir of love that was creating an ever-larger pool in my divine heart. I practiced adjusting the new receptors until I found the setting where I could still feel the new kind of love, but it didn't distract me from the physical reality that I was living. Then, singing praises to God, I climbed down a ladder to the ground to find out where I was.

I noticed a silence so tense that to hear it was like running into a wall. Then I saw a group of people sitting in a circle under some oak trees beside the house where I had slept. This house was in the outskirts of a town, surrounded by juniper bushes and oak trees that provided plenty of privacy. Plates of bread, fish, and seasonal fruit were spread out as a picnic breakfast on a cloth. The people were seated around the food, but they were not eating. Their faces lit up when they saw me, and they all greeted me:

"Rabbi, did you pray all night long?"

"Come and eat with us."

I remembered they were my first disciples. I counted five of them. Their names had not yet come into focus, but their words were clear.

"We didn't know if we should go up and get you, or wait, or eat without you."

"Look, the landlord brought us all this food! He said to thank you again for sharing your wisdom."

Two of them scooted apart to make room for me. I sat down, and one of those next to me whispered in my ear, "Rabbi, I said no to one of these guys last night! I have to tell you all about it."

Mary. Now I remembered exactly who I was with, where I was, and what day I was living. Her face was triumphant. I looked at the others, the men, and saw the opposite emotion: defeat. James looked the most bedraggled—he must have been the one whose sexual advances were rejected. I sighed. The task of teaching them felt heavy for a moment, like picking up a burden, but the previous night's vision gave me a lot of motivation and patience.

I addressed them loudly as a group. "If anyone has something to say now, you will say it in front of everyone. Otherwise it will have to wait. I'm going to teach you how to live together as my disciples."

Now *all* of them looked defeated. I went ahead and blessed the meal. I broke the bread—fine quality wheat bread—and gave each one a piece. Gazing right into their eyes, I made sure that their souls were feeding from me. We ate quietly for a while. The silence opened up somehow and became a stillness before God. I let my human mind become still, too, so I could speak directly from my divine heart. I wanted to nourish their minds as well as their bodies and souls.

"I give you a new commandment: Love each other. Love each other in the same way that I have loved you. People will know that you are my disciples because you love each other," I said.

They still didn't say anything, but I could tell they were thinking about it as they ate. I watched how they selected food from the plates in front of us. They took care to leave the best of everything to me: the most succulent pomegranate with the fewest blemishes, the biggest slice of melon, the most perfectly formed loaf of bread, and the most evenly roasted piece of fish. Peter got the next best piece, and so it went through a little hierarchy that they had already established with Mary at the bottom. I watched her cheerfully choose the only fig that was partially rotted, leaving many better figs and pomegranates in the dish.

"If you want to be great, you must become a servant, just as the Son of Man came not to be served, but to serve and give his life for others."

They stared at me, uncomprehending.

"Give your life?" John, who was seated on my other

side, creased his already wrinkled brow. His bewilderment bordered on alarm.

"You don't get it, do you?" I took the best pomegranate, the one they had obviously left for me, and handed it to Mary. I had to place both her hands around its round, red form before she would take it. The others watched in horror that was quickly turning into rage. "Somebody say something," I urged.

Peter exploded, "Surely you don't mean to make a *woman* into a disciple like the rest of us!" He spat out the word "woman" with disgust.

"Why not?"

"A rabbi shouldn't even talk to a woman in public."

Now all the other men spoke at once, so I couldn't tell who said what.

"Women get contaminated by childbirth and all that. If a man touches one of them at the wrong time, he gets dirty, too!"

"Women are so unreliable that they can't be witnesses in court."

"Or start divorce proceedings."

"They can't be priests either."

"And *this* woman was a prostitute. Just by being here, she tempts us to fornication and adultery."

It was hurting me to hear their blame and hate. Clever arguments to refute them crowded my mind. I struggled to remind myself that my purpose was not to prove them wrong, but to teach them to love—by my example as much as by my words. Let them experience for themselves the truth about women, and about power itself. Meanwhile, to ease my pain, I only half listened for a while as they expressed more prejudices and recited more laws at length.

I turned to Mary. Hanging her head, she stared at her plate, mute and immobile. I caught her attention by touching her hand once lightly. When she looked up, I met her sad gaze with a smile. The wind rustled the leaves and blew through my hair. I rebalanced my energies, opening more to the new kind of love coming to me from my future followers. Refreshed, I returned my full attention back to the men.

Peter was still droning on. "In the Temple at Jerusalem, there is a separate court for women, farther away from the Holy of Holies."

"The Temple?!" I exclaimed. "Our own bodies were created to be a temple for the Holy Spirit. God gave each person varying proportions of male and female. Every one of us needs to fully express both. You believe that gender limits what a person could or should do, but whatever you think is a limitation is not. Everything is possible—including life after death."

"Do you prefer her to us?" Peter cried out. "Are we to listen to a woman?!"

He was in such emotional pain that I carefully checked to make sure his soul was still drawing divine love from me. It was, as were the souls of all the others at the meal. The conflict was all occurring at more superficial layers of being.

"My beloved rock." I reached across the food and placed my hand over his for a moment. "I'm not without compassion for what you suffer as a result of following me. You're upset by the contrast between God's law of love and the rules that govern the world in which we live. We are in the world, but we don't belong to the world."

They were all genuinely struggling to understand what I had said and how it applied to the debate about women's role and the practical question of how my disciples would relate to each other, male and female.

"So you want us to judge people based on their character, not their gender," Andrew ventured.

"Actually I don't want you to judge people at all. That's God's job. God is your judge—your *only* judge."

"But that would lead to anarchy! We need courts to punish criminals," James protested.

"Don't judge, and you won't be judged." I was trying to answer as directly as possible, but I think they found my reply off the subject.

"What I'm saying about women applies to every kind of power imbalance," I continued. "I don't want you to exalt me, either. You know I am the Messiah, but I don't want you to tell anyone. Just because I am the son of God, doesn't mean I came to earth to be worshiped or to start a new religion."

I think this idea was the hardest of all for them, because they couldn't even discuss it. Peter changed the subject back.

"I just want to be sure that I understand what you're saying about women," Peter said. "You want us to live in a way that is significantly different even from the Baptist's disciples."

"What do you know of the Baptist's approach?" I asked.

"Andy said that at the Baptist's camp, women were allowed to listen to the teachings and be baptized, but they still kept in their place, silent and separate."

"Oh, *Andy* said." I leaned back, crossed my arms, and studied him until he squirmed. "That's a little different from the story you told me, Andy. Is that what you said?"

"Well, it *was* like that—most of the time."

I cocked my head and kept looking at him. "If you want to be the expert on what happened between men and women at the Baptist's camp, I think you should tell us all more details. Go ahead. Everyone seems quite interested."

This was an understatement. All eyes locked onto Andrew. The longer he kept silent, the more intensely they bored into him, drilling for clues as to what had happened between him and Mary.

I put an end to the silence. "Maybe I should tell them—"

"No!" Andrew interrupted. His eyes pleaded with me, as did his soul. I offered his soul a richer, denser form of my love than it was already drinking, but it would have to leave its comfort zone, "lower" itself in a way, and worship my divine heart in order to receive it. His soul hesitated, poised between fear and longing, between hunger and the pain of reaching for food.

"I would never betray something that you told me in confidence," I assured him. "I only meant that maybe I should tell them how men and women did study together at the Baptist's camp, since I spent at least as much time there as you did. Would you like to tell them about it, or should I?"

He just looked at me, uncertain.

"Or Mary could tell us," I continued.

Fear made Andrew speak abruptly. "Oh, no, I'll do it! Basically, women kept quiet and separate while John was teaching, but otherwise we could mingle. It was informal, kind of like a big family. I met Mary then, and I began to teach her the scriptures like we learned as boys in synagogue."

"You *taught* her?! Why?" Peter expressed the outrage and disbelief written on all the men's faces. They would have been much less offended if he had admitted having sex with her.

"It was before I knew she was a demon-possessed prostitute," Andrew said defensively.

"The demons are gone," I reminded them. "I cast all of them out of her. And she's not a prostitute anymore, either. You're all just my disciples now, nothing more. Andy, maybe you should tell them what you told me about her mind. What kind of mind did you say she had?"

Andrew looked sullenly at the half-empty plates in front of us. "A brilliant mind."

"What?!" None of them, Mary included, could believe their ears, but Peter was the one who pressured his brother. "What did you say?"

Andrew glared at Peter and raised his voice in anger. "I said she has a *brilliant* mind. That's why I taught her. She's very eager to learn scripture, and she can memorize it *and* analyze it extremely well. Much better than you ever could, Simon!"

Mary's startled face softened as her spirit began to soar. She sat up taller. It was obvious to me that she was not used to being praised like that.

I looked right at her and repeated it slowly so she

could savor it. "A brilliant mind. That's right, God gave you a mind that shines like a bright light. Nobody lights a lamp and then hides it. They put it on a stand so it can light up the whole house. In the same way, let your own light shine so that others can see your good works and thank your Creator."

She had said nothing throughout the entire discussion.

"Please tell us what you've been thinking, Mary," I urged. "You are one of my disciples, so you really must speak up when I'm teaching like this. It's for everyone's benefit."

It was as hard for her to speak before this group of men as it was for them to stop and listen. "Well," she began, "I was thinking how grateful I am to Andrew for teaching me. Thank you."

She looked right at him, but he stared into space as if he hadn't heard.

Then she quoted the end of a rather obscure psalm: "Blessed be God who has not rejected my prayer or stopped loving me!" She watched the men to gauge their reaction, but they seemed not to even recognize the scripture. She could tell that I knew she was showing off a bit. She gave me a conspiratorial smile.

"We can worship God together by taking turns choosing a line from the prophets or the psalms and singing them as a group," I explained. "Magdalene, I want you to start today. Choose another scripture for us."

"Oh, I don't know many scriptures," she said with false modesty.

"Yes, I can see that," I played along. "You don't have to know many. You just have to know one."

Her eyes flashed with intelligence as she thought for a moment. "The Baptist used to quote a prophecy from Isaiah over and over. It went like this: 'Prepare the way of the Lord in the wilderness and build a highway for our God through the desert.'"

All of us were transfixed by her delivery. With an almost musical voice, she stressed certain words to bring the passage alive in a way that was gorgeous, authentic to its original meaning, and best of all, resonant with Mary's own deep faith. It was rare for a woman to quote scripture to a group of men. I wasn't sure if I had ever experienced it before in my earthly life. I, too, had heard the Baptist quote this text often, almost as a threat, but in Mary's mouth it became a breath of fresh air, scented with budding hope.

I sang it back, composing a new tune to try to express how pleased I was with her and with the others for listening to her. Then John played a flute accompaniment while we all sang it together, then again and again in pairs, trios, and every different combination we could imagine.

As we sang, I enjoyed observing a long and varied parade of feelings cross Andrew's expressive face. His soul, like all the others, continued to nestle against me and nurse steadily, but wave after wave of contrasting emotions seemed to well up in him, then ebb away as he let go of them. He was still attracted to Mary—spiritually, intellectually, sexually—and he resisted it on each level. First he felt anger, then regret. He flipped through many memories, each one leaving him sad-

dened, and then freer. When that was done, future possibilities presented themselves, provoking dread or else
a longing that was even more frightening. What if he let
her get away with everything? As we sang the scripture,
he let its light fall on his fears and they melted away one
by one, leaving one last dull ache. He was *still* attracted
to her.

His soul dared to bow down to my divine heart and
accept the enriched love-milk that I had been offering
him there. He and I both raised our voices in relief as
his soul began to feed on the new formula. The others
sensed the energy shift, for we were all in tune with one
another then. We stopped singing after that chorus. We
were ready to move on to the next scripture.

Andrew spoke up. "Mary, do you know what comes
right before the scripture we just sang?"

"No, sir."

"Sir! You don't have to call me 'sir.' Call me Andrew.
Or Andy, like in the old days."

When she heard him say "Andy," she looked at him
in surprise, and their eyes met, really met, for the first
time since her arrival last night.

"I'll sing it for you," he offered. Andrew's voice
throbbed with passionate tenderness as he chanted, "'O
give comfort to my people, so says your God. With tender whispers, tell Jerusalem that her war is over and her
mistakes are forgiven.'"

Mary seemed to see Andrew for the first time, focus-
ing on who he was instead of who she could make him
become. Watching her listen to him was like watching
a flower blossom. His song stirred her soul and set up
a vibration that caused her heart, her mind, and then

her whole body to unclench and become receptive. The physical change in her was subtle: She smiled slightly and repositioned herself so her clothing emphasized the lines of her body. A similar change came over Andrew.

The other men watched them, and I sensed a kind of "thud" when all of them understood at once the true nature of what had gone on between Andrew and Mary. Actions, even sexual misconduct and taboo teaching, could be understood and prevented, but such transgressions paled in light of the powerful emotion that had caused them in the first place: wild, unexpected love that was growing stronger and evolving before our very eyes.

Because we were deeply bonded as a group at that moment, the rest of us were not only witnesses, but also allies or perhaps accomplices. It made the others uncomfortable. They fidgeted. Peter balled his fists, furrowed his forehead and was about to speak, but I cut him off by singing the verses again. I made sure we kept singing, in different configurations as before, hoping the meaning of these words would penetrate every mind.

Peter refused to sing with the rest of us for a long, long time. When his anger passed, he watched me, trying to fathom what I had in mind and what possible good might come of following me. He stayed silent as stone while the rest of us sang and John played flute.

On a human level, I felt sorry for Peter, because I, too, was protective of my younger siblings. I remembered how hard it had been for me to let go of my brother Jim during my wilderness fast. I had to be on the brink of death before I could trust God to take care of him. I made a conscious effort to turn Jim over to God once more, and to release each of my disciples, too.

When I turned my attention back to our song circle, Peter was singing his forgiveness to Andrew, who sounded it back to him. Every soul present was lapping at least some of the dense mercy-milk that I had offered first to Andrew, and forgiveness flowed freely back and forth among us all. We stopped making music as one body, feeling a sense of peace and completion.

"We are ready to begin teaching others about the kingdom of God," I announced.

John played a quick, dramatic trill to applaud my remark. As John played his final notes, I noticed his gnarled fingers were beginning to move more nimbly. Without any conscious effort on my part, we had entered into a healing process. I acted so ordinary when I healed people that Mary was the only one of my disciples with first-hand knowledge of my curative powers. The others hadn't noticed. I thought it was time to acquaint all of them with this side of me, so I decided to make a show of it.

"John, I see that you have trouble moving your fingers when you play the flute," I noted.

"Yes. I have some arthritis. I think it was caused by a fishing injury and the wear and tear of pulling in the nets. Plus I'm not as young as I used to be. Some days are better than others. Today is turning out to be a good day." He wiggled his fingers and smiled.

"Do you want to be healed?" I inquired.

"Of course."

Without my asking, he placed his knobby hand in mine and waited to see what would happen. For me, our touch was electric. I liked the wrinkled skin and calloused, muscular strength of a hand that had truly *lived*. As I rubbed my thumb over the misshapen, bony part of his hand, I let my divine heart re-ignite the multicolored jewels swirling in his soul. It wasn't so much that I personally healed him as that my presence crystallized his faith, clearing the pathway between him and God. "Your faith has made you whole," I announced.

He took back his hand and studied it as he flexed his fingers. Their rugged appearance had not changed. "I can move every finger more freely now. Praise God," he said with quiet awe.

The others smiled vaguely at us, puzzled about how to interpret what they had just witnessed. None of them had paid attention to John's ailment before. I saw no reason to explain further.

John rested his newly healed hand on my knee and I let it linger there. We were touching in the familiar way of people who have already kissed. Mary noticed instantly. Her eyebrows shot up in surprise as she cast a questioning glance at me.

I confirmed her suspicions with a smile. She looked around and saw that the others were already used to the little intimacies that passed between me and John. Mary settled back, at ease with our group for the first time now that she knew the lay of the relationship landscape.

"Let's go find some more women to join us," I proposed.

Resistance rose in every man's face, then washed away. Tranquility prevailed as they loaded the few remaining pieces of bread and fruit into a bag. Mary hesitated over her big, perfect pomegranate, still uneaten. She held it with her fingertips, feeling its ripeness, then added it to the communal food bag. Andrew looked more pensive than usual.

Peter, standing beside him, couldn't wait any longer to talk to him. He made his tone of voice the gentlest I had ever heard from him. Still, it was loud enough for all of us to hear. "So, I see why you wouldn't marry that nice girl we picked out for you."

"Oh, *Simon!* Leave me alone!" Andrew, who had thought himself beyond embarrassment, was embarrassed once more as Mary looked down with a shy smile, obviously trying not to make him feel any more self-conscious.

Andrew turned to me. "Can I walk ahead?"

"Sure. Take the road to Nazareth. I need to talk with someone there."

Andrew took the south road out of Magdala with me behind him and the others further back. Soon Mary scampered past me to catch up with Andrew. They were close enough for me to hear them.

"Andy, you forgave me before I had a chance to apologize. I'm sorry for hurting you. I didn't mean any of those awful things I said."

"I didn't forgive you because you were sorry or because you have changed or for any reason having anything to do with you. I forgave you because I'm trying to follow the path of forgiveness that the Rabbi teaches." After a pause, he added, "I hope you'll forgive me, too."

"Forgive you?!" She sounded shocked. "For what?"

They lowered their voices and walked closer together, so the rest of their conversation was too soft to hear.

chapter nine:
break with the past

I FELT A SENSE OF DISSONANCE as my disciples and I approached my family home in Nazareth late that afternoon. Everything looked the same, but I felt different from before. We rounded the last curve in the dirt footpath and saw the house where I had grown up.

The first to greet us were the animals. The few sheep and goats that my family kept trotted up to me. I made clucking noises at our chickens. They cocked their heads and strutted over to me.

Next came some of my nieces and nephews who were playing in the courtyard. "Uncle Jesus! Uncle Jesus!" We hugged and kissed each other.

Older members of my extended family poured out of the house and nearby woodshop to embrace me, including Jim, the next oldest brother after me. His soul reminded me of an unsprouted seed: hard-shelled, but full of potential. His soul hadn't changed much since childhood, but physically Jim had grown to look so much like his father that for a moment I thought he *was* Papa-Joe. People said that Jim and I were both handsome, with our earth-tone brown skin and dark eyes, hair, and beards, but my look was more refined and androgynous. Jim had Papa-Joe's sturdy build, distinguished features and ready smile—except Jim wasn't smiling now.

"What took you so long?" he challenged. His whiny, accusatory tone meant that he had missed me a lot.

"I am here now," I said and began gesturing to each person with me. "I want you to meet my friends: John, Andrew, Mary Magdalene, Peter, James, Susanna, and Joanna. I just met these last two today when we were walking here from Magdala." The ripeness of their souls had attracted us to each other, but I had paid attention and made sure that the next people to join us were women.

My family welcomed them all easily. They were used to new people following me around, wanting to get to know me and enjoying the atmosphere of camaraderie that I created.

Before I could start naming all my relatives, Jim intervened.

His jovial voice showed how much he enjoyed performing the role of host. "Everyone is welcome to eat with us and stay here if you need lodging. We'll have a welcome-home party for Jesus tonight. Kids, go tell the rest of the family that Jesus is back and invite them to celebrate with us tonight."

Some of the older children dashed off, while others clung to my hands and cloak. I heard a newborn baby crying in the house. I didn't recognize the voice. "Who's that?"

"Debbie had her first baby while you were away," Jim announced.

"Oh, I've got to meet my new niece!" I exclaimed.

"She's inside with Mom. She just finished the first stage of her days of purification after childbirth, so you can go ahead and hug her if you like," he explained.

As I proceeded to the house, Joanna sidled up to me and spoke under her breath. Her soul was like soil rich in natural resources. She bore the fine clothing and manner of the wealthy. "I know that everyone is supposed to offer hospitality, but it looks like it might be a hardship for your family to feed so many guests. I don't want to insult them by offering them money, so do you think I should go buy some extra food? I'm a woman of means and my husband even works for King Herod. I'd like to use my wealth to support you and your ministry."

I paused and looked at her. Joanna was masking her age through the skillful use of cosmetics around her eyes. She probably had never entered the home of a carpenter, nor of anyone else belonging to the middle class.

"This looks like poverty to you," I stated.

Joanna glanced at our house nervously. "I wish I could do something to help."

She was right that my family would have to scrape together the resources to hold a party in my honor. I was on the verge of worry when I remembered that I could trust God to provide for all my needs, including this one. I drew on the deep well of assurance in my divine heart. I felt a sudden, brief surge of certainty. It was stronger—or perhaps more physical—than I had ever felt.

"It's okay," I assured Joanna. "You can help by accepting the hospitality that's offered to you, even if it seems way below your usual standard."

I went right in to see the new baby. Almost everyone followed me and squeezed into the house. The large, single room had two levels: The ground level served as a stable for the animals, while a platform built on a low stone arch made a living area for people. The walls were coated with white plaster. The few windows were barely big enough for an adult to crawl through. Most of the household items were neatly organized on shelves or hanging on the walls, where I saw rings of dried figs, skins filled with wine, and a familiar assortment of pottery, baskets, bedding, and utensils for cooking, spinning, and weaving. The space was packed with everything the people and animals needed to live, but still it smelled clean, like figs and olive oil.

"Hey, Jesus!"

"Welcome!"

I recognized the souls behind the voices: one pure-white light, the other small and birdlike. Mom and my youngest sister were sitting together in the corner.

"Debbie! Congratulations!" I cried out.

Debbie smiled at me through the noise of the baby. She was trying unsuccessfully to comfort her child.

"May I hold the baby?" I asked.

She seemed reluctant. "Well, okay. Let me show you how."

"I *know* how! I held you all the time, starting when you were even younger than this little darling."

"But she's sickly and cries a lot. Mom and I give her medicinal herbs and pray every day for her healing," Debbie chirped. Her face and mannerisms had always reminded me of a sparrow.

Moving cautiously, Debbie demonstrated how to support the baby's head with her hand, then handed me the crying infant wrapped in bands of cloth. "Anna, meet your Uncle Jesus."

"Anna!" I couldn't contain my joy. Baby Anna looked right in my eyes and stopped crying. I kissed her tiny hands and let her grasp my beard. "Isn't she a honey? A brave, sweet new soul ready for the world!"

Then I cradled her near my breast, rocking her as I searched her whole energy system for the source of her illness. I noticed that her soul was still relying on an energy apparatus like an umbilical cord to connect to God through her mother. I used my divine power to gently disengage her soul from her mother and guide the soul-cord directly to God, where it plugged in naturally and began drawing energy. Anna evoked a wave of healing tenderness in me, which I sent vibrating through her. She fell asleep in my arms.

"How did you quiet her?" Debbie asked, amazed. "She never looks so peaceful."

"Love finds love," I replied.

Mom and I exchanged glances. She understood then that I had just healed the baby. She sat in our simple hut with the same dignity as if she were seated in a palace. Her face was shaped like the moon and her round eyes glowed with inner peace. She had the wrinkles and silver-streaked braid of a woman her age, but her smile was girlish. I smiled, too, and looked away quickly, proud but also shy at displaying my new healing ability before Mom.

My family was used to my maternal side, but my disciples reacted strongly to my obvious comfort with babies. They hadn't seen me—or any man—display such expertise with infants before. My female disciples were charmed, while most of my male disciples turned away to admire a cedar chest, intricately mitered and carved around the edge with intertwined triangles and Stars of David.

"Rabbi, I've never seen a chest so beautiful. Did you make it?" John asked.

When my family heard him call me "Rabbi," they all stared at me, including the children.

I tried to act casual. "Yes, I made that chest."

Jim interrupted their exclamations of praise. "Jesus, I need to talk to you in the wood shop."

"Just let me say goodbye to Anna." I cuddled her, not wanting our first meeting to end.

"Rabbi, may we come and see the wood shop, too?" Peter asked.

Some of my other male disciples repeated his question, eager to do something that they considered manly. Again all eyes in my family turned to me, questioning why people would want to call me "Rabbi" and why I would allow it.

"Yes, yes, you can see the shop. In a moment."

I poured my full attention on the baby. "Anna, beloved by God," I cooed.

Then from somewhere near me I felt a pang of longing so sharp that it broke my concentration, which was almost impenetrable, and sent a quiver to the core of my divine heart. I relied on my divine senses to find its source: Mary Magdalene. She had pushed through the crowded room to stand at my elbow, watching my interaction with the infant. Her eyes brimmed with unwept tears. Nobody had ever, *ever* loved her like that when she was a baby, not even for a moment. Never. It made me want to cry, too.

I handed sleeping Anna back to her mother and

slipped my arm around Mary's waist. I let her snuggle close to me while my divine tears fell on the places in her soul that had been stunted since infancy by lack of love. My divine tears spattered uselessly against undeveloped receptors that should have been able to absorb them.

Still, I was awed by the strength of Mary's soul. Even when it had been so severely neglected, the power of its soul-longing was strong enough to pierce my own concentration, my own heart. Or did the neglect it had survived actually strengthen her soul? My human mind struggled to figure out why God had allowed Mary to suffer when she was just a baby. Then my divinity broke forth like the dawn and suffused me with an understanding that was complete and yet fleeting. I could no more capture it in my human mind than I could hold a sunbeam in my hand. I, too, needed faith in order to face the mysteries of God's will. I accepted that God's mercy was so great that it was sometimes invisible to the human mind. My divine tears kept falling on her soul.

"It's not too late for you, Magdalene," I whispered so that only she could hear. "With God nothing is impossible."

She leaned on me, unsteady on her feet from what was passing between us at the soul level. I looked at my Mom. I could see her soul much more clearly than I had been able to do before my baptism. Its crackling, crystalline beauty astonished me. No wonder my Father chose her to bear His child.

"Mom, I want you to meet someone. This is my disciple Mary Magdalene. Mary, this is my mother. Her name is Mary, too. She's the one who first taught me that God can make anything happen."

Out of weakness as well as politeness, Mary dropped to her knees and bowed her head in a posture of greeting a superior. "God honors you, and so do I. You are fortunate to have carried God in your own womb."

"Oh, my," Mom chuckled. "We don't usually talk like that. Is *that* what you're teaching people?" She shot me a disapproving look.

Mary looked up. "Oh, no, he didn't teach me that. It came from my heart."

"From your heart?" Mom looked thoughtful.

Their eyes met in instant rapport. "Nobody has said anything like that to me since I was pregnant with Jesus. This is how I look at it: A Power greater than myself has empowered me."

While Debbie busied herself with the baby, Mom seemed to know the right words to say to Mary. "Come, my beloved daughter, and sit here with us." When Mom smiled wide, she revealed the slightly irregular outlines of her teeth, which only added to her cuteness and charm.

Mary acted as if the words "my beloved daughter" were three precious gems that Mom had dropped into her unsuspecting hands. Mary clutched her hands together at her heart, treasuring the intimacy that had just been bestowed upon her and also trying to still her beating heart. She was too overcome to speak.

"Come, come, daughter," Mom chided her, just as she spoke to my sisters when they didn't obey quickly enough. She took Mary's arm and half-dragged her until they sat side by side.

They were dressed the same, in the simplest possible style with their cloaks adorned only by basic embroidery and their hair in a single braid beneath a head covering—and yet on the physical level they gave the impression of being opposites: One was old and the other young. One was serenely, supremely confident and the other desperate for approval and trained to please. Mom's posture was motherly, while Mary was still sexy somehow, just by the way she tossed her head and gathered her robes around her ankles. Seeing them side by side like that, I was fascinated not by their differences, but by a kindred spirit they shared. They were both exceptionally intelligent, but it wasn't that. My divine senses revealed that their orientation toward God was almost identical: ready to love even through suffering. I had an eerie sense that they shared a similar future...involving me. I found them both utterly beautiful. Mom smiled at me and nodded.

I left them like that and went to the wood shop as Joanna joined Mom, Mary, and a group of my aunts, sisters, and their daughters. On my way out, I heard one of my nieces ask, "Grandma Mary, did you bake a lot of extra bread today? I just checked and found that we already have enough bread for Jesus' welcome-home feast!"

I realized with a start that my concern for feeding everyone may have actually caused the bread to multiply. But I wasn't sure. I hadn't *tried* to do it. All I did was trust my divinity. Maybe my Father had told Mom to prepare for our arrival.

"Jesus, come on!" Jim said. "You're still as much of a dreamer as ever, I see. Some things never change." He yanked me away from the conversation and out toward the woodshop. I could tell from his urgent manner that filling my place in the household had been harder than he expected.

✛ ✛ ✛

Jim and I walked side by side to the nearby wood-shop and the men followed. Susanna, one of my new disciples, ran up from behind us. "Rabbi, may I come, too? I've always wanted to learn carpentry, but nobody would teach me."

"Everyone's welcome," I replied.

Jim stared at her with open, disparaging curiosity.

"What's *your* problem?" Susanna asked him rudely.

Jim was so surprised at being confronted that he answered meekly, "It's just that I've never seen a woman with a man's short haircut. I've never met a woman who wanted to know about carpentry, either."

"Get over it, Jim," I snapped. "It's like you see a speck of sawdust in her eye, but you don't notice the log in your own eye."

He glared at me. "You and I need to talk in private," he said, then addressed Susanna. "You're welcome, of course. I never said that you weren't."

His mood brightened when he began giving a tour of the shop to Susanna and the others. Wood chips crunched under our feet as Jim and I showed them the carpentry tools I knew so well: saws, mallets, chisels, and planes to shape the wood as well as rule sticks, squares, and a plummet and line to make sure our lines were true. I could tell from the neatly arranged tools, piles of fresh lumber, and works in progress that Jim was running the business well.

"Jesus and I will demonstrate how to use the bow-lathes," he declared without checking to see if I was willing. "I can entice the customers almost as well as Jesus did, but nobody can do the fine detailing that he does. Wait, I'll show you the menorah he built for the synagogue over in Capernaum."

Jim rummaged in the woodshop and returned with the beautiful seven-armed lampstand. I had created this unusual menorah by turning the seven spindles on the bow-lathe and then carving them with delicate patterns of Hebrew alphabets intertwined with vines. It was held together by an elaborate system of dowels. I had finished it with a high polish.

While my disciples marveled over my workmanship, Jim turned to me. "The synagogue hired us to replace the whole balcony railing with banisters to match this menorah. We've got all the wood ready. Let's make some banisters."

"Well, okay." I had come to tell him something that he didn't want to hear, and our best conversations usually occurred while we worked side by side in the carpentry shop. Jim took the necessary lumber to our main work area while I gathered the tools we would need: two bow-lathes and a set of various chisels. We knew each other's strengths and weaknesses so well that we didn't even have to discuss how to divide up the tasks.

He prepared to do the rough cut by dropping the first log into two Y-shaped braces set in a heavy plank. He fastened a leather strap around the log. Then he started turning the wood by pulling on a bow attached to the leather strap. His rapid back-and-forth movement propelled the lathe. With his other hand, he cut the wood.

When the log was trimmed down to size, he passed it to me for the decorative, detailed work. I ran my fingertips over the log and used my divine senses to probe the character of its grain. The pleasant scent of sawdust filled the air as I began spinning and shaping it. My disciples' admiring eyes made me feel self-conscious at first, but I lost myself in the creative process as I cranked out one banister after another.

Jim interrupted my train of thought. "*Rabbi*, is it?" he asked with a touch of sarcasm.

I looked up and saw that my disciples had all wandered away with my brothers, nephews, and uncles. I was alone with Jim and his questions.

"You've turned yourself into an expert on God?"

"Something like that." After my cousin's opposition, I wasn't surprised that my brother was hostile to my new life.

"Well, at least you're back," he sighed. "It's been a real hardship for me to cover for you while you were away. You were gone longer than I expected. I had to hire two people to fill in for you in the shop."

I just kept working, so he continued. "King Herod is accepting bids through tomorrow on a big construction job in Sepphoris. I did some research on the project. It's a government building, located close to the theater and one of the bathhouses. Remember all the fun we had when we worked construction together in Sepphoris?

We used to quit early, grab a bath, and then go to the theater."

"We had a lot of fun together," I agreed cautiously.

"So you should go to Sepphoris tomorrow and talk to the contractor. You can always sweet-talk them into accepting our bids."

I felt like I was suffocating. I tossed down the bow that tied me to the lathe and let the truth fly out of me: "I've gotta get away from all this!"

Jim stopped working and really looked at me for the first time that day. "What?"

"I tried to tell you before I left, and I came back to make sure you understood. I'm through with this life."

Genuine concern shone on his broad face. "You can't be serious about leading that bunch of losers!" he exclaimed. "Look, you're my big brother and I accept you just as you are, but don't you think you might be too...*gentle*...to head a group of disciples? There's always a lot of betrayal and back-stabbing inside religious cults. You'll face opposition from the religious leaders, too. You know how the chief priests and scribes are out to get the Baptist. He's going to end up arrested, imprisoned, probably even whipped and tortured. Are you sure you have what it takes to be a spiritual leader?"

"I am *absolutely sure* that I have what it takes."

I was so definite that he gave up and tried another approach. "Don't think I don't know what's going on," he taunted, already irritated with me again. "It's like what happened with you and that shepherd you fell for. Or that Pharisee that you thought was such hot stuff. When you started seeing prostitutes, I thought you had outgrown all that shit. There's a law against what you're doing with that tall, scruffy guy who's always next to you."

"John isn't scruffy!"

"Nobody really cares if you commit abominations with men, as long as you do a regular job, get married, and continue the family bloodline."

"I have other plans for my blood," I said coldly. "I'm a lot more like my Father than you realize, and I'm not going to hide it anymore."

Jim stared at me in stunned silence. All my brothers and sisters had grown up hearing the story of my birth—both Mom's version and the ugly rumors from the neighbors who called me a bastard. Jim and my other siblings had heard me refer to God as "Father" ever since I was a little boy. However, we all pretended that my divine ancestry made little difference. I certainly had never said anything to imply that my Father had given me special power or purpose—until now.

Jim's shock gave way to anger. "You just want to keep your status as head of this household and dump all the work on me! You expect me to work my ass off so you can waltz around the country indulging all your grandiose religious fantasies."

His attitude made me mad. "You can have the status and authority as head of this household!" I had intended to offer him this honor as a gift in the context of how much I loved and respected him, but now I threw it in his face.

"Do you mean it?" he asked.

"Yes, yes," I said impatiently.

This arrangement pleased him. Jim spoke so softly

that I could barely hear him. "We'll go with the spiritual solution then," he muttered, as if talking to himself.

He resumed his woodworking, and I did the same. As the late afternoon shadows lengthened, the only sound in the woodshop was the whirr of the lathes and the chipping of wood. After Jim finished prepping the last leg, he handed it to me and watched. I sensed his respect for the speed and expertise with which I sculpted it.

"I'm not going to bid on that Sepphoris job if you won't be here," he said. "We're going to be swamped just trying to keep up with the work that you were supposed to do. With baby Anna we have another mouth to feed. I'm going to have to work a lot harder, cut expenses, turn down all the jobs requiring fancy detailing—and I'll still have to hire extra help."

I hung my head lower over my lathe.

Jim noticed and softened his tone. "Oh, it's okay. Just help me finish these banisters. I tried subcontracting with a master carpenter, but the quality of his work was far inferior to yours. We'll lose our contract with the synagogue if I can't match the fine detailing you did on their menorah. I know how fast you can work when you try. You'll be done in a few days."

"I can't."

My casual manner made his face flush with anger. "It's for the synagogue, damn it! Isn't that holy enough for you? Won't you do one little thing to help me out?"

"You don't get it. I'm leaving tomorrow and I won't be back."

Jim crossed his husky arms. His heavy beard seemed to bristle as he scowled at me.

I put the finishing touch on one last banister with a long, skillful sweep of my chisel. Then I set it down. "I'm doing my Father's work now," I said.

This time Jim turned purple with rage. "Your Father?! Jesus, I'm so sick of hearing you blather on about your Father. I'm doing *my* father's work, too. But you don't give a damn. I can't believe you won't make these banisters."

"The way I live my life is my best teaching tool. I can't just stop trusting my Father and whip out some wood products because you're afraid that you won't have enough money."

"Yes, you can!"

"Nobody can work for two bosses. You have to give priority to one or the other. You can't devote yourself to God and to wealth," I insisted.

"Don't preach to me!" Jim was so enraged that he took the menorah I had built and slammed it to the ground. It splintered apart. At the soul level, no interaction had occurred between us at all throughout the entire conversation.

The pieces of the ruined menorah lay scattered at our feet as he yelled, "Go ahead and play God! See if I care!"

chapter ten:
lower temple

BY THE TIME AUTUMN TURNED to spring, my disciples had grown in number and in understanding. I decided to take some of my closest disciples—John, Mary, Andrew, and Peter—with me to the Temple shortly before the weeklong festival of Passover. On the way, we entertained each other with stories of our past visits to the Temple and, like many others on the road to Jerusalem, we sang psalms about the glories of the Temple.

Religious Law required Jewish men to make a pilgrimage to the Temple for Passover every spring to celebrate our people's exodus from slavery in Egypt. Visits to the Temple at Passover time were a beloved tradition for each of us, including the women, who often accompanied the men on the pilgrimage. This was the first time for me and my disciples to go to God's house together, with our fresh understandings of God, so all of us were looking forward to it.

We approached the Temple from the east, moving through the dry, almost uninhabited Kidron Valley and up a fairly steep cliff that led directly into the Temple grounds. As we drew near, my human mind was filled with memories of happy times at the Temple. Even as a boy, I liked to pray and study there with others who loved God as I did. Now that I was wed to the Holy

197

Spirit and publicly baptized, I expected to feel even greater joy and connection with God while I was at the Temple.

It was easy to see the Temple complex long before we reached it because it was an immense set of structures built on the highest spot in Jerusalem. The tallest and most holy building was constructed of snow-white stone partially covered with massive plates of gold. It looked like a golden mountain, so blindingly bright as it reflected the day's sun that I had to keep turning my eyes away. Smoke billowed from atop a cube of unhewn stone that was larger than a two-story house. This was the altar, where offerings of oxen, sheep, goats, pigeons, grain, and frankincense were burnt all day long to atone for sins. Though we were still far away, I could already smell the savory goodness of roasting food and sweet incense, a scent that had always pleased me.

The Temple was as magnificent as ever, but it didn't evoke the same emotions in me. I felt empty. My human side was so stunned by the unexpected void that I became disoriented.

"Is that the Temple?" I asked, even though I knew that it was.

"Of course." Andrew sounded exasperated that I should ask such an obvious question.

Peter, who was the most protective of me, came and wrapped his arm around my waist as we started the final ascent, just as he did when he was helping me move through crowds of people all wanting to touch me. His steady embrace grounded and soothed me. The crowds around us now took no notice of us as they headed toward the Temple. Some of them were even being healed as they brushed past me, but they attributed it to their proximity to the Temple. Peter continued singing psalms of pilgrimage while I fell silent, listening to the songs of the people and turning deep inside for God's guidance as we climbed upward.

I began to walk alone when we reached the steeper pathways and staircases close to the Temple. Shouts of jubilation filled the air when we arrived at the high perimeter wall of huge stones perfectly carved to fit together. "Hosanna! Hooray! Hallelujah!" people cried out as they walked through what was called the Beautiful Gate. We passed through the double doors of the monumental brass gateway to set foot on the pavement stones of the Temple complex.

We were in the Court of the Gentiles, a vast open space where everyone was welcome. It entirely surrounded the rest of the Temple complex. The baaing and bellowing of animals mixed with distant music and countless human languages. Nobody was paying much attention to each other. People were so enthralled by the building and its rituals that they had forgotten about the God that it was built to honor. My disciples began handing out coins to some of the beggars who always waited at the Temple gateways.

Memories came flooding back as I looked around the Court of the Gentiles. It was bordered on all four sides by a series of magnificent columns supporting a roof. The sheltered porticos behind these colonnades served as inspirational open-air classrooms where I had spent many pleasant hours listening to preachers, discussing with teachers, and debating the Law with scribes, all within glorious view of the Temple itself.

Visitors from as far away as Rome always crowded the Court of the Gentiles, but today was especially busy because Passover was approaching. Along with more pilgrims, there were more police. Roman soldiers dressed in helmets and armor plate carried swords and clubs as they patrolled among the crowd. Some rode on horseback. Pontius Pilate, the Roman governor, beefed up security in Jerusalem during our nationalistic holiday by deploying extra Roman soldiers, both local mercenaries and troops sent from Rome. I was part of a bustling crowd, but I continued to feel lonely and I was getting a headache.

I raised my eyes to what was called the Holy of Holies. I had to squint because the light reflecting from the Temple's gold-plated pinnacle seemed more brilliant than the sun itself. The Holy of Holies stood at the pinnacle of the Temple complex, which was organized as a series of spaces nested inside one another—each one smaller, higher and more exclusive than the one before. In earlier Temples, the Holy of Holies had contained laws carved on stone tablets, but those were lost centuries ago. Now the Holy of Holies was basically an empty room intended to be God's dwelling place. It was hidden behind clouds of smoke rising from the altar, plus an outer curtain and an inner veil. No human being ever visited there except the high priest, who entered once a year on the Day of Atonement with burning incense and the blood of sacrificed animals to make atonement for the sins of all Jewish people.

I had never been there in the flesh. Because I wasn't a priest, I wasn't even allowed to enter the courtyard closest to it, the Court of the Priests. It was odd to think that I would receive the death penalty if I physically entered the Holy of Holies, since I had visited it many times in my meditations. I remembered how Satan took me up there once, too, during my wilderness temptation. My stomach churned when I thought of how he had almost convinced me to jump off.

I kept my gaze on the Holy of Holies, knowing how my Father liked to rest there. I let my consciousness float upward and linger before the veil. I hadn't paid much attention to the veil before, but this time I was drawn by its vivid blue, purple, and crimson yarns. Two figures were skillfully worked into the veil's tapestry. With a warm flush of surprised recognition, I saw that they were a couple of cherubs entwined in a sexual embrace. They mirrored the holy wholeness of my union with the Holy Spirit.

A breeze rippled the cherubs and carried me to the other side of the veil. I sensed myself in a windswept room with sunlight pouring in through a narrow window. Shaded from the glare of sun and sin, I rested in unspeakable peace. The air was slightly hazy, perhaps from the incense and offerings burning on the altar outside, and filled with a strong sense of potential energy, raw power relaxing between actions. It was like being the chamber of a human heart as it pauses between heartbeats.

To be in the Holy of Holies with God as God was to feel peace and be peace, to feel potential and be potential, and yet...it was almost *too* peaceful and remote. Today I sensed and shared my Father's longing to be with the people who loved Him, not towering above so high and mighty. Out of that longing, my Father had decided to send me into the world.

I began to lower my human eyes. The next thing I saw was the enormous Fortress of Antonia looming behind the Temple at the northwest corner of the Temple complex. The Roman soldiers who occupied Jerusalem lived there. In the past I had ignored the fortress, preferring to focus on God's house. Now I looked and saw soldiers surveying the Temple court-yards from atop its towers and from narrow windows in the tower walls. If they saw anything that threatened the Roman government, hundreds of soldiers could rush down stairways that opened directly into the porticos of the Court of the Gentiles.

I dropped my gaze to ground level. I couldn't help seeing what everyone saw when they first crossed through the Temple gates: moneychangers. Row upon row of tables were set up for moneychangers to do business. These men, many with half-shekel coins in their ears to denote their trade, cried out lustily to lure customers, "Welcome! Come here to exchange your dirty Roman coins for holy Temple coins!"

Every adult male Jew had to pay an annual tax to the Temple of a half shekel, which was roughly equivalent to two days' wages. This tax and any other financial offering to the Temple had to be made in Temple coinage. As Jews, we hated the Roman coins because they were issued by the conquerors who had occupied our land and because they bore a picture of their god Caesar. We considered it sinful idolatry to make any kind of likeness of people or animals, let alone a pagan deity. Crowds of people were lined up at every money-changer's table to trade in the repulsive heathen coins. When I was a student here, the rabbis had confided to me that the high priest received kickbacks on profits from the currency transactions.

Nearby the sellers of sacrificial animals were trying to outshout the moneychangers:

"Get an unblemished lamb now for your guilt offering before we sell out!"

"Unleavened bread on sale today! The perfect burnt offering for people on a budget!"

"Attention new moms! God will be pleased if you purify yourself with our pairs of pigeons!"

Their cries mingled with the sounds and stench of the sacrificial animals trapped in pens and cages behind each seller's table. Some pilgrims had brought homemade bread, heads of barley from the current harvest, and animals from their own flocks to sacrifice, but many more stopped to haggle over the price and buy. In the past I thought all this fuss over coins and sacrificial animals was silly. Today it made me sick.

The people's longing for God was like a powerful river that almost sucked me into its current as it gushed past me. I yearned to satisfy them and to assure them of my love, too. Instead of flowing directly to and from God, as soul energy should, the flood of human longing was being diverted into all kinds of unnecessary side channels. The crosscurrents left me dizzy both in my divinity and in my physical body.

My head throbbed. In my pain and loneliness, I looked to my disciples. We were still standing just inside the entry gate. They were bickering while wave upon wave of people pushed past us.

"No, we should save at least enough to buy food for tonight." Mary tended to be the most practical.

"But people give us food and donations everywhere we go. Where is your faith?" Andrew challenged her.

"If we're going to spend all the money, let's just buy all lambs instead of pigeons for our guilt offerings," Peter proposed.

"But that only benefits those who sin the most!" Andrew argued.

The sins that concerned them were small infractions of the Law done unintentionally, such as uttering a rash oath or accidentally touching a menstruating woman. Crimes such as theft might require financial restitution as well as sacrifice. Under the system of Temple sacrifices, no atonement was possible for the most serious sins done on purpose such as idolatry, murder, or adultery. For people convicted of those sins, there was the death penalty.

I felt a chill even though the sun was hot as I understood, as if for the first time, that the Temple was not just a center of worship but also the courthouse where these laws were administered. Trials were held in courtrooms in the Court of the Gentiles. The accused could be sentenced to death by the Sanhedrin, our ruling council of seventy priests, scribes, and elders. Before the Romans occupied our land, we Jews usually administered capital punishment by stoning. Now when a death sentence was issued by the Sanhedrin, it had to be approved by the Roman governor and was often carried out via the Roman method, crucifixion. Both methods killed the body, but Jewish tradition said that crucifixion also cursed the soul.

I began thinking about the cup that my Father kept offering me in my meditations. Long ago my Father gave the Law to people so that God and humanity could get closer, but sometimes the Law became an impediment. If people thought sacrifices were so all-fired important, then God was going to provide a sacrifice that would atone for human sin once and for all: His beloved son, me.

I understood the need for blood sacrifice. People were afraid that they were too sinful to approach God just as they were. I had gotten sucked into that dynamic when I was a student at the Temple. My teachers believed that following the purity code would unite humanity and divinity. I thought I would give it a try. I had to block my divine awareness almost entirely in order to follow the purity laws to the letter: Don't eat this, don't touch that kind of person, never on the sabbath, kill this kind of creature if you make a mistake.... Maybe I should have known that suppressing my divinity was not a path to God, but at first I didn't. I felt the thrill of following rules mercilessly to prove my worth—I forgot that I was already worthy. Only when my divinity rose to the surface and took the initiative was I able to put an end to it and move on.

Peter interrupted my thoughts. "Rabbi, do you want us to buy any sacrificial bread or animals for you?"

"It's not necessary," I replied.

They all looked at me in surprise for a moment, then resumed arguing.

"I still think that we should spend all the money we have," Peter insisted. "Whatever we don't need for buying sacrificial bread and animals, we should exchange and give to the Temple as an offering."

"Remember, the Rabbi taught us to give away everything we have to the *poor*—not to the Temple," John snapped back.

After more debate, they finally worked out some kind of compromise and agreed that John, Mary, and I would go change money while Andrew and Peter went shopping.

"Afterwards we'll all meet at that empty table." Peter pointed to the one table that stood vacant among the moneychangers.

People kept jostling us as we waited in the slow-moving line. Some tried to sneak in front of us. Others just wanted to hear the deals being struck ahead. The moneychangers used scales to weigh the Roman coins presented to them and sometimes refused to give full value in Temple coinage, claiming that some silver had been shaved from the coins' edges. They seemed to work in pairs or teams with one man handling the transactions while others packaged the Roman money, brought fresh supplies of Temple coins, and shouted out a sales pitch to potential customers.

"Change your money here and secure God's blessing!"

"God will love you if you use our money!"

Rage boiled up inside me. I couldn't take it anymore. "I'm going to that empty table now," I blurted to John and Mary.

I shoved my way through the crowd, climbed atop the table and began shouting my own message: "It is written, 'My house shall be called a house of prayer,' but you have turned it into a hotbed of thieves and scam artists."

That got their attention. Even many of the money-changers paused in mid-transaction to look at me out of curiosity. Some lost count of the money they were exchanging and had to start over.

"This Temple will be destroyed so it can be rebuilt in people's hearts. Don't forget the words of the prophet Hosea, 'I want true love, not sacrifice, and knowledge of God instead of burnt offerings,'" I continued.

People in the crowd listened with astonishment as I went on and on like that for a while.

"If you want to know more, I'll be teaching here at the Temple all week," I concluded and jumped down from the table. My disciples had all gathered there with their Temple coins, sacrificial bread, several cages of twittering birds, and even a lamb. They looked frightened, for none of them had ever seen me so angry, and they weren't sure what to do.

My headache was no better, and I was breathing heavily. My glance fell on the lamb they had purchased. I felt a deep empathy with the sacrificial lamb far beyond any I had experienced before. I picked up the lamb, remembering that day in the cave when I joined Old Snake and the other animals in one peaceful pack.

While my disciples watched in silence, I let myself be comforted by the lamb's soft, white fleece and playful spirit. She basked in my love, holding nothing back. Although she was not aware that she was about to sacrifice her life, she was perfectly willing to offer her whole future to me. I let her model for me how to feel lamb-feelings of innocence and trust. Then I thanked her for her valuable lesson and for her life by pouring a special blessing through her entire energy system while I petted her wooly body.

As the lamb wriggled in my arms, I looked at my disciples' worried faces. Each of their souls was still nursing steadily from my divine heart. I fed all of them an extra dose of love as I tried to explain, "I am the good shepherd who is willing to die for the sheep."

I could tell from their blank expressions that they didn't understand. I had meant to reassure them but, if anything, they looked more troubled. After an uncomfortable silence, Mary spoke. "Rabbi, we could leave right now if you don't want us to make any offerings or sacrifices today."

Glad for a plan of action, the others voiced their agreement. They sounded disappointed, but eager to please.

"Yes, we could take the birds and lamb with us overnight and bring them back tomorrow," Andrew said.

They searched my face for a sign of approval and found none.

"Or we could give them away," John suggested.

I said nothing.

Mary tried again to guess what would please me, stretching her mind to think of what was almost unthinkable. "We could let the birds fly away free right now."

"What an idea!" Peter exclaimed, expressing the shock that was on all their faces. Then they turned to me and waited for some sign as to what we should do.

I actually wanted to leave the Temple right then and there, but I could tell they would be sorry to turn away

now after our long, festive pilgrimage to the only earthly place they had ever thought of as God's home. They
hadn't been with me long enough to understand the
true nature and location of God's kingdom and how to
enter it. Besides, I didn't want to force them to give up
the only path to God that they knew. I had not yet
made the personal sacrifice that would clear a new way
for them.

"It's okay if you want to offer these gifts to God here
today," I said.

With relief, they gathered their bread and birdcages,
and we started leading the lamb toward the next courtyard, the Court of Women. They didn't realize that they
had already pleased God with a sacrifice: their willingness to give up this ritual if I had requested it. All of
them, especially Andrew, chattered cheerfully.

"Rabbi, you were great! You sounded just like the
Baptist!" he crowed.

Steps and ramps led us to the entrance to the Court
of Women. The reason for the name was that this was
the highest level women were allowed to enter. Armed
Temple police stood at the entrance, ready to enforce an
inscription carved into the stone gateway in Hebrew,
Latin, and Greek. It forbade entry to all Gentiles and
ritually unclean Jews on penalty of death.

The rule didn't require us to be physically clean.
Many of us, myself included, were dirty and sweaty
from the journey through the desert to the Temple, and
that was acceptable. Those who needed ritual purifica-

tion could dip themselves in pools set up for this purpose. Some people were also rinsing pots, mattresses, and even saddles that had come in contact with ritually defiled persons or substances. We bypassed the pools and stepped into the Court of Women, which was much smaller than the last, with materials and workmanship that were more refined. Despite its name, there were plenty of men here, too.

My head ached even worse as we waited in line to drop our offering money into one of the Temple treasuries. These bronze receptacles were shaped like inverted funnels to ensure that funds flowed in only one direction.

"Mary, remember how you rubbed my neck the other day to make my headache go away?" I asked. "Would you do that for me now?"

"Oh, no! Not in this holy place!" she exclaimed. Out of piety she had veiled her face so only her eyes showed, but the expression of horror in them was plain to see. I felt rejected. It must have showed because she looked stricken and stammered, "I mean, if that's what you really want, I'll do it."

"Do you feel our touch is unholy?" I asked her.

"I just didn't want to defile you or embarrass you."

I had forgotten the petty prohibitions on touching again. The purity code listed so many ways that a woman could ritually contaminate a man that cross-gender touching simply didn't happen at the Temple.

Mary hung her head, looking miserable. "Do you really want me to touch you while we're here, Rabbi? I'll do what you want."

I sensed that she saw my request as some extension

of her former work as a prostitute, using her body to please a man. That wasn't my intention at all. Since we were in God's house, I personally had felt that I could relax and be casual with my friends just as I did when we visited my family home in Nazareth. "Forget it," I told her. "I only asked because I think of you as a healer."

While trying to get my physical needs met, I had accidentally reopened an old wound in Mary's soul. It was bleeding and in pain. With my divine heart, I rubbed some healing oil on her soul-injury and let myself love her without restraint. Her soul flinched at first. When the rest of her soul had relaxed, I focused my love only on the wound, trusting that this time it would knit together with her faith and heal into a stronger source of compassion and further growth.

I tried rubbing my own neck, but I couldn't reach it very well. I remembered that touch between two males was considered much less defiling. I looked at John expectantly, hoping that he would offer to massage it for me. His spiritual path sometimes led him to initiate an ecstatic kiss with me, but today he didn't seem to notice me. The distractions and formality of the Temple had put a distance between me and my disciples. Usually we were so tuned in to each other's needs that we helped one another long before anyone asked for assistance. More than wanting my neck rubbed, I had longed for the sense of connection that human touch gave me. Now I felt more isolated than ever.

I began watching the people around us, comparing their clothing to their souls. Lots of well-dressed scribes scurried past us. They were experts in the Law whose duties included teaching, legal interpretation, and recording the minutes of Sanhedrin meetings. The higher their status, the longer their sleeves and hem-lines. In contrast, their souls were relatively unkempt. Many of those ahead of us in line wore the brightly col-ored robes of the wealthy, but their souls were dull. As they poured their donations into the treasury, I heard the sound of countless coins jingling and clinking against each other.

Soon we added our own coins to the treasury, recit-ing the standard prayers and receiving a perfunctory blessing from an official who droned the same words for donor after donor. Lest my disciples think the mon-eychangers were the only robbers at the Temple, I tried to explain my opinion to them as bluntly as I could before we moved on.

"Watch out for the scribes. They just love parading around in long robes, being greeted with respect in the marketplaces, and getting the best seats in the syna-gogues and at banquets. These hypocrites devour wid-ows' savings and cover it up with long prayers."

A jaunty, well-groomed soul caught my attention. It belonged to an elderly woman who hobbled past us and plunked two copper coins into the treasury. She was dressed in sackcloth, woven from the bristly, black hair of goats. Her garment meant she was a widow, and it was so ragged that she must have been a poor one.

My voice swelled with emotion. "Look, this poor widow has put in more than anyone else. They gave part of their disposable income, but she is so poor that she put in everything that she had to live on."

"Do you mean that displeases you?" Andrew asked.

"I said they devour widows' savings! Do you think that pleases me?"

My disciples stared at me for a moment, trying to take in my teaching. The sacrificial lamb, now in John's arms, bleated.

"Let's go," I said.

We walked toward the Nicanor Gate, the bronze gate leading to the Court of Israel. It was enormous, but not quite as wide as the gate before it. Stairs and rampways for leading oxen and other large sacrificial animals reached to the gate itself.

When we arrived at the top, Mary spoke up. "I'll meet you *right here*. I'm going to offer my pigeons down in the Court of Women, but I'll do it quickly and come right back here and wait for you."

I had forgotten that we would have to separate.

chapter eleven:
upper temple

AT THE ENTRANCE to the Court of Israel, yet another multilingual inscription warned us that any woman who passed beyond this gate would be killed. Women were getting a good view of the altar, though, by standing behind the bronze bars that stretched along the porch on both sides of the Nicanor Gate. The next court was narrow, so there was not much physical distance from here to the altar. Under the watchful eyes of Temple police, many women and girls were crowded along this viewing platform to observe and pray as priests burned offerings atop the stone cube of the altar.

"Magdalene, I'd love to stay here with you," I said. "But I need to go into the Court of Israel to look for a member of the Sanhedrin who used to be my favorite teacher. He can get me access to teach here."

I looked at my male disciples, hoping one of them would volunteer to stay here with Mary. Instead their eyes glittered with even more desire to proceed.

"Rabbi, we had no idea that you knew one of the big shots here!" Peter burst out. "Is he a priest or a Pharisee?"

John answered with his own eager speculations. "He can't be a priest. They're all upper-class snobs who can't see past the written Law. Surely the Rabbi knows one of the Pharisees. They're more like us, regular people who consider the oral traditions, too."

Without comment, I studied Mary. She looked panicky.

"You won't forget me, will you?" she asked. "If you leave me here, I won't be able to find you again because we haven't decided where to spend the night. It's too late to go all the way back to where the other disciples are tonight. I'll be left all alone here in the big city with hardly any money." Her voice quavered, and she blinked back her tears. The implication was clear: She would be tempted back into prostitution. Her soul tensed, grasped, and dug itself into my divine heart with a viselike grip. It held on so tightly that it choked off the very comfort it was seeking: my continued love.

"We'll be back for you," Peter assured her.

"We won't forget," John added.

"I promise you I will not leave this Temple without you—no matter what!"

Andrew's more impassioned promise made the edges of her eyes crinkle as she smiled slightly, but they still brimmed with tears and fears.

"And as for money, you can keep all that we have," Andrew continued. Peter jumped as Andrew actually reached into the folds of Peter's belt where he kept his money and helped himself to all the coins there. Andrew also collected John's money and mixed the coins together with his own. I didn't bother carrying money. Then he poured all of our cash into Mary's hand, being careful not to touch her. The coins were copper, so it amounted to almost nothing.

As the coins hit Mary's hand, Andrew's well-intentioned gesture suddenly reminded both of them of another time when Andrew had paid Mary and of the estrangement that had followed. Their eyes met. Then they quickly looked away. Each recognized in the other the fear that they were doomed to repeat the past even when they were trying to live free in God's kingdom. Andrew looked helpless as he realized that he had made Mary feel worse instead of better.

"I'll just stand right here and watch everyone who passes, so you won't be able to leave without me seeing you," Mary proclaimed with bravery that hid anger that hid fear.

We all looked at the Nicanor Gate. It was so wide and the crowd was so thick that it would be humanly impossible to see everyone passing through it.

I decided to speak. "We don't have much money because we chose to trust God. Remember?" I looked at all of them. Then I turned to Mary. "We'll find you on our way out. I can locate you wherever you are, like a shepherd seeking a lost lamb. I can and I will. I've done it before. Remember?"

The healing that I began earlier in her soul now rippled to the conscious level, and her eyes glowed with the strongest faith I had yet seen there.

"Of course, I remember, Rabboni." It was the first time she or any of my disciples had used the diminutive form of rabbi, transforming the word for teacher and master into a term of endearment.

I responded by paraphrasing a psalm for her, knowing how she enjoyed that kind of banter. I changed it so it sounded like it was addressed directly from me to her, and I spoke in a half-teasing tone that let her choose whether I was affirming my human love for her or revealing my divinity—or both. "Where can you hide from my spirit or where can you escape my presence?"

Sure enough, she knew the psalm and continued the quotation, matching my light tone. "If I fly to heaven, you are there. If I burrow down to hell, you're there, too. If I ride the wings of the morning to the farthest edge of the sea, even there you uphold and guide me."

Peter, Andrew, and John watched uneasily as I did what could be construed as teaching a woman—right at the gate marking women's exclusion. "Okay, let's go," I told them.

We stepped past more Temple police into the Court of Israel, which was half the size of the courtyard before it. Even more expensive building materials were used: bronze instead of wood, iron instead of stone. The mood was serious. At this level the most important sacrifices were received, and the Sanhedrin met in executive session. Amid the somber tone was a sense of brotherhood. We were all Jewish men here, all ritually clean before God, so we could be more relaxed about touching each other. Priests and worshipers were chanting prayers loudly and in earnest. The priests wore white linen hats and white checkered tunics tied with long, colorfully embroidered belts that hung almost to the ground. They were intoning a special blessing on those whose ritual cleanliness depended on the sacrifice that they were in the process of making.

We were engulfed in the varied sounds and scents that wafted down from the Court of the Priests right above us. A huge choir was singing to the accompaniment of trumpets, harps, and cymbals. The death cries of animals could be heard, too. They squealed and bellowed as they were sacrificed in the slaughterhouse, which was also located in the Court of the Priests.

The altar was so close that sometimes we could hear blood sizzling as priests splattered it on the altar with its burning fires. Depending on the type of offering, the meat would be eaten by the worshiper or the priests, or else it would be burned entirely. The blood was carefully drained and poured onto the altar for God. Since childhood, I had been taught that blood was especially sacred because it carried the essence of life, and life itself is sacred. Blood was considered so holy that consuming it was another crime punishable by death. Gusts of smoke scented with incense blew into our faces. Today the smoke of the offerings made me feel nauseous as my head began to pound even harder.

My disciples and I stood in yet another line. This time all of us in line chanted prayers while we waited. I felt strange as I watched the priests in their fancy outfits blessing people on behalf of God. In one sense, they seemed overly aware of their power, and proud of their wealth and social status. On another level, they were eerily oblivious to the soul-saving power in the ritual of forgiveness that they repeated. I would get bored with the prayers, too, if I recited them so often. Thinking they already knew God's mysteries, the priests had stopped seeking God, and those who do not seek do not find. Their numbness moved me no less than the heartfelt desires of the masses. To me, the parade of soul-hungry seekers felt like the whitewater torrents of the Jordan River at the foot of the mountains of the north, threatening to drag me underwater and drown me if I tried to rescue them all. Like them, I began to long for God's help and guidance.

Peter interrupted my reflections by nudging me. "Rabbi," he said. It was our turn to offer our sacrifices.

I joined my disciples in the ritual and prayers until the time came for us to place our hands on the heads of the animals and birds who would be sacrificed for our sins. I let them do that without me. I had come here to offer my own life to God. I had no intention of asking some other creature to do it for me.

The priest looked at me with curiosity. Nobody came up here empty-handed. They all had at least a handful of flour to offer to God. The priest let my breach of protocol pass, and we advanced to an area where worshipers could finish their prayers by kneeling, crouching, or lying face-down in supplication.

Mats were provided to make these prayer positions more comfortable. I lay prostrate, and the fresh straw-like scent of the mat filled my nostrils. I was shocked by how good it felt just to lie down. I was much more tired than I had realized. With a sigh of relief, I rested my body. The hubbub of prayers being chanted around me seemed to fall away.

Drawing on my previous meditations, I visualized myself holding a gold cup filled almost to the brim with my own blood. In my imagination, I was careful not to spill it as I slowly climbed several flights of stairs until I reached the top of the altar. I had entered the Holy of Holies many times in meditation, but even in my dreams I had never visited the altar of life-shattering, life-giving sacrifice. The intense heat of the flames burned away all but my purest intentions as I walked right through the fires to the middle of the altar. A red line was drawn around the place where blood sacrifices were received. I emptied the cup of my blood there.

"Father, I give my life to you," I said aloud.

Nothing happened. I became aware that my head and belly still hurt as I lay face-down on the mat, waiting to find out how God would respond. Eventually I sensed the Holy Spirit breathing in tandem with me. I could not hide the severity of my headache and nausea from Her like I could from my disciples.

She began to speak, partly by whispering words, partly by evoking emotions and images in my mind. "My Beloved Bridegroom, let it feel good," She urged.

"But it doesn't feel good," I protested silently. The hope that She would heal me flickered in my mind, but that was not Her purpose.

"Let it *feel*," She amended. "Pain and love travel on the same channel." She paused between the repetitions so each phrase became a meditation.

When I was ready, She proceeded to the slow, steady repetition of a new concept: "There's no need to push your body so hard."

My human side shrank from Her, sorry that by trying too hard to please God I had displeased God. I saw how it might be easier to die for God than to live a human life well for God, day in and day out. My subtle movement allowed Her a new access port for feeding me forgiveness. In a heartbeat, I felt more deeply loved than ever. This new position gave me a model that I could use to relate to my disciples, too.

"No need to push," She kept repeating, until I understood it as an affirmation that I was exactly where I was meant to be: down among the people instead of above it all in the isolated Holy of Holies. I felt Her compassion for how hard and lonely human life could be.

She offered me another thought and let it resound: "I *will* take your life, but not now."

The assurance that God accepted my sacrifice relaxed me and flooded all my sensibilities with feelings of gratitude and well-being.

"Let me decide the time and circumstances," She continued. "Let me decide.... Let me...."

She lulled me with a long litany of let-me's. My muscles loosened and even my blood vessels opened wider. I noticed a pleasant sensation as my body began to increase the blood flow toward my genitals.

I sensed the Holy Spirit's approval. "Do you want to make love?" She asked me.

"Here?!"

My sudden concern for propriety was answer enough. She laughed indulgently and withdrew without stirring me to join Her in the seamless union that I actually did desire.

A priest drowned out Her laughter by chanting a prayer as loudly as possible right beside me. He was trying to tell me that I had spent too much time in prayer. He wanted me to make way for others who wanted to pray in the limited space available close to the altar. I scrambled to my feet and tried to make eye contact, hoping to show him that I was okay and that I didn't mind his interruption. I never intended to hog the holy space. He looked right through me, numb to the bottom of his soul. His only concern was maintaining the orderly flow of traffic.

I sighed and felt my head aching the same as before. I descended down one staircase to where Peter, Andrew, and John were waiting for me patiently. Each of them met my gaze with a smile. I was pleased to see that, like me, my disciples had been refreshed by their interaction with the divine during the ritual of sacrifice. Their souls were drinking more deeply from my divine heart than before, even though I had made no conscious effort to encourage or reposition them. It confirmed for me what the Holy Spirit had implied: I could let go. I smiled back at my disciples.

"We can go now," I said.

"But don't you want to look for your friend on the Sanhedrin?" Peter asked.

"No. I'm not feeling well, and I need to find a place to rest until tomorrow. There's no reason to go to all the trouble of hunting for anybody."

My disciples exchanged disappointed glances as I set off down the next staircase. I moved so quickly that they had to hurry to keep up with me.

"Rabbi, slow down!" Peter cried. "Wait for us."

I kept moving, slowing my speed just enough so that they could keep me in sight if they stayed alert while we rushed through the multitude of people. They got to experience firsthand how they, like Mary, could get lost in the crowd if they allowed their eyes to wander from me.

As I moved through the crowd, I sensed the unripe soul of the very same teacher I had planned to seek out. His special long-tasseled cloak announced that he was a Pharisee. He also wore the insignia of a Sanhedrin member. My beloved teacher's long, white beard showed his true age, while he had the unlined face of someone much younger. A special turban denoting his high status partially covered his bald head. He strode past me quickly in the opposite direction.

"Nicky!" I shouted. "You're just the one I wanted to see! Wait!"

He whirled around and surveyed the crowd with contempt mixed with curiosity. He was angry at being addressed in such a familiar way by someone far beneath him in the hierarchy of the Temple, and yet I had used his nickname, the one known only to those in his inner circle.

When I realized I had offended him, I rushed through the crowd and knelt at his feet to give him the proper salutation for such an occasion. "Hail, Nicodemus, blessed by God." I took his right hand in mine and kissed it. His fingers smelled of incense. He wore a tasteful gold signet ring with a pattern of wavy parallel lines.

My kiss sent a shiver of delighted recognition through

his soul and then his body, long before his mind identified me.

"I give thanks in all my remembrance of you," I added, "for you were my favorite teacher when I studied here." That was all the greeting that politeness required, but I decided to go further. Still kneeling, I closed my eyes and lay my cheek on his hand in a gesture of genuine affection, allowing him to see and recognize my face.

He ran his other hand over my hair, lingering almost imperceptibly, and down to my shoulder. There he took hold of me and pulled me to my feet. "I remember you! Stand up. You're Jesus of Nazareth, aren't you? You used to call God your 'Father.'"

"He is my Father." We smiled at each other.

"You were one of my most promising students! I thought we would be serving together in the Sanhedrin by now. Did you know that some of your classmates are now on the Sanhedrin?"

"It doesn't feel like that much time could have passed," I replied.

"Why, it must be more than ten years since I last saw you. I've never forgotten what you said when you told me you were quitting your studies. You told me, 'Don't judge, and you won't be judged.' You said that the way I judged others was the way I would be judged, and the sentence I imposed would be imposed on me. It seemed like nonsense at the time, but over the years I've found that it has helped me."

"It has helped me, too," I concurred.

In that moment, we switched roles and we both recognized that he had a lot to learn from me. His soul moved into a posture of submission, sort of like a bow. I was pleased. From this position, his soul would be able to receive divine love and instruction from me. I didn't offer it anything yet. I just let his soul stretch itself and get accustomed to its new position.

"Tell me, what have you been doing with yourself?" he asked.

"I was baptized in the Jordan by the Baptist. I am preaching the same good news that he did: Repent, for the kingdom of God is at hand. These are some of my disciples." They had caught up with me now and they were crowded around me, eager to meet Nicodemus. I gestured to them.

Nicodemus barely glanced at them. "The Baptist.... I was part of a delegation from the Sanhedrin sent to listen to him and investigate what he's doing. He's a good man, but he needs to be more diplomatic. Reform comes slowly to institutions, so he has to learn patience."

"The Baptist is my cousin."

"Your cousin!" He was shocked. "Your blood cousin?"

"Yes."

Fear made Nicodemus widen his eyes and lower his voice. "You should keep quiet about that around here. The Baptist has made many powerful enemies."

I took a wide stance and stood taller, letting him see the fullness of my manhood and my divinity. "I did not come here to hide who I am." I said it loud.

He stared at me, admiring my bravery and acknowledging my willingness to live according to God's word, whatever the cost.

"Well, I suppose you came here to teach," he said. "I will talk with the people in charge of the porticoes in the Court of the Gentiles and arrange for you to teach in one of the best places, over at Solomon's portico where I used to teach you."

"Good. I'll start early tomorrow morning."

"Okay." He swallowed. He was going to have to work fast. "I'll do whatever I can to help you behind the scenes. I'd love to hear you teach, but it will be difficult for me to go down to the porticoes to listen to you. My responsibilities on the Sanhedrin are much greater than they were when I was teaching you. I'm on many committees and sub-committees, so my schedule is very busy and, well, you know...."

Yes, I knew. He had a reputation to consider. He was afraid to be seen with me. I said nothing.

Nicodemus licked his lips nervously and continued. "If it's all right with you, I can come to you at night and we can talk privately. Where are you are staying?"

I couldn't remember. I turned to the nearest disciple and put my hand on his shoulder to draw him into the conversation. "John, where are we staying?"

"We haven't found a place yet, Rabbi."

As Nicodemus observed my gesture, a pang of longing crossed his face and passed through his whole being down to his soul. He and I had once shared such intimacies. His favorite students, myself included, had served as his personal assistants. I used to wash his feet, straighten his clothing for him, bring him snacks during Sanhedrin meetings, and run other errands for him. I remembered how much he had taught me about the Law and how merciful his legal rulings were, by human standards. His kindness to me then had proven how open-minded he was. The other leaders at the Temple had kept me at a distance because I was nobody from nowhere: only a carpenter's son from way out in uncivilized Nazareth.

I opened my divine heart to Nicodemus' soul, inviting it to nurse. His soul was undamaged, but also small and immature, as if it had been sheltered from the life experiences that prod souls to grow, or as if it had not yet been born. After a lifetime of loving God from a distance, the soul of Nicodemus received its first direct contact with divine love. It shuddered for joy as it began to drink.

Meanwhile, I looked in his wide-open eyes and spoke aloud. "Come with me now," I urged.

He knew what I meant. I was inviting him to join me not just for the evening, but permanently. Indeed, if Nicodemus walked away from his Temple responsibilities to hang out with me then and there, it would have been the beginning of the end of his career on the Sanhedrin. Such behavior would not be tolerated by the men with whom he wielded power. He hesitated.

"Come on, Nicky. Follow me."

"I can't." He looked away.

My heart ached: another rejection today at the Temple.

He kept talking. "I'll send one of my assistants down to the porticoes tomorrow to ask you where you're staying. I promise I will come and talk with you there one night this week—even if I have to skip the Sanhedrin banquet." Glancing around cautiously, he lowered his voice to a whisper and added, "I'll have my assistant carry my signet ring with him so that you know you can trust him." Then he scurried away.

I didn't even have a place to stay yet. It hadn't occurred to me that I might need to keep its location secret for my own safety. A fresh wave of nausea washed through me.

I shifted my focus from the people around me to the distant landscape. This high courtyard of the Temple provided an incredible view. I looked eastward far across the Kidron Valley to the uneven ridge atop the Mount of Olives. At times like this, I felt soothed by resting my eyes on the horizon, on the place where earth and sky touch. Eventually I let my gaze drift downward to the land. On these slopes lay olive groves and the towns of Bethany and Bethphage. Streams of pilgrims continued to follow the same route that we had taken through the valley. From where I stood, the people way down in the Court of the Gentiles seemed to lose their individuality. They looked like a flock of sheep, moving aimlessly.

Then my eyes were drawn to a single pair of eyes, shining at me from under a veil and behind the bars of the Nicanor Gate. It would have been impossible to pick out Mary with just my human vision, but I recognized her soul-sparkle. She seemed to feel my attention, too, because she raised her arm high and waved at me. I waved back.

"I'm ready to go," I said to the men with me. We began to retrace our steps out of the Temple.

When we were reunited with Mary, she was standing with a couple whose souls were connected to each other in a symbiotic relationship. "I've made some new friends," Mary announced. "This is Martha and her sister Mary of Bethany. We have the same name, so we agreed to call her Mary-Beth to avoid confusion."

I enjoyed the unusual triangular pathways taken by divine energy as it flowed between my divine heart and the souls of the two women. They didn't look like sisters. Martha, who was slender, curtsied gracefully before me while Mary-Beth bowed her stocky body in a casual, but no less genuine show of respect. Their souls greeted my divine heart in unison.

"Rabbi, Mary told us that you need a place to stay," Martha murmured. "We would be honored to offer you hospitality at our home. We live in Bethany with our younger brother Lazarus. It's only a short walk."

Mary-Beth's voice was brash, almost boisterous. "All of Mary's friends are welcome!"

I smiled inwardly to see my male disciples' discomfort at being designated merely "Mary's friends."

"Thanks," I said. "We'll accept your hospitality."

chapter twelve:
manifestations

"COME WALK WITH ME, ANDY." I held my hand out to him. My disciples and I were just beginning the journey to Jerusalem from the house in Bethany belonging to Martha, Mary-Beth, and Lazarus. Bird songs filled the sky that was still blushing from dawn.

Andrew had been asking to talk with me individually since the evening of our first visit to the Temple together, but a couple of days had already passed since then. My teaching at the Temple was drawing large crowds every day, including some new people who needed my time. I was also taking the Holy Spirit's advice to heart and giving myself more leisure hours. I spent every night relaxing with my disciples and then resting in the embrace of the Holy Spirit. Now I felt centered, confident about my teaching, and ready to focus on Andrew's soul as my presence made it grow.

Our sandals made a slushy sound because last night's rain had left the path muddy. "You wanted to talk to me. Now is a good time."

Andrew looked uncomfortable. "It's a private matter."

"I know. We'll let the others go ahead of us. You can have my full attention all the way to Jerusalem." I paused to calculate the distance. It was about two miles.

"But you'll be mobbed by people along the way," Andrew said, accurately describing what had happened on the previous days.

"I can make it so they won't see me."

Andrew shot me a surprised look. I had been experimenting with ways to cloak myself energetically so I became unobtrusive, perhaps almost invisible. I couldn't subject myself to the whims and fantasies of every passerby, nor did I want to make Peter and my other disciples into my bodyguards.

Andrew nodded his agreement. When the others were out of earshot, we began hiking down the Mount of Olives. He kept silent for a long time. We could see Jerusalem gleaming on the hilltop across the valley. The sun washed the city's domes and the many flat-roofed buildings, all densely packed on the hill. Their small, square windows seemed to squint as the daylight roused them. I sensed the enthusiasm of the olive trees waking up around us as their roots drank in the night's rainfall and their leaves stretched to the day's first sunlight.

I inspected Andrew's soul and made sure he was still accepting optimum quantities of divine love through every pore and receptor. His continued silence began to make me feel impatient, but I let it pass. This time with me was my gift to him. Let him use it as he wanted. I listened to his silence.

We were almost halfway to Jerusalem when a torrent of words broke loose. "It's about Mary. I love her. I desire her. I want to protect her. I've prayed about it a lot, and I'm going to ask her to marry me. I know she's going to come to you for approval, so I thought I'd talk to you about it first."

"Are you sure she's ready?"

"Yes, I'm sure she'll have me."

"That's not what I asked. Are you sure that she's ready?"

"She's older than I am. She's actually past the ideal age for marriage."

"I didn't ask how old she is. I asked about readiness."

Andrew paused and furrowed his brow before replying, "How do you mean?"

"Well, you know she was a prostitute until recently. That means she has had a lot of degrading, damaging sexual experiences."

"But you cast all the demons out of her. She's fine now."

"All the demons are gone, but she's still learning to live as a whole person. As are *you*." I looked in his eyes for emphasis, then turned my eyes back to the path we were walking. We were starting uphill now. "Her spirit was wounded through her sexuality. Even after the wounds heal, there will be scars. When you become one flesh, her strengths become your strengths and her scars become your scars. Are you sure you are ready for that?"

"You are the one who encouraged me to love her!" Andrew wailed.

"*Love* her, yes. That's what I'm getting at. Accept her as she is. If you marry Magdalene, it's not going to be easy between you sexually like it would be if you married a virgin and let your sexualities mature and blossom together."

"It's not like I've never had her! I *know* how good the

sex can be between us! It was fantastic, much better than what I was able to describe to you. And she thought so, too."

"But it wasn't like that every time, was it?"

"No." Andrew looked away.

We were passing tombs that had been carved in the rock face. Near the road was one of the Roman execution grounds where they crucified criminals. I was relieved to see that nobody was dying there this morning. It looked like a forest of dead, branchless trees waiting for the next time when a cross beam and a condemned man would be hoisted onto them.

"Andy, you're too good and too innocent to be able to imagine the sexual horrors she's experienced, but if you decide to marry her, then you're going to find out about those forms of suffering. God who reigns in both of your bodies will use that relationship to reveal truths to the two of you. You'll have to learn what triggers her painful memories and how to avoid those behaviors even in the throes of sexual passion. You will have to remember, so she can forget—forget long enough to entrust her body to you."

Andrew was silent for a while. More people crowded around us now that we were climbing the steps near Jerusalem, but they left us alone. "How do you suggest I find out if she's ready—I mean, if *we* are ready to marry?" he asked.

"Pay close attention when you're with her. Notice how she acts when you are near her and notice how you feel, too. See if you can perceive how she's feeling when you touch her in different ways. Just stay alert."

Andrew became agitated. "But shouldn't we at least be betrothed before I touch her like that? I don't want her to get the wrong idea."

I laughed. "It's all or nothing with you, isn't it? I didn't mean you should have sex." Still chuckling, I wrapped my arm around his waist and drew him to me so we walked side by side. For all his talk about sex, Andrew was rather uncomfortable in his body. He did not enjoy my touch as much as my other disciples did. Instead of just letting him pull away, on this occasion I tried to do for him what I had asked him to do with Mary. I began searching for the touch that would allow us to relax and be ourselves together.

"I only wanted to know what you thought," Andrew said defensively.

"I *told* you what I thought." Using my divine heart, I located that easy place between us much faster than could be done through the trial and error of human senses. I draped my arm over his shoulder and into his comfort zone. He relaxed and we laughed together. Then, modeling what he could try with Mary, I kissed him lightly on the cheek. He gave me a startled look as the love that I constantly poured into his soul was manifest physically. Then I released him. We were at the gate to the Temple. "We can talk more about this later," I promised, then walked through the gate.

As soon as we entered the Temple compound, I stopped cloaking myself, and we were mobbed by throngs of people with every imaginable type of disease, deformity, and demon possession.

"Have mercy on me!" they cried.

Others, not quite so pushy, were shouting and singing praises for the many healings that had already happened in my presence that week: "Blessed is the one who comes in the name of the Lord!"

Andrew wrapped his arm around my waist and did his best to help me move through the crowd, although he wasn't as strong or aggressive as his brother Peter. Lots of healings had occurred by the time we neared the prime portico location where I had been teaching all week. Crowds were gathered here, too, but they were more subdued because they included the people who were too lame or weak to come chasing after a miracle, as well as the impartial majority who just wanted to hear me teach. My audience overflowed into the areas where others were supposed to be teaching. I have to admit I thought it was fun to cause this kind of disruption. I used my personal power and my growing skills in crowd control to part the multitude. I went to the raised platform where I could sit while I taught.

The people jammed around the platform. They included some of my disciples and two souls who were both tied up in knots, so they could not respond freely to divine love. I studied them with my human eyes and saw that they were both well-groomed men about my age. Their long-tasseled robes indicated that they were Pharisees. They wore badges of office proclaiming their membership on the Sanhedrin. I sat down next to them.

"So it's true," said the more handsome one. He crossed his arms and sneered at me. "You're the one who is causing this mess. I had to come and see for myself and hear what swill you are spouting to attract all these swine."

"Hello, Caleb," I responded casually. "Hello, Amos."

The other man nodded back to me, his eyes chilly. He looked dumber and heavier than his companion. I recognized them from my days studying at the Temple when we were all just reaching manhood. They didn't like me back then either.

"What are you now? Shepherd to the scum?" Caleb asked. "You could have escaped Nazareth. You were almost as good as I was at interpreting scripture."

He was one of the best, but I was better. I let it pass.

"You could have become one of us," he continued. "Instead you brought the dregs of Nazareth here with you to pollute this holy place. How can you *stand* it?" At least the disgust on his face was sincere.

Amos spoke up. "I might have invited you to my home for dinner, but I can't now that you've allowed yourself to become defiled by letting all these filthy lepers and cripples touch you."

"You've got it wrong," I answered. "Their touch doesn't make me dirty. My touch cleanses them." I held my arms open to emphasize my point.

I hadn't intended to humiliate my old classmates with a public demonstration, but the Holy Spirit had another idea. I sensed Her sweep into the well-scrubbed soul of someone who was sitting at my feet. The person seized the opportunity to grab at my arm while hiding inside a tattered cloak. Through the holes in the cloak, people could see a face that was disfigured, discolored, and pocked with oozing sores.

"Look, it's Simon the Leper!" they gasped. The crowd backed away. He was a leper who had broken the purity code by coming out in public.

Simon bowed to me, moving awkwardly because of his stiff limbs. "If you are willing, you can cure me," he pleaded.

As he clutched his cloak over his face, I saw that some of his fingers were misshapen, while others were missing altogether. His soul opened and showed me a clean central niche it had prepared as a home for my divine heart. I couldn't resist. I stretched out my hand and touched him.

"I'm willing."

Even I was impressed by the dramatic effect. The healing took place right before our eyes while my divine heart eased into his soul. Simon the Leper stood up and let his shroud fall away. The sores quickly dried up and then the scabs fell off to reveal skin glowing with robust health. His face became as unblemished as baby Anna's. Simon held up his hands and laughed in wonder as his remaining fingers straightened.

He wiggled them and began shouting, "Hosanna!" The crowds cheered with him. My disciples were clapping for joy because this healing was my fastest and most sensational yet.

Only Caleb and Amos sat stiffly silent. My eyes met theirs. I saw they were badly shaken. I felt awkward, for I would gladly have healed their souls, too, but they could only see my exercise of power as their defeat. Anyone in their position would have had a hard time accepting an offer of help from me in that moment.

To give them a chance to save face, I ignored them and sternly charged Simon to follow the rules of the Temple by having the priests verify his healing.

I quieted the crowd and used my divine heart to establish a connection with each person there, sending rays of multicolored light onto and through their soul-skin. In return I received signals that informed me about what they needed to hear. This technique enabled me to address the increasingly large crowds around me in the most intimate, effective terms possible. I included Caleb and Amos in my rainbow embrace.

They couldn't deny the reality of the healing they had just witnessed, so they decided to challenge me on other grounds. "Who gave you the authority to these things?" Caleb demanded.

I studied him and Amos. They didn't really want to know. Witnessing my healing power had caused their minds to close, not open. They seemed to think that their relationship with God depended on mine being wrong. Their soul-knots tightened, clamping down on the energy conduits that should have pumped divine love. I chose my words carefully so that I could teach the whole crowd and protect myself while at the same time leaving an opening for Caleb and Amos to change their minds.

"I have a question for you. Answer my question and I'll answer yours. Was the Baptist doing God's will when he baptized people, or was he just satisfying a human need?"

Caleb and Amos exchanged glances in surprise.

"The Baptist?"

"Is *he* behind this?"

The guilt on their faces told me that they were somehow part of an official program of harassment against my beloved cousin. Now I knew that there was truth behind the rumor that the Sanhedrin was plotting to have the Baptist arrested. Anger crackled through me like lightning, then disappeared. Caleb and Amos argued with each other under their breath about how to answer.

"If we say it was God's will, then he'll ask why we didn't believe the Baptist," Caleb said.

"But if we say God had nothing to do with it, the crowd will stone us. They're convinced that he is a real prophet," Amos countered.

They looked nervously at the crowd, sensing the danger. Caleb spoke for both of them in a loud voice so everyone could hear. "We don't know."

"I'm not going to tell you where I get my authority, either," I concluded.

"We could have you arrested," Amos threatened. He certainly wasn't as clever as Caleb at word play.

So now it was official. The ruling elite saw me as their enemy. It felt good to stand up to them and let them see me for who I was.

The debate continued like that for the rest of the day, with other scribes and Pharisees in the crowd joining Caleb and Amos to try to trip me up. I found the hostility exhilarating. I discovered that I could use love to deflect the negative energies they directed at me and thereby use their attacks to propel the discussion forward. Most of the people in the crowd listened with quiet fascination. My courage made them even more eager to understand what I had to say.

Later that week John tagged along with me when I went to the Mount of Olives to pray one night. John didn't say anything as we roamed through the olive groves, but I wasn't concerned because we often enjoyed the freedom of mutual understanding without speech. In some ways our prayer sessions had become even more intense since I started trying to keep my sexual desires under wraps.

We settled down under the boughs of an ancient olive tree whose lifetime spanned many human generations. The half-moon was shining in a way that highlighted John's silver-streaked curls and the wrinkles etched on his unusual yet attractive face.

I began by chanting, "Our Father who art in heaven." The words helped bring me into rhythm with God. I made more room for the light shining from my divine heart. It cast an invisible circle around us.

Normally John would have either repeated the phrase or moved on to chant the next line in the prayer that I was teaching him and the others. When we returned to ordinary consciousness, we usually discussed our visions and helped each other figure out how to integrate them into our lives. Tonight I sensed sadness in his silence.

"Do you want to just talk?" I asked.

John could be shy and somber, capable of accompanying me on my own darkest moods. He spoke with difficulty. "You healed a lot of people this week." He didn't sound happy about the fact.

"I didn't do it by myself. Their faith made them whole."

"Oh, not that again!" he snapped.

"What's wrong?" I continued to feel serene, with a strong desire to help him.

"That's what you said back when you healed my hand. Ever since then, I have been able to move my hand freely, but the pain has never left me. It still hurts."

"Oh, *that*," I sighed knowingly.

"I talked to the people you healed at the Temple this week, and their pain went away. I've tried confessing all my sins to God. I even confessed and repented some things I didn't think were sinful. But nothing stops the pain. The reason it still hurts must be because I don't have enough faith to heal completely."

"You don't understand. It is not that you sinned or lack faith, but that the works of God might be made manifest in you."

"Then I feel like a failure for not healing," he wailed. "I've failed you!"

"Why? How?" Sometimes human logic made no sense to me.

"I should have healed to show people all the good that comes from following you."

"Oh, no, you don't have to do that," I said, adding the full spectrum of kindness to the mix of colors that I was using to feed John's soul. "That's not what I'm looking for in those who represent me and teach my ideas. Your pain is not due to lack of faith. It is inherent to your faith journey. Open to the pain, for love and pain travel on the same frequency."

While John took a moment to reflect, I remembered how hard it was for me when the Holy Spirit first started teaching me this truth during my headache at the Temple.

"Do you mean," John asked slowly, "That you and your Father could heal my pain—but you won't?"

"Well...." My human heart pounded. John had more faith now than he realized, but I knew that the answer to this question could make him lose his faith, as it had caused many other people to turn away from God. My mind raced in search of the perfect explanation.

The Holy Spirit came like warmth rubbing away the tension in my back between the shoulder blades. "Everything's okay. Just tell him the truth," She advised.

"Well, *yes*," I answered simply. "God can end your pain, but God won't."

"But that's cruel and sadistic!" He was so angry and horrified that he dug up some handfuls of dirt, then stood and hurled them back at the earth right next to me with as much force as he could muster. Specks of dirt rebounded into my eyes and mouth. It tasted gritty and bland, but I went ahead and swallowed it as I wiped my eyes.

"A sadist uses pain to separate himself from others," I said, with mud still on my tongue. "God uses pain to melt away separation. I feel your pain as intensely as you do. I have ever since we first met. For example, I know your fingers are hurting a lot worse now from jabbing them into the earth."

"If you felt the pain like I do, you would make it stop!"

"I didn't come to give people a painless existence," I emphasized. "I came so people could live—really live to the fullest extent possible."

"Wipe that smug look off your face!" he snarled.

John's words stung me like a slap in the face and I turned away. I couldn't help feeling self-conscious about my unmistakable inner peace.

John stomped around for a while, muttering profanities and stopping now and then to glare off in the distance. I thought he might leave.

When I was sure he was going to stay, I spoke again. "I'll massage your hand if you like. It's not going to cause a miraculous cure, but I might be able to ease the pain some, as one man to another."

He threw himself down next to me and gave me his hand, which was caked with dirt. I moved my fingertips over the spots that hurt most. His hand and fingers were extraordinarily long, despite the places where life's stresses had thickened his bones.

"You *do* know where the pain is," he admitted.

I felt awkward as I massaged the length of his hand with my palms and thumbs. Since my healings occurred through my divine heart, I hadn't bothered to develop the simpler healing skills inherent in my human body. "I think I could do this better if we lay down. Then I could put your hand right over my heart," I said.

"I'll get you dirty," he warned.

"I don't care."

We lay side by side, as we often did during our

private prayer sessions. I loosened my robe and placed his hand on my skin directly over my human heart, which became the focal point of my divine heart. I let my heartbeat provide a gentle massage while I used my hands to exert strong pressure on his. I liked the feeling of his muscles, his calluses, his dusty skin, and even the misshapen parts of his fingers.

I spoke softly. "You've seen me naked now; you know that I allow suffering. It takes a lot of faith to see that and not reject God. You're afraid that you lack faith, but you actually have tremendous faith."

"Maybe I just love you." He made a fist and spat out the words as if it were a crime. "Maybe I'm just stupid."

I stroked his fist in silence, easing the knots out of the muscles until his hand opened and relaxed. Something like that began to happen in his soul.

"Maybe you just didn't know that it would hurt when I loved you back," I told him. "I *am* healing you. It just doesn't feel like what you expected."

The Holy Spirit swept over me then in a way She had never done before when I was with another person. I was wrapped and rapt in Her love. Slowly She spoke both to me and through me. The words came out of my mouth, but they were Hers in style and content: "Let me carry you through the dark and fog..."

John moved under the crook of my arm and snuggled closer.

"...to a beautiful place where you would never go on your own: the depths of my healing heart."

"Why wouldn't I go there?" John asked.

"You would never find the way...and even if you

stumbled upon it by accident...you would slip and fall without me."

The Holy Spirit showed me places like gateways in John's soul. I knew they led to rooms created for God to inhabit, and I longed to open them, but they were fused shut, as if some fire had melted and scarred them. My divine heart ached with compassion and confusion as it explored these closed doors and tried unsuccessfully to open them. Then the Holy Spirit let me know that my own future actions would restore and open the gates. She showed me how to enfold John just as he was. As One, We surrounded John. He seemed to become every soul, cradled in the depths of Our healing heart. We stayed in this state of rapture for what felt like forever.

"Rabbi?"

I opened my eyes, but all I could see were the dazzling stars strewn across the night sky above me. Someone was cuddled against my chest. I reached over to feel who it was with my fingers, and was happy to discover John's tight curls and wrinkled face.

"Rabbi, I just received a beautiful vision from God."

"So did I."

Sometimes we tried to explain our visions in detail, but tonight John sat up and announced cheerfully, "My hand still hurts."

Then he laughed until I started laughing, too. We had a long laugh together before we returned to the group.

chapter thirteen:
changer of people

I WRAPPED UP THE NEXT day's debate at the Temple when lunchtime arrived. I motioned for Peter to come to me. "See that person looking at us from the back of the crowd?" I whispered to him.

I pointed and he followed my gaze. "The skinny man with the tapered beard who is leaning against the pillar?" Peter asked.

I had been concentrating on the stranger's hungry soul, which was riddled with holes because malnutrition had forced it to feed on itself. The soul was shining a fierce light straight into my divine heart, hunting for me, beckoning me. Now I tried to see him as Peter did. Yes, he did have a pointy beard, sharp facial features, and an angular body. He was about my age. "That's the one. I want you to go invite him to have lunch with me. Tell him to wait there while I dismiss the crowd and come to him."

While Peter did as I asked, my other closest disciples started to eat lunch—all except John. He was at the back of the crowd talking to someone with a drowsy soul that had been awakened by my teaching, but was falling back to sleep. I looked with my human eyes and saw John conversing with an athletic-looking young man dressed in the simple, stately uniform of the high priest's servants. Each was focused on the other with the unwavering intensity of a marksman zeroing in on a target.

Peter returned and joined the meal of bread, dried fish, and olives. I had one more request of him before I left. "May I take your water skin and bag with me?" As usual, I had been traveling with nothing.

Peter swallowed the mouthful of fish he was chewing. "You can have them, but there is only one barley loaf left in my bag."

"That's enough." I grabbed his beaten-up belongings and waved goodbye. "Don't wait for me. I probably won't see you until tonight at the house in Bethany."

As I approached my lunch companion, he continued to lean casually on one of the Temple pillars, just as he had while I was teaching. His only acknowledgment that he had been waiting for me was to turn his eyes on me, cat-like, while his body maintained a posture of pretended indifference. Some would have thought his behavior rude, but I found it refreshing after being surrounded by crowds of people who begged and grabbed for everything I had. His hazel eyes were keenly intelligent and sensitive, as I suspected they would be. I could tell that he was a moneychanger because he had a half-shekel coin stuck in his ear.

"You look hungry," I stated. "Let me feed you."

"I'm famished," the moneychanger agreed. "I know a great place just inside the Damascus Gate where we can buy the finest, most delicious bread in all Jerusalem. It has a crisp, flaky crust with an incredibly tender, chewy inside. We can get it while it's still steaming hot and then go right next door for goat cheese from the city's best cheese maker. The cheese melts right into the bread, and it's fantastic!"

"Mmm, it sounds good." I had an idea. It took a moment to form a complete image in my mind of the flavors, aromas, and textures of the meal he was describing. It became so real that it made my mouth water. Then I let go of it completely and submitted it to God's will.

"But the marketplace at the Damascus Gate is awfully noisy," I said. "I know a quiet, shady place here on the Temple grounds where I thought we could talk while we ate. I have some food with me that I think you will like."

Still leaning on the pillar, the moneychanger looked doubtful.

"Let's take a look," I said as I held Peter's bag open. With wary, feline movements, he stepped closer and peeked into the bag with me.

"That's unbelievable!" he exclaimed. "You have the very same bread and cheese I was telling you about."

I just smiled. This was the first time I had proven to myself that I could transform matter and multiply food. I took it as an affirmation of my relationship with this particular moneychanger.

"So you'll join me for lunch here?"

"All right."

We walked toward a secluded corner of the porticos. My divine heart sensed his soul drawing near. It was soft and pliable as a soul should be, but it had many empty holes. In order to function, it had propped the holes up with hard measuring devices, sort of like sticks. The mind could access them for making judgments. I had seen these soul-sticks often, for Satan was always eager to supply them to anyone who had a gap to fill. The soul-sticks do prop up a soul in danger of collapse, but divine love could fill those holes much better, for love has the same flexibility and texture as the soul and actually heals the soul while supporting it. The brittle sticks had left all kinds of leaks and demon-infested wounds in the moneychanger's soul, which did nothing to diminish its iridescent, resolute beauty. I paused to let my admiration fall on his soul in a way that it could feel and understand as a leaf feels and understands sunlight.

"What's your name?" I asked as we walked.

"Judas. Judas Iscariot."

I considered it, searching for the right nickname for him. None came to mind, so I tried my all-purpose variation: "Beloved Judas."

He burst into laughter. "Even my wife doesn't call me that!"

I had a strange feeling when I said the nickname. It felt like an arrow hitting a target. "Still, the name Beloved Judas suits you. Someone else must have called you that."

"My mother. She died when I was four years old and that's one of the only things that I remember about her." Judas dropped this information casually, as if it were of much less importance than what we ate for lunch.

We sat on a stone ledge, blessed the meal and began to eat. The fresh bread and melted goat cheese were just as delicious as Judas described. I let myself savor the food and the pleasure of his company. It amused me to watch him act like it was no big deal for him to have lunch with me. I could see that he was never going to ask me why I invited him to lunch, so I raised the topic.

"I noticed you standing in the back of the crowd, and I thought you might have some issues you'd like to discuss privately. It impresses me that you, a money-changer, would come to hear me teach after I denounced what the moneychangers are doing in the Temple."

"You were right when you said we had made it into a den of thieves. We do cheat people, not only the pilgrims, but the priests, too, when we can get away with it. Some cheat more than others, but all of us do it, myself included." He looked me right in the eye.

I liked his frankness.

"I wonder what solution you propose," he continued. "Don't you think we provide a service that is pleasing to God? Surely you don't want to profane the Temple with dirty Gentile money and its pagan pictures?"

"The sacrifice pleasing to God is mercy, not money."

"Yes, of course. But He must have money, too. It takes money to run the Temple."

I gestured toward the Temple complex. "See these enormous buildings? They're all going to be rubble."

My answer shocked Judas into a momentary silence. He pressed his lips together and blinked. The magnificent, seemingly indestructible Temple was the pride and joy of the Jewish people, admired by Gentiles from throughout the world.

He searched my eyes, trying to understand how I could predict such catastrophe for our people without shedding a tear. "You're a Jew," he said quietly. "I'm sure you respect the Temple, but it is like a home to me. Since you are a Galilean, you only visit here a few times a year at most, but I have come here to work and worship almost every day of my life. Even when I was a boy, my father brought me here. He was a moneychanger here before me. How do you think we can turn away God's wrath and save the Temple? Do you think God wants us to move the moneychanging business outside the Temple walls? Is that your theory?"

"Don't worry about tomorrow. Let tomorrow take care of itself. Today is the real challenge," I responded.

He narrowed his eyes, struggling to figure out how my answer related to his question. I interrupted his train of thought. "Would you like some more bread?"

"Yes, actually, but it's all gone."

"Oh, I don't think so." I reached into the bag and pulled out another cheese-laden loaf. I tore it in two and handed half to Judas.

He looked puzzled. "I thought I took the last piece. Oh, well." He smiled as he took another bite.

"Will you tell me something?" I asked.

Judas nodded his agreement.

"Why have you come to listen to every word I've taught since I arrived at the Temple this week? You stand in the back from the moment I start speaking in the mornings until the last word passes my lips every single day! Taking all that time away from your business must be hurting your profit margin. Why are you doing it?"

He dropped his cool manner now that I had exposed how much he cared about me. "How could you possibly have noticed my comings and goings among such a vast multitude of people?!" he exclaimed, raising his voice in outrage: "How could you?!"

I kept my tone even, but let it resonate with the love I felt for him. "Oh, it's very obvious to me when someone is truly seeking God."

"You must have mistaken me for someone else!"

I gazed right into his eyes. "I haven't mistaken you for anyone else, Beloved Judas. I can see you quite plainly right now."

"But I am not a holy man!" he declared.

Outside Judas' consciousness, his soul turned itself inside out in order to show me all its holes, an act that requires a tremendous amount of trust. Meanwhile, he kept talking. "I told you I cheat people when I change their money. I cheat the priests, too. I love gossiping and getting involved in Temple intrigues behind the scenes. I cultivate friendships with powerful men on the Sanhedrin and even among the Roman oppressors. I flatter them all with lies, then I betray their confidences. Instead of giving alms, I buy luxuries for myself. I use the loot I get by cheating to get drunk and cheat on my wife with the best prostitutes that money can buy."

I liked the dispassionate tone he took as he listed his faults. It was obvious to me that he had spent time and effort trying to see himself clearly without making excuses.

"I've had to seek the Lord's forgiveness many, many times," Judas concluded.

"So you admit you seek God?"

My question made him pause. "Well, if you mean seeking God's forgiveness, then yes." The forlorn expression on Judas' face and in his soul made me long to pour myself out for him.

I considered how best to do it. I could feel the Holy Spirit beside me and inside me, encouraging me to risk a relationship with Judas even as She showed me that he could cheat and betray me just as he had done to others.

"Aren't you going to answer my question?" I asked Judas.

"What question?"

"Why did you come to hear every word I taught?"

"You teach with astonishing authority and bring the scriptures to life."

"That can't be the reason. There are many great teachers here at the Temple." I frowned and took another bite of bread.

"People say you are the son of God, the Messiah who will gather our people and free us from the Roman bastards who oppress us. When I see how the crowds adore you, I believe you could win that kind of power."

"Come on. There's got to be more to it than that!" I retorted. "You yourself said you know lots of the powerful men who run things around here right now. You don't have to chase after a nobody who might *someday* lead a successful revolution."

Judas gazed at the Temple while he considered what to say next. When he turned to me again, he spoke in a new way, unguarded and direct. "The people who know me would laugh if they heard what I'm about to say," he began. His eyes searched mine, anxious for any sign of encouragement or disapproval.

I met his gaze without judgment and waited. The

holes in his soul gaped wider open before me. He had my full attention.

"Well," he continued, "I suppose this may be my only chance to talk privately with you like this, so I might as well tell you everything."

He paused. I waited.

"The thing is..." he said and looked down as if he were about to say something shameful, as if he expected to be ridiculed or slapped. "I like the way you love people. I thought that if I could learn to love people the way you do—I mean, just a *fraction* of the way you do—if I could do that, it would be a great thing."

"I can teach you to love like that." I tried to say it with the complete confidence that I felt, but tenderly enough to honor his sense of vulnerability.

He looked up and immediately began to argue with me. "You don't know how hard I've tried. I've done everything—resolutions, prayers, and every kind of Temple sacrifice—and nothing ever works. Even when I do love someone, I end up hurting them. If I don't turn against them, I come across as cold or manipulative. I can't seem to show gratitude. For example, you've been extremely kind to me, and I haven't even been able to say thanks for lunch. Something inside suppresses my ability to love, and I've tried everything to overcome it."

"You haven't let *me* try."

My answer startled him, stilling and distilling his thoughts. "Go ahead and try, Rabbi," he said softly.

This was the permission that I had been waiting and praying to receive. He was seated next to me, and now I gazed into his eyes while I placed my hand on the space where his neck and shoulder met. "I am the bread of life. Come to me and you'll never be hungry. Trust me and you'll never be thirsty," I promised.

Our first touch both jarred and attracted me, like the taste of spicy food. I knew I would affect him—I felt that with everyone whom I touched—but in Judas' case, I also sensed that he would have a profound effect on my human life. I stretched my conscious mind open wide in order to foresee my future with Judas, but the Holy Spirit clouded it.

"Be human, be patient," She said playfully, managing to chide, tease, and reassure me all at once in the tone that was unique to Her.

Pressing the palm of my hand against Judas' neck and shoulder, I opened my divine heart to his soul and let it see my longing to know and nourish it. I wasn't sure how fast I could move with this soul without causing it to turn away from me completely. If I let my love flow right into its most serious wounds, Judas would feel an unbearable burning sensation in his soul that that would lead to physical illness and erratic behavior.

I let the Holy Spirit guide me to where and how I should begin. With a sigh of compassion, I carefully removed one soul-stick. It had left calluses as hard as the sticks themselves. I concocted a mixture of divine love, calibrated to the exact needs of this stiff, hollow place in Judas and let it flow in—slowly in soul-time, but instantly in human time. I was pleased that his soul began absorbing the love right away. It curled up against my divine heart and entered a resting state. Using my human eyes, I saw Judas perk up and look at me intently.

"God hears and answers your prayers, Judas," I said aloud. "Your sins are forgiven."

He stared at me. My statement demanded a decision: Believe me or not. I watched him struggle to determine whether my forgiveness was blasphemy or a blessing. Only God could forgive sins and, as far as he knew, only the Temple priests could announce God's forgiveness. The recognition began in his soul and spread through his being. I felt goose bumps on his skin beneath my hand.

"You *are* the son of God," he whispered in awe. Judas showed neither terror nor joy at his discovery.

I kept looking in his eyes without changing my facial expression, but inside I felt satisfaction. I was thrilled to be accepted for who I was in that moment. I had already discovered that people often changed their minds later.

We just kept looking at each other face to face. He observed me closely not only with his eyes, but with his mind and soul, too. I held my divine heart open for him and let his soul sniff me to glean whatever information it could. At least it could become acquainted with my soul-scent and with my good will.

Finally he voiced the question in his heart: "What do you want from me?"

Judas' muted response pleased me. He was not making any assumptions about how to please me. He was going to verify what I wanted before he did anything. I liked his simple yet sophisticated form of deference. "Please tell me what you want me to do," he asked again.

I looked him right in the eye. "Come, follow me."

"You mean leave my job as a moneychanger, my home, my wife and kids? Leave everything and become your disciple?"

"Yes." I said it like a sigh, filled with all my hopes for him. "Instead of changing money, you'll be changing people."

Judas met my gaze. Without ever taking his eyes from mine, he began to smile broadly, then reached to his ear and removed the half-shekel coin that was a symbol of his profession. He tossed the coin at the Temple. We laughed as one. I stood and he followed me through the Temple precincts, past the moneychangers, and out of the Beautiful Gate. We walked through the Kidron Valley and up the Mount of Olives. We explored the orchards there together.

Judas and I spent the whole afternoon together on the Mount of Olives, praying and getting to know each other better. After nightfall I took him to the house in Bethany where my closest disciples and I were all staying. A dirt path led us to a cluster of one-room houses built from limestone blocks. Martha, Mary-Beth, and Lazarus lived in a simple stone house with an interior stable much like the one in Nazareth where I grew up. I opened the door to their house and ushered Judas inside.

Their goats welcomed me first. They sniffed and nuzzled me while I petted them and called them by name. As the man of the house, Lazarus was supposed to come to the door to greet guests, but he stayed seated next to John. Lazarus and I had already moved beyond formalities into an easygoing friendship. While his soul bounced merrily around my divine heart, Lazarus clowned with me like the young man that he was.

"I'm at your service, m'lord," he called out with a dramatic flourish, imitating the formal speech of a royal courtier.

I saluted him back. Then Mary Magdalene came over with a bowl of water and a towel to wash my feet. Most of my disciples followed the custom in which the women washed the men's feet and each other's feet when they arrived at home. Some of the women considered it a treat to get to wash my feet, so they had devised a system of taking turns to give all of them equal access to this sought-after chore. Tonight must have been Mary's turn. When she noticed that I had brought a stranger with me, she decided to offer her service to him out of hospitality. She had a reputation as the best foot washer, so it was like offering the finest morsel of food to a guest.

She signaled with her eyes to Joanna, one of my newer disciples. Joanna was sitting with the others around a lamp, chatting and munching on some bread and a stew that smelled of beans, onions, and cumin. At Mary's signal, she came over to tend my feet.

Meanwhile, Mary knelt before Judas. She removed his sandals and began pouring water and oil over his feet. Joanna was too matronly to catch Judas' interest, but I watched his eyes widen as he experienced Mary's expert touch and observed the sultry beauty of her symmetrical face and figure.

When my disciples and I were alone together, as we were at that moment, we spoke and dressed even more informally than members of one family. For the women, that meant they abandoned their veils and head scarves and let their tunics show and flow. Sometimes they even unbraided their long hair. Mary was dressed in just such a carefree style as she stroked Judas' feet. She didn't intend to be provocative, but she had spent so much time naked with strangers that she had lost the habits of modesty. Now her glossy black hair fell onto Judas' feet. She was completely unselfconscious as she tossed her head to send her hair flying out of the way.

The sensuality of her gesture was not lost on Judas. He, too, was feeling carefree, perhaps even careless, after an afternoon of feeding on God's unconditional love. Now he leered at me and laughed. He knew that Mary's lavish foot-washing techniques were usually practiced in brothels as a prelude to sin.

"I thought you were an ascetic!" Judas teased me. "I know plenty of men in the Temple hierarchy who would pay a small fortune to take this one to bed!" He indicated Mary with a quick nod of his head. He spoke as one might about a fine specimen of livestock, never expecting it to understand or respond.

Mary's face turned red with rage and humiliation. She glared at Judas and raised her voice. "Here we live by the Rabbi's teachings: If you want to be great, then serve everyone."

A stunned silence filled the room. Everyone looked at me, waiting to see what I would do. I had to stop and figure out why they were so shocked. Then I remembered that our customs said women must defer to men, especially strangers of unknown status. My disciples knew I disregarded this custom, but until now no woman among us had ever spoken so boldly. I noticed something else on the faces of my male disciples: horror at seeing their past in a new light. Now they knew what was on Mary's mind every time they had smugly enjoyed the male privilege of her foot washings. All the while she was thinking that she was the superior one—and according to my teachings, she was right.

I was still closely attuned to Judas. I sensed his soul cringing at the punishment it expected me to inflict on Mary. Judas had no doubt that I was going to punish her. But I didn't.

"Judas, this is Mary, who is called Magdalene," I said simply. "Mary, everyone, this is Judas Iscariot. He is one of us."

Mary pressed her lips together in frustration when she heard that she was going to have to put up with Judas for a long time to come. Just as he recognized her as a prostitute, she knew a whorehouse customer when she saw one. She looked at Judas' feet, and I knew she was tempted to "accidentally" on purpose wrench a toe out of joint or to exact revenge in the manner even more familiar to her: by making him lust after her, then spurning him later. Instead, she finished washing his feet simply and efficiently.

I caught her eye as she and Joanna stood to return to the others. "Whatever you did to him, you did to me." I said it loud enough so everyone could hear my approval.

Judas offered no apology. He didn't want to cause

trouble again, so he said nothing. But he shot me a look that told me he felt lost, utterly lost, in my world.

I slipped my arm around him and drew him into the circle of my disciples. They were seated in a way that was casual to the point of being unorthodox. Many of them leaned against the person to whom they felt closest: Mary and Andrew, sisters Mary-Beth and Martha, their brother Lazarus and his new friend John, and so on.

John slid up against Lazarus to make room for me to sit beside him. I pulled Judas down next to me on the other side. After a quick blessing, we took some bread, dipped it in the bean stew, and began to eat.

"Aren't you a moneychanger?" Peter asked. He offered a bowl of olives to Judas.

I answered for Judas. "He *used to* be. He doesn't change money anymore. He left his past and his old job behind just like the rest of you did."

Judas' eyes darted toward Mary, comprehending that she was a *former* prostitute. As their eyes met, they formed a truce.

Then a look of wonder softened his face. "The rabbi says I will be changing people from now on."

Peter chuckled, remembering how I made a similar promise to him when we first met. "Will you be traveling around the country with us then, Judas?"

Judas looked to me. "Rabbi?" We had not yet talked in concrete terms about what I meant when I asked him to follow me.

"Yes, Judas Iscariot will be with me to the end," I confirmed and watched him try to hide his smile of pleasure. "This afternoon Judas took me to a beautiful olive garden that he knows. What did you say it was called?"

"Gethsemane," he answered.

Martha and Mary-Beth exchanged a shocked look.

"What's the problem? Speak up," I urged.

"We've never heard anybody describe Gethsemane as beautiful," Mary-Beth replied. "Most people think it's too wild and desolate."

"Oh, I like wild and desolate," I smiled. "I'm planning to go back there and pray often. I'll take all of you there. For now, introduce yourselves to Judas and make him feel at home. I need to get some sleep." Ensuring that my mind and body got enough rest had become a new kind of spiritual discipline for me.

"John," I whispered to him, "Will you be my pillow?"

"Of course." He slid a muscular arm protectively across my chest as I lay my head on his lap. I closed my eyes and listened to my disciples introduce themselves. As they said their names, I made sure each soul was nursing steadily from my divine heart.

"From your accents, I would say you are all from Galilee except for the three people who live in this house," Judas surmised.

There was a general chorus of agreement.

"All of you are country folk, and I'm a city boy raised in Jerusalem." The edge in Judas' voice told me that he was dismayed to find himself involved with an odd assortment of disaffected women and hicks who were beneath him in social status.

"If you don't mind my asking, how the hell do you finance this operation?" Judas wondered aloud.

"I succeeded in business in a man's world. Joanna and I use our wealth to support the Rabbi and his ministry. So do many other women." This gruff, confident voice belonged to a lovely striped soul full of paradox and promise. She was Susanna, another of my newer disciples.

"I hope it helps to give the Rabbi some of what I have," Joanna quavered almost apologetically. "I come from a well-to-do family, so I don't even need to draw on what my husband earns as King Herod's steward." In her voice I read anxiety diverted into generosity.

"*Women* can pay for all this?" Judas asked in disbelief.

"What's the big deal? You admit Queen Herodias is a woman of wealth, don't you?" Susanna countered.

"Herodias! That bloodthirsty monster who divorced her husband and married his brother to get power?!"

Mary rose to the queen's defense. "I say she's smart. Women have to do stuff like that to get ahead sometimes."

I dozed off.

chapter fourteen:
secret visit

"RABBI, RABBI, WAKE UP!" I was jolted awake by the urgency in John's voice and the tension in his body as he lifted his knees, twisting my neck painfully.

My disciples had been relaxed when I fell asleep not long before, but now they were all in an uproar, bustling around the Bethany house and issuing orders to each other. Mary was braiding her hair so quickly that it looked sloppy and uneven, while the other women were digging through our belongings for their head scarves. Veils fluttered in the air as they flung them on.

"He's here!" John exclaimed.

I looked at him. "Who's here?"

"That old friend of yours from the Sanhedrin."

I sat up and watched my disciples, marveling at how one person's arrival had changed them from a relaxed, family-like group into a storm of anxiety. Some were so agitated that they interrupted the flow of divine love into their souls. Mary-Beth and Martha were each washing one of Nicodemus' feet while others peppered and pestered him with obsequious greetings.

John stared at me as I continued sitting where I was. "Don't you care that he's here?" It was more of an accusation than a question.

"There's no reason to panic. Where's your faith?" I replied. I walked over toward the doorway to bring peace to the situation.

"Nicky, welcome," I said calmly and greeted him as a beloved equal with a hug and a kiss on each cheek. I let my hands rest on his hips while he placed his on my shoulders. He had the blank expression of a baby still in the womb. I was close enough to see that he did have some new wrinkles, especially around his eyes. I touched a few of the wrinkles with my fingertips, enjoying and respecting these marks of age. Then I ran my hand down his long beard. "You've grown older. I like your wrinkles and your distinguished white beard."

"You've grown up." He squeezed the muscles of my arms appreciatively. We smiled at each other, pleased by where each of us was in the cycle of life.

"Come sit with me and my disciples. We don't have to be formal, do we?"

"No...." Nicodemus' reluctant tone informed me that he preferred ritualized courtesy and polite manners, but he would go along with my wishes while he was visiting me. "I brought a small gift for you and the head of this household to thank you for receiving me. Please accept this humble offering." He reached for a basket with a cloth covering that he had set on the floor. He was upset to see that one of the goats had already stuck his nose into it and was helping himself to a date.

"My animal friends appreciate your gift, too," I laughed as I accepted the basket. I removed the cloth to reveal a sumptuous arrangement of premium dried fruits and honey cakes. A fruity scent perfumed the air.

I led Nicodemus over to where I had been sleeping on John's lap. I snuggled against John and had Nicodemus sit beside us there while the rest of my disciples arranged themselves much as they had been, except nobody else touched and the women hid behind their veils.

I set the gift basket down where everyone could reach it. Lazarus brought Nicodemus a bowl of water for ritual purification, and Nicodemus went through the Pharisees' rather elaborate procedure of washing and prayer before we could eat.

Mary-Beth began bringing bread and dishes of vegetables, goat cheese, and condiments while Martha, whose manners were more refined than her sister's, poured wine for each of us, beginning with Nicodemus. She held her hands prettily, careful not to spill a drop as each person muttered their own individual wine blessing.

"Nicky, I want you to meet my disciples." I popped a sweet, chewy date in my mouth and gestured to indicate all those seated in the circle with us. Most of them bowed and did their best to invent suitable greetings, for nothing in their lives as fisherfolk and such in far-off Galilee had prepared them for a high-society occasion like meeting a member of the Sanhedrin.

Some of the women gave appropriate salutations, but Judas was conspicuous because he knew exactly what to say, and then embellished it. "Hail to you, most excellent Nicodemus, faithful minister of God's justice. We always thank the Lord when we pray for you because we have heard of your faith in the Lord and of the love which you have for the people of Israel."

"I know you!" Nicodemus exclaimed as if this were a crime. "You are a moneychanger."

Judas altered his demeanor, switching to a quiet new poise that I assumed was his imitation of me. "I used to be a moneychanger, but now Jesus of Nazareth is teaching me to become a changer of people."

Nicodemus snapped his head toward me. "But I've seen this man at the Temple scheming with—"

"Stop!" I cried out. Nicodemus may have thought he was doing me a favor by warning me about Judas' past, but it made me angry that he was already criticizing my choice of disciples.

"You don't need a doctor if you're not sick. I came to call the sinners, not the righteous," I explained.

Nicodemus peered warily around the lamp-lit room, actually looking at each of my disciples for the first time now that he thought they were sinners. He had forgotten that I had called him to follow me, too, and therefore he also must be a sinner in my view. His fear was not so much that they might betray me, but that they might betray *him* and leak word of his secret sympathies with me.

He scowled at Judas. He eyed John in a knowing way that made me uncomfortably aware of how the two of us leaned against each other.

Then Nicodemus noticed that I allowed Mary-Beth to sit at my feet and listen, a breach of the etiquette that kept women separate from men and religious education. I'm sure he found it vulgar, if not downright sinful. His eyes dwelt on Mary-Beth for a long, uncomfortable moment. Then his upper lip curled in distaste when he spotted Susanna's unconventionally short hair.

I had already overheard Susanna defending herself when some of my disciples pressured her to conform to gender norms.

I raised my voice to protect my disciples. "Be careful not to look down on these little ones. I'm telling you, angels in heaven are protecting them," I said bluntly.

Judas gasped at my rudeness while the others, including Nicodemus, stared at me in shock. This was no way to treat a member of the ruling elite who had honored me with a visit. Still, I had meant it kindly enough. Nicodemus' soul perceived my intent and moved once again into a position of surrender, bowing before my divine heart and giving me access to the receptive places where I could feed it. Meanwhile, I nibbled a piece of bread dipped in olive oil.

Nicodemus used his diplomatic skills to change the subject. "Rabbi, I see that you are sent by God because you have done miraculous healings this week at Solomon's Portico."

"Listen, nobody can see the kingdom of God without being reborn," I replied. My divine heart caressed his soul and urged it to nurse, but it was too immature and lacked a sucking reflex. For now it had to feed as if through an umbilical cord.

My comment made Nicodemus start spouting childish questions. "How can anyone be born once they are old? Can we get back into the womb?" he asked.

"Don't be so surprised. You can hear the wind blowing, but you don't know where it came from or where it is going. It's that way with everyone born of the Spirit." The same Aramaic word meant wind, spirit, and breath. I let Nicodemus puzzle over which meaning was primary in my wordplay while I prayed for his soul to be born anew.

"How can that be?" he asked.

"You're a high-ranking rabbi, and you don't understand this?" As we batted ideas back and forth, my divine heart stood ready like a midwife to deliver his soul, but it would not come. Nicodemus was stuck.

Martha had finished refilling our wine glasses and now set down a cucumber-and-yogurt salad a little too noisily, glaring at her sister. They bore no family resemblance, but instead seemed to be opposites: Martha was thin with silky hair, while plump Mary-Beth had kinky hair. All week long each of them had been paying a lot of attention to me and my disciples. Each had expressed her hospitality in her own way: Martha by anticipating and tending to all our needs, and Mary-Beth by hanging out with us and entertaining us with stories of her life. Martha exuded a subtle sadness, while Mary-Beth was quick to anger. Both were loving women of integrity. Usually they created a nice balance, but their difference caused conflict.

"Rabbi, don't you care that my sister has left all the work to me? Tell her to help me," Martha whined as she refilled my cup.

"Martha, Martha, you're worried about many things. Only one thing is needed. Mary-Beth has chosen what's best, and it won't be taken away from her."

She accepted my words with a resigned nod and retreated to the kitchen area. I followed her. She was so intent on measuring flour into a bowl that she didn't notice I was right beside her.

"Martha." I briefly touched her hand, which was

dusted with flour. "You misunderstood what I said. I didn't mean that you should serve while Mary-Beth listened. Everything is done. Come, join the feast."

"But they're running out of bread. I thought I'd make some more."

"Let me take care of that."

"You!" she exclaimed. She couldn't imagine me cooking or humbling myself to serve when an important man had come to hear me teach. She opened her eyes wide and looked right at me. I reached for her soul, stroking it so it relaxed and let me guide it into a better feeding position.

I moved closer to Martha and spoke quietly so only she could hear. "Surely you've noticed that you never run out of food when I'm around. Other people don't pay attention to these small differences in the quantities of food, but I thought you did."

"Yes, the other night I was *sure* I had just enough fish for everyone to eat one, but I then saw some of you take a second helping. And there were other times...." Amazement dawned on her face as she grasped my meaning. She searched my eyes for confirmation. I smiled back at her, happy to be recognized.

"Come on, let me feed all of you," I whispered in her ear, gesturing back to the group.

Martha slapped her hands together to shake off the flour, then came and sat in the corner where most of my female disciples were.

I resumed my seat between John and Nicodemus. It may have seemed like I was still speaking to Nicodemus, but I knew he couldn't absorb any more of my teaching that night. I had something that I felt inspired to say to my disciples, and Nicodemus just happened to be there.

"For God so loved the world…" I began.

Everyone looked at me intently, their eyes glowing. The house was absolutely silent. Even the animals stopped munching their straw. It was one of those magical moments when each person in a room shares a mutual understanding and time seems to stand still. My disciples and I were each remembering the particulars of how I had gone out of my way to draw them to me: catching that enormous mountain of fish with the fishers, casting the demons out of Mary, and just today feeding and leading Judas away from his life as a moneychanger.

Judas gazed at me, surprised and transfixed by the gratitude he felt for being invited into this gathering. Martha's eyes bored into me, too, as she dared to consider the full significance of my ability to multiply food and why I had revealed it to her. I could feel John's muscles tense as he twisted to get a better look at me. Even Nicodemus, who came here in secret because he wanted to hold onto his power and riches—even he glimpsed my divinity and marveled as it cast a whole new light on the personal care I had given him in the past.

Each person there had his or her own unique journey with me, but as I spoke, we all felt that God had carried us for a purpose to that very moment in that one particular house in Bethany. I felt it, too. Out of that understanding, I was able to reveal my divine side to them with humility in awe, saying words that otherwise would have sounded absurdly boastful. There were very few times in my earthly life that I was able to explain my mission so clearly, and this was one of them.

"For God so loved the world that He gave His beloved son, so that whoever trusts in him will not die, but have eternal life. God didn't send the son into the world to condemn it, but to save it," I said.

I felt the Holy Spirit pulsing through and among us. Excited by my Bride, I began to repeat my words, but this time I chanted them in the sing-song fashion usually reserved for holy scripture. "For God so loved the world..." I intoned, rocking my upper body back and forth in small bows as was the custom when reading scripture. I selected the cadence, pitch, and sounds in our Aramaic language that would open up a resonance among us so that everyone present would be able to feel the vibration of divine love, not just in their souls, but in their bodies as well.

"For God so loved the world..." I lingered over this phrase, my personal favorite, as I repeated it more times than they could count. Then I moved on: "...that He gave His beloved son so that whoever—whoever— *whoever*...trusts in him will not die, but will have eternal life." One by one they joined their voices to mine until we were all chanting as one body. I'm sure it was an erotic experience for at least some of the people there. It was for me. On and on we chanted like that until silence surfaced and left everyone else satisfied.

Transcendent moments like that one never last, and this one didn't either. Soon my disciples started asking what I meant. To me, our chanting felt like foreplay and I didn't want to stop until we reached the ecstatic climax with the Holy Spirit that I knew was possible. I tried to answer their questions, but the more I explained, the less important my ideas seemed. Words diminished the mystery I was trying to convey.

Sensing my frustration, the Holy Spirit whispered in my mind. "It's okay, Newlywed. I'll take you all the way later tonight."

Her promise motivated me to bring the gathering to an end. I had Nicodemus lead us in a closing prayer, and my disciples bid him farewell. I walked him out the door so we could say goodbye alone.

As soon as I stepped out of the Bethany house, I was overwhelmed by the velvety allure of the night sky. I savored the quality of the air, which was humid from receding rain. I resolved to sleep outdoors that night.

I almost forgot Nicodemus was there, but he drew my attention back to him by slipping his arm around my waist affectionately. "What always impresses me about you is your dignity," he said.

I thought it was a strange comment. Did he think I would lose my human dignity just because I was a penniless nobody from nowhere, lacking social status and surrounded by sinners?

"I'm going to keep on helping you behind the scenes," he continued. "But please don't do anything that would force the Sanhedrin to take a public vote on you. I won't be able to protect you then."

"I never asked you to protect me. I asked you to follow me."

Nicodemus embraced me and spoke softly in my ear. "I will follow you—in my own way."

"I am the way," I reminded him.

I felt helpless. As Nicodemus held me, I smelled the sweet Temple incense on his beard and clothes. As a devout Pharisee, he must have prayed for God's blessings every day of his adult life. Now that those blessings were within his grasp, he wanted to go his own way. I could heal strangers who came to me in faith, but I couldn't move this man whom my human self had loved for years. His soul stubbornly refused to be born. I felt at a loss.

"You study the scriptures because you think they will give you life—and they do bear witness to me. But you refuse to accept life from me," I lamented.

Nicodemus squeezed me tight and in a moment of audacity kissed me on the lips, then fled into the night.

With a hollow sensation inside, I went back indoors. I was shocked to find everyone celebrating and congratulating each other as if we had won a great victory.

Peter rushed up to me. "Nicodemus is very open to your teaching," he grinned.

John was right behind him. "We can do a lot with him."

Of the others, Judas looked especially self-satisfied, as if he had won a long-shot gambling bet. "I know Nicodemus by reputation. He is well respected on the Sanhedrin, and he has amassed a lot of wealth. You have made a powerful ally." Judas commended me with a clap on the back.

"Why would I need a so-called powerful ally when almighty God is my Father?" I asked, incredulous at their lack of understanding. "It's easier for a camel to squeeze through the eye of a needle than for a rich person pass through the door to God's kingdom."

Everyone fell silent and looked at me, baffled. "Do you mean you don't think Nicodemus can go to heaven?" Andrew asked. "Then who can?"

I considered. "For mortals it's impossible, but God can do anything."

With that, I grabbed a rolled-up mat and carried it back outside. I climbed up the ladder to the roof. I tossed the mat in a corner and went to the eastern parapet to rest my eyes on the horizon, noting the difference between the earth's solid darkness and the black vacuum of the sky.

The rooftop location helped me slip back into the almost-romantic mood that I had experienced while chanting that night. In silent prayer, I asked my Bride, "Are you ready to finish our lovemaking? How about here?"

I barely noticed the sound of two more people climbing to the roof.

"Rabbi?" It was Mary-Beth. "Tonight is cold, so Martha and I brought you some more bedding. Okay?"

"Thank you," I answered, but the Holy Spirit held my attention.

I felt Her playful touch deep inside my chest as She asked me, "How about *here*?" My heart beat faster as I lost myself in Her infinite willingness.

I let my human senses become quiet again as the variations among the stars began to grow more distinct and faint stars seemed to pop out of nowhere. In this space of subtleties, the Holy Spirit was very tangible to me. "My Beloved," I prayed. I breathed in the divine rejuvenation that came as a response: in, out, over and over. I let myself slip into Her consciousness and dissolve.

Then I heard whispers. "We should tell him."

"Yes, but not now."

The sisters were *still* making my bed. I realized that they were dawdling over the task in hopes of talking with me. As soon as I tore myself away from direct contact with the Holy Spirit, the women's longing for me drew me like a magnet. Tenderness toward them welled up in me, and I decided that I had time for one more human conversation that night. I walked over and saw Martha smoothing out every wrinkle from a woolen blanket spread over my mat, while Mary-Beth was arranging and rearranging a pillow for me.

"Thanks," I said again as I sat on the blanket and looked in their eyes: Mary-Beth's dark and generous, Martha's just as dark, but receptive. It was the first time we three had been alone together. Divine energy traced pretty triangles at it poured from me into Martha and from her to Mary-Beth, then back to me. Sometimes it reversed its course, repeating the cycle in the opposite direction. The Holy Spirit reigned over us, providing a kind of filter that purified our energies and prevented one person's disturbances from merging into the others. The flow of sacred love between Martha and Mary-Beth was always strong, no matter which way it traveled.

"Your teaching tonight was *fantastic!*" Mary-Beth said, clapping her pudgy hands together for emphasis. "Martha and I have been hoping and praying for years for God to guide us to someone like you. You are going to lead our people to true liberation. You are the *best* on earth!"

I smiled and let it feel good as she went on like that for a while. Mary-Beth's words kept growing louder and faster. "We want you to know that you are always welcome in our home. In fact, please treat this as your own home."

Martha managed to slip in a sentence. "We discussed it with Lazarus, and we all agreed."

"That's right," Mary-Beth enthused. "Please come here whenever you want and stay as long as you want. You can come even if you just need a quiet place to pray. We won't interrupt you."

"Even though we're interrupting your prayers right now." Martha's sly wit made us all laugh.

"I feel at home with you. I'll be back," I agreed.

A not-quite-satisfactory silence stretched among us.

"I thought there was something more you wanted to tell me," I prompted them.

There was, but there wasn't. The sisters looked at each other, unable to speak. They had longed for my attention and approval, but now that they had it, the intensity of my love was almost unbearable to them. They had invited me into their house, and here I was, knocking at the door to their hearts.

The goodness of who they were, of who God had created them to be, was hidden from them behind layers of shame. Their silent, futile struggle to hide the full extent of themselves and their beautiful relationship moved me to speak in compassion. "Everything hidden will be revealed, and everything secret will come to light," I assured them.

Fear made them convert to a closed, vacant politeness that they thought would appease me. "We have to go," Martha said preemptively. "We'll get you some more bedding."

I put a hand on her shoulder for a moment, holding her back. "No. Enough serving me. Enough listening to me. Go ahead and *speak* to me."

An awkward silence arose as each sister waited for the other to speak up. Mary-Beth was full of bluster, but when it came time to say something difficult, Martha was the braver one.

She took the lead now. "Well, you've been so open with us that we thought we should be more honest with you about who we are. Lazarus isn't our biological brother. We all decided to move in together and be a family because none of us wants to get married. We all look after each other."

Martha drew a deep breath and began to stammer as I gave her my kindest look. "Mary-Beth and I told you that we were sisters, but we're not sisters by blood. We're...sisters...by love." Unable to find any more words, Martha took her sister-lover's hand and held it in my lap.

"If people knew what we do, they would say that we gave up natural intercourse with men and are consumed with passion for each other," Mary-Beth explained.

I had sensed their real relationship from the start, but their honesty opened a floodgate between us. I couldn't find words that would convey my feelings to them, either, so I held their hands in mine and bowed my head to place a long, gentle kiss on their clasped hands. Divine love surged powerfully among the three of us. Now their souls invited my divine heart into their relationship and we forged a stable triangle with me at the apex. Their souls began a lifelong kiss.

When I looked up and saw their bright eyes, the right words came to me. "May nobody separate what God has united."

chapter fifteen:
boredom strikes

LIFE FOR ME BECAME ONE LONG PARTY. I traveled all over Judea and Galilee, including many interesting places I had never visited before. Everywhere I went, more people got healed and more disciples latched onto me. I became famous for healing. The crowds kept getting bigger and more enthusiastic. I developed the ability to connect my divine heart with larger and larger numbers of souls simultaneously, so that nobody ever felt lost in the crowd. I spoke as personally to each listener, as if we were alone together. Then I moved on to let my ideas percolate. The crowds around me were filled with lively conversation groups as people debated my words and applied them to their own lives. The scribes and Pharisees criticized us, but it seemed like fun to taunt them and their silly, overly rigid religious ideas.

When we had had enough of the crowds, we would hang out in Bethany at the home of Mary-Beth, Martha, and Lazarus. The Baptist and I communicated back and forth through his disciples. We scheduled several visits, but he always sent a message postponing the date.

The love between me and my disciples deepened as I fed them with my words and my divine heart. We spent a lot of time singing, dancing, laughing, and feasting. We all fell in love with each other as a group, so that even when conflicts arose among us, we felt joy in resolving them. My disciples and I fell into roles as we found comfortable ways to relate to each other: Peter protected me, Andrew sought my protection, Judas pushed me to hone my ideas. Mary and John were my most frequent prayer partners, the ones with the greatest openness to mystical states. Each of them also shared prayerful kisses with me, but in different ways. For Mary, kissing was almost instinctive when she felt God's love. She liked that I accepted her kisses without asking for more. John would have gladly gone further, but I never let us climb to the level of sexual arousal that we had reached on the night we first met, so he found other sexual outlets.

They all got used to referring to God as my Father, and they were coming to know Him as their own Father, too. They tuned me out when I spoke to them about the Holy Spirit. Mary was the only one who really understood that God could and did come as a lover.

My beloved Bride melted away everything in me that didn't serve love and we became One, a more blissful experience each day. As She unfolded, We unfolded. I stopped having visions with the cup of my blood and I rarely thought anymore about my upcoming death. I dreamed that my death could be delayed or even averted entirely by teaching people to love. My life went on like this for months, or perhaps more than a year.

Then came a certain spring day in Galilee. I was sitting on a grassy plateau with my back against an olive tree while my closest disciples chattered in a group nearby. Enough people were there to fill many villages, but nobody approached me. Everyone who wanted to be healed that day had already been healed. For the moment, all the children had been blessed and all the critics silenced. I felt that I had been exceptionally eloquent when I taught the crowd that day. The hills around me formed a natural amphitheater that glowed red, gold, and purple with wildflowers at the peak of their blossoming. A tumult of fruit trees bloomed on the lower, more accessible parts of the hillsides, creating a subtle rainbow of pinks and pastels. I smiled at them and thought: perfect. Just then a strong wind arose from a new direction and blew the perfume of innumerable flowers under my nostrils, past my ears and through my hair.

"I want to make love to you tonight," the Holy Spirit whispered as She mussed my hair.

I blushed and swept my hair out of my eyes. Anticipation prickled my body. I knew I would receive a lot of pleasure that night. I also understood from experience that She wanted to tell me something that my human mind found too upsetting to accept in an ordinary state of consciousness. We would think it together when We had become One. Now I wondered what it could be. I scanned my surroundings, alert for signs of unmet need. My disciples' conversation caught my attention.

"I wanted the Rabbi to tell the story about the prodigal son today," Mary said idly. I noticed how robust her soul looked compared to the day that the demons left her, although the wounds were still not fully healed.

"My favorite is the story about the good Samaritan. He didn't tell that one, either," Peter responded.

Boredom made them bicker. "The one about the rich fool is better," Judas argued.

"No," blurted John. "His best one is how he will separate the sheep from the goats at the end of the world, although he didn't tell it as well today as he did last week."

Peter shoved him playfully. "Oh, you *would* like that one!" They all started laughing.

I looked away uneasily. Unexpected twists in my stories were supposed to shake people into new ways of thinking. I hadn't realized that many retellings had made my stories routine and predictable.

Then I noticed some young women approaching. Their hair was wild and free, except for a few tiny braids interwoven with lilies picked fresh from the fields around us. Their heavily embroidered robes were new and drawn tightly to reveal their curves. They gamboled and then grouped together like frisky young lambs.

"Mary, can we meet your new man?" They all giggled.

"You mean the Rabbi? Sure." She got up and led them over to me. Each one tried to hide behind the others as a playful way to honor me. Finally they all bunched together behind Mary and peeked over her shoulders with unabashed curiosity.

"Rabbi, these are some of the women I used to work with: Delilah, Sheba, Phoebe, and Tamar."

I remembered Tamar from the brothel. "Hello," I said.

They all tittered and hid their faces in mock shyness. "Come on, Mary." They began pulling her sleeves.

"I'll see you later." She waved goodbye to me.

They pulled her away, but not far enough away to show me much respect before they began asking rude questions. I could easily hear them bubbling with excitement.

"What's your new man like?"

"He's cute! Almost as cute as our Reuben."

"Tell us what he's like in bed."

"Yes, is he sweet and full of love like he is in public, or is he the type who makes you do nasty things in bed?"

"He's not my man," Mary retorted. "There's actually another guy that I kind of like."

"You know better than that! You have to stick with the top billy goat."

"Jesus is my rabbi," Mary insisted. "He teaches me."

"Oh, Mary, you're not in love with him, are you?" Now they all clucked in disapproval.

One raised her voice in shock and horror as if she had just heard of a death. "Oh, Mary, not *you!*"

"We've never had sex," Mary stated.

This they plainly could not believe. A mean tone crept into their voices when they realized she wasn't going to gossip with them about my sex life.

"You're protecting his reputation—and for what?"

One of them grabbed the neck of Mary's robe and rubbed it between her fingers, assessing its quality. It was crudely woven and frayed with age. "Is *this* the best he can do for you?" she sneered.

Mary looked down at her shabby robe, surprised. "He says I have treasure in heaven," she said, but the hurt showed in her voice.

"Oh, Mary!" they all cried out in exasperation. Their mood shifted again as they began to mother her.

"Don't worry. We'll help you win him over. Let us braid some flowers in your hair."

"Come on. When he sees how beautiful you look, you'll be able to *make* him buy you a new robe."

They pulled her away while my attention was drawn to a new stream of people who came to me with various needs for healing, wisdom, and love. I didn't think of Mary again until sunset when Andrew approached me.

"Do you know who that is with Mary? I don't like the way he looks at her." He pointed to the middle of the crowd where I saw Mary, Martha, and Mary-Beth. They were chatting with a man who sat close beside Mary. Her old cohorts were nowhere in sight. The iridescent purple flowers in Mary's hair accentuated the eager, exhilarated expression on her face and made her look all the more alluring. The man turned from her to study Martha's svelte figure and the animated way that Mary-Beth moved her hefty body.

"Your accents tell me that you come from Judea," he said to them. "I'm surprised that your husbands let you come so far chasing after a preacher."

"Oh, we've never married," Mary-Beth asserted.

"We haven't found the right man yet," Martha added, tossing her head disingenuously.

Martha caught me watching. She must have read my surprise and hurt at their denial of the woman-to-woman marriage that I had blessed, because she looked away quickly. Her nervous laughter rankled me.

The man's eyes glinted with lust—not for the

women, but for their capture. "Maybe I could help you find a man," he wheedled.

Andrew tugged my sleeve and his voice grew more urgent. "Who is that creep?"

"That's Reuben, Mary's old pimp."

"Her old pimp! Are you just going to let her talk to him?"

I studied them a moment. The women's souls were unchanged, still drinking in an even flow of divine love. Reuben's soul had added more chains to its self-imposed prison. It was a dangerous situation, but dangers confronted every soul around us. "The women are free to do as they please. If I force them to stay with me, I become just like him, and then he wins anyway."

"Well, I'm not putting up with it!" Andrew stormed and began marching over.

I let him go. I did not see them again that day.

✛ ✛ ✛

When everyone else settled down to sleep that night, I left to be alone with the Holy Spirit. I climbed to the top of one of the flower-covered hills where the wild-flowers themselves welcomed me. I could understand their meaning as they called out to one another and to me with their fragrances: "A bridegroom! A newlywed!"

Flowers have a special affinity for weddings and were quick to pick up on this aspect of my being. I knelt among them and spent some time admiring the different blossoms: succulent lilies and the tiny yellow flowerets of the mustard plants. By relaxing my mind, I got back in touch with how it felt to create their kind back before I had a separate identity. My divine heart had expressed some of its delicacy and extravagant generosity by concocting these transient little lovelies. Then I began to pray, using the same words and ideas that I had been teaching my disciples.

Pleased, the Holy Spirit drew near. She listened a long time, then encouraged me to lie down in the natural flowerbed. I could discern the aroma of each individual flower as they wove a lacy blanket of scents over me. I thanked the Holy Spirit for everything in pairs of opposites, starting with what easily aroused my gratitude and moving toward what my human self resisted. She coaxed me to let down my resistances one by one. The floral perfume was so strong and close that it seemed to massage me. I thanked Her for absolute love and absolute suffering, for absolute trust and absolute helplessness.

She entered me. Then at Her urging, I entered Her. My heart bloomed. It made me feel both vulnerable and powerful to be in Her like that, to feel Her cast a bright light of total acceptance on even those parts of my being that society had told me were unacceptable or dirty. We balanced each other, we mirrored each other, we enthroned each other, and we always encouraged each other to express ourselves more completely, even the wildest corners of ourselves. Especially those.

We romped along the range of genders, stopping to play at ultra-femininity, hyper-masculinity, and every other way station that pleased Her/Him. Then we left the male-female spectrum altogether and stretched our gender games into other dimensions where we could match and counter each other in delicious freedom.

My feet and hands throbbed and the edges of my lips burned as my mouth gaped open in our whirlwind of ever-changing gender configurations. I broke out in a sweat. My tension mounted until I could no longer stop myself from giving Him/Her my whole life. In a burst of trust, I gave all of me, *all* of me. I gave and gave and *gave*. In the giving, I received bliss without limit and sent it shining out through the universe.

I reached my zenith and We merged into One. Together we touched every star, every heart, every being. We remained One even after We came to rest. In that Oneness, We spoke ideas that I didn't know I had, while my human mind listened in silence and let Us utterly love it. We communicated slowly with lengthy pauses because my human mind needed a long time to digest the enormity of each divine thought.

"I love your disciples, your friends," We said. My human mind remembered them one by one, and We cherished them, carefully checking the soft sucking places where they were drinking in divine love at that moment. We enriched the nutrient content for them just slightly and treasured the unique ways that each one expressed love back to Us.

Our love evolved into extreme yearning. "I want to live in them—but they're not ready!"

My human mind had never known the Holy Spirit to feel such anguish.

"Prepare them," We commanded. "Send them away."

As soon as my human mind heard this idea, it seemed self-evident. We displayed the idea in such a way that my human mind could wordlessly examine its many facets. Gradually the Holy Spirit allowed my human mind to move into a more interactive mode in which it could ask for and receive a few specific answers. I floated into peaceful sleep as the Holy Spirit's ideas hatched in my mind.

The songs and buzzes of flowers woke me the next morning. "A bridegroom! A newlywed!" they twittered in their soprano voices.

"Buzzzzz."

I hadn't known flowers to buzz before. I opened my eyes, and it seemed that some flowers had taken wing and were fluttering in the sunshine above my face. I reached for one, and it landed on my finger—a handsome butterfly! We admired each other for a while. A bumblebee buzzed by, and I sorted out the source of the buzzing sound. I tuned into the insect conversations of vivid praise for each blossom around us. Nobody could describe the variations in floral colors, scents, and nectars as precisely as butterflies and bees.

I had brought some grapes with me, and I savored them as the bugs inspired me to focus on the material world. At last I remembered that it was time for me to send my disciples away. Without further thought, I hiked downhill to find them.

Peter and Susanna saw me when I was still far away and came running. "Rabbi, Rabbi, we're glad you are back!" Susanna shouted. "A demon has entered into Mary again!"

"A demon?" I looked squarely at Mary's soul, which had never been far from my conscious thoughts, much less my divine heart, for the whole time I was gone. There was no demon. It was jarring to switch from the hum of bees back to the shouts and sensibilities of human community. My human ears began to hear Mary squealing in the distance.

"Andy is with her. He's trying to calm her down," Peter panted, for he was out of breath from running. A sudden shriek from Mary told us that Andrew wasn't having much success.

As they led me to her, I could begin to make some sense of what she was wailing. "How sick is that?!" she kept saying.

She and Andrew were sitting under the same olive tree that I had leaned against the day before. The crowds were gone, but a large group of my disciples were bunched together on a hillside, looking alarmed. They knew Mary could be loud and dramatic, but none of them had seen her this distraught. I sent Peter and Susanna to join the group while I sat down beside Mary and Andrew. I looked Andrew in the eye first, to let him know how much I appreciated his willingness to be with Mary through her personal storm. The helplessness in his eyes made me rub his arm in reassurance.

Then I turned to Mary. She looked bedraggled. The purple flowers that had once complemented her beauty had wilted into dead weights. Tears dampened her face. Her soul was bleeding from several long, clean incisions, a type of soul-wound that was not yet familiar to me. They looked easy to heal. I stroked them with my divine heart and they instantly closed up and scabbed over, leaving almost no trace.

"What's the problem?" I asked them both. I felt completely calm.

"I'm attracted to people who abuse me." Mary began quietly and grew louder and more agitated as she explained. "I almost went back to Reuben last night. I knew he was a pimp who had used me, but he said this time it would be different and I wanted to believe him. The old lies still enticed me. How sick is that? It's scary! He's such a con artist and a seduce-aholic. I sent Andy away and I let Reuben grope me. How could I be so stupid?!"

"You're human," I said evenly. "It's okay."

She really looked at me for the first time that day. My acceptance startled as it soothed her.

"Come on, I have a new idea I want to share with a bunch of the disciples together. It will help you handle your feelings, too."

"But...." She looked doubtful and I saw that Mary was still at war with herself.

"Your soul is like a lovely oasis that mirrors the image of the most high God who created you," I explained. "The attractions you are feeling are an integral part of the sacred landscape that is you. Maybe you can feel them more clearly now that you are on the healing path with me. The trusting places inside you are beautiful. They were designed for God to inhabit. You haven't forgotten that God's kingdom is inside of you, have you?"

Tears streamed down her cheeks. "But you said that feeling lust is the same as committing adultery. You said that no one who looks back is fit for the kingdom of God. I'm not fit for God's kingdom," she sobbed.

Now I knew the source of her unusual soul-wounds. "Listen to me. My word is *never* to be used as a weapon—not against yourself and not against others." I put my hand on her shoulder and waited for her to raise her eyes to meet my gaze. "Yes, I said those things, but I've also said over and over that God's kingdom is inside and all around you."

I looked over at Andrew to make sure he heard, too. "My word is very powerful, and it can inflict a lot of damage. It was never intended to be used against people. You are not to judge yourself."

"But *you* will judge when you come in your glory," she said.

"Yes, and I judge with mercy." I used my sleeve to wipe away her tears. "You live under the law of love now: Do *with* love and *for* love and when you don't, there is forgiveness—more love. Nothing should ever make you stop loving yourself. Nothing! Nothing can separate you from God's love. Nothing!"

"But what if I hadn't just lusted in my heart? What if I had really had sex with Reuben last night?"

"Then I would still forgive you."

"But if I hadn't come back here and repented? What if he had gotten me to stay with him?"

"Then I would go and find you like a shepherd who leaves his whole flock to search for one that has gone astray. I've done it before." I cocked my head and looked at her.

"I know." As she remembered the day I found her at the brothel, she smiled a little for the first time, and her soul glowed warmer. My divine heart radiated warmth to match.

"Let's go join the others." I was about to get up, but Andrew stopped me with his words.

"I can tell you exactly what happened."

"That's not necessary," I answered.

"Aren't you going to cast the demon out of her?"

"There isn't any demon." My tone was definite.

They looked at each other, struggling to understand the forces at work in their lives. It gave me an idea.

"Magdalene, I saw how beautiful you looked yesterday with fresh wildflowers in your hair," I smiled. "But now they're all dead. Would you let me and Andy undo your braids and take out the dead flowers?"

She glanced quickly at Andrew to gauge his reaction, since it was considered erotic for a man to touch a woman's hair. If anything, he looked intrigued. She nodded agreement.

I scooted closer to her and began to untwist one of several tiny braids that lay half-hidden in her ebony hair, most of which hung in long, loose waves. It was thick and glossy to the touch. Her old brothel-mates must have sprinkled her hair with perfume for it smelled strongly of the sweet-pungent roots of the spikenard plant, a much heavier scent than the wildflower breaths that had surrounded me the night before.

Working my fingers in her hair reminded me of how I used to braid my little sisters' hair when we were growing up. They liked to show affection for each other and their girlfriends by fixing each other's hair. Mom and the girls let me join in this fun, even though I was a boy. They accepted my eccentricities, and besides, my braids were the best: tiny and neat. I tried to get them to braid my hair too, but they refused because I was a boy.

I pulled away from the memory and looked over to see how Andrew was doing. He was sitting in the same spot with his face screwed up from inner strife. "You don't have to help, Andy," I said.

"I want to, but I don't know how."

"Come on over and I'll show you." I had him sit down closer to Mary than he had been since becoming my disciple. "It takes a lot of skill to weave flowers into this kind of tiny braid, but it's easy to undo them. Watch me." I deftly untwined a lock of Mary's hair and tossed aside the drooping flower that had been bound there. "You just have to be careful not to pull too hard or you'll hurt her."

Andrew lifted a braid gingerly, as if the hair itself had nerve endings. He chose the one closest to Mary's face. With supreme kindness, he placed his other hand on Mary's back and bent over so she could see his puppy-dog eyes. "You let me know if I hurt you, okay?"

"Okay."

For a while I lost myself in the human pleasure of doing the simple task with my friends. I combed my fingers through Mary's luxuriant hair, searching for more braids to unwind. Eventually they were all untangled, except the one that Andrew was working on. I was surprised to see that he was still only halfway through his first braid. He worked clumsily, for he was struggling with sexual arousal, tenderness, passion, and all the other colors of love that were provoked and evoked by touching Mary's hair. In contrast, she was at ease to the point of near-numbness. Mary was used to having different men handle her.

Andrew noticed me watching him and realized that we were waiting for him to finish. Embarrassed, he felt he had to explain. "I'm good at mending fishnets, but this...!"

His remark roused Mary. She sized up the situation and giggled a musical little laugh. "Fishnets! Oh, Andy." She leaned her shoulder against his chest. That was all she said, but the way she said it communicated a symphony of loving emotions.

Andrew raised his hands in surprise, but when Mary didn't move away, he let his arms fall lightly around her. Still laughing, she tilted her face up toward his while he looked down at her. Their eyes met. They reached an instant understanding that their feelings for one another were mutual. I felt their heartbeats register a series of shocks and aftershocks to this truth. Mary parted her lips. I think they would have kissed if I weren't there.

Their souls turned to face each other. Now that they had each put God first in their lives, their soul-situation was radically different from the way it was during their previous sexual encounters, back before they became my disciples. Their souls beheld each other and saw the majesty and protection that was now available to them if they chose to become one in the flesh again. Each soul allowed itself to be explored by the other, and they rejoiced together as they discovered new areas of healing, growth, and possibility that were not there the last time their souls touched. The touch between their souls really was a kiss of sorts.

To my human eyes, Mary and Andrew both looked

flustered and breathless, like two people who have just kissed passionately. By some unspoken mutual agreement, they both sprang apart simultaneously and resumed their previous positions. Andrew lightly ran the palm of his hand down the full length of Mary's hair from the crown of her head to the middle of her back. Then he pursed his lips and began trying to untie her braid again. He worked much more efficiently this time. Mary stole a glance at me, wondering how much I had been able to observe.

"It is finished," Andrew announced as the last braid unraveled.

Mary shook her long locks, then gathered them and quickly wove them into one modest braid which she twirled into a bun at the back of her neck. Andrew watched with new appreciation now that he knew more about braids. Then we three stood up and went to join the other disciples.

chapter sixteen:
sending forth

ALL EYES WERE ON MARY when she, Andrew, and I rejoined the rest of my disciples. As soon as they saw that she was back to normal, they crowded around to congratulate Mary and me. Andrew got ignored. He stood near the edge of the group, staring at the ground. His soul had grown exponentially during his latest encounter with Mary. The love he had given her was now illuminating a previously empty swath of the universe with Andrew's own unique palette of colors. I walked over and slipped my arm around him.

"What you did for Mary today was beautiful," I said. "I hope you don't think your efforts were ineffective and then I came along and fixed her, because that's not how I see it at all. We healed her together. Someday, beyond Beyond, you'll see all the incredible ripple effects of your kindness. It can't have been easy to stay with her while she talked about lusting over another man."

"I didn't know what to say."

"That's okay. Love heals, not words. You entered into her suffering with her, and what you did for her, you did for me." Overcome by gratitude, I kissed him on the forehead. "I just wanted you to know that *your* suffering is not invisible to me, and I will stay with you through it just as you did for Mary."

I released him and addressed the whole group. "Listen up! I want to talk with some of you under the grove of trees on that hilltop over there." I pointed. "I'll choose those who are supposed to come with me." I smiled at Andrew. "See you there."

The Holy Spirit and I had agreed upon a few people, such as Mary and Andrew, the night before. My bride had promised to reveal the rest to me this morning. I sent Her a short silent prayer to let Her know I was ready. She engulfed me and I let my human consciousness fall away. My divine senses guided me as I moved among my disciples without really seeing their earthbound identities. Instead my attention was drawn to a lovely golden light from the Holy Spirit Herself that rested like a lion's mane about the heads and shoulders of some of the disciples. I felt the Holy Spirit shining deep in the core of my own heart, too. She beamed encouragement each time I sought out one of these illuminated disciples, looked in their eyes and indicated with a touch or nod that they were invited to the hilltop. "*You*," I said sometimes. "Yes, *you*."

For me it was a dreamlike interlude of divine bliss fraught with significance, but nobody else seemed to sense anything out of the ordinary. I often taught in small groups, and they must have assumed this was just one more lesson. I didn't think I could teach in my buoyant, enraptured state of mind, so I dawdled as I walked up the flowery hill to meet those who had been chosen.

The Holy Spirit laughed lovingly at me: "Clumsy new Bridegroom!"

The wildflowers, all yellow and purple, bowed in the wind as they echoed the refrain: "A bridegroom!"

Even as She teased me, the Holy Spirit obliged me by dimming the glow in my heart and on each disciple. It had paled by the time I sat under an acacia tree atop the hill. John flopped down next to me, confident that he belonged there. I looked at the faces of the people seated around me and was surprised by some I saw there and by some who were absent, such as Martha and Mary-Beth. The last remaining gleam of light enabled me to confirm that these were indeed the ones picked by a wisdom greater than my human reasoning.

"You're all bored with hearing me tell the same stories over and over," I began. They objected, but not enough to convince me that I was wrong.

"Why, just yesterday I discovered a new meaning in the one about the house built on rock and the house built on sand," Joanna protested.

"I didn't say you had fully understood the stories. I said you were *bored* with hearing me tell them!" I retorted sharply.

I had their attention.

"I want all of you to tell the stories to people," I said. "Make them *your* stories. Tell the ones that you want to hear and leave out the rest. Change the details or make up new stories to illustrate the same points. All you have to do is stick to my basic message: love."

"Do you mean," John asked, "that you are going to sit with the crowds and listen to us, so that you can critique us later?"

"No, not at all. I'm not going to critique you. I trust you with the stories. I mean I'm going to send you away, two by two, to preach the kingdom of God to the people you meet."

I could tell they were excited, so I gave more details. "Travel light. Don't take food, money, or even a change of clothes. Live on people's hospitality."

"What if people won't listen to us?" Susanna asked.

"It's not a question of 'what if,'" I replied. "You will be ignored and even attacked. You have all heard how people insult me when they run us out of town. If they call me the devil, just think how they'll bad-mouth my followers."

People looked to Peter, depending on his take-charge personality to show them how to react.

"Rabbi, I will gladly face their insults for you," Peter declared.

"Just don't force my teachings on people," I added. "The purpose is to help all of you grow as much as it is to help your listeners."

"Fine," Peter said. "You can count on me."

Many others voiced their agreement and exchanged bright-eyed glances. My challenge had energized the group.

"I'm going to call you apostles because you are my authorized representatives, my messengers. I think I'll also call you 'the Twelve' for the twelve tribes of Israel." I felt playful as I made this reference to our common ancestry as Jews, but nobody else seemed amused.

They grimaced as if they had eaten sour grapes.

"What's the matter?" I asked.

Judas was scanning the group, counting everyone with his finger. Then he leaned forward and darted his eyes at me like he did when he was really irritated. "But

Rabbi, there are many more than twelve of us! There are sixteen men, plus you have chosen as many women as men! There are exactly thirty-two people here."

This struck me as funny since I hadn't even noticed the discrepancy. "You don't have to take everything I say so literally!" I laughed. "It doesn't matter if there are more than twelve. Numbers mean nothing to me. The Twelve will not be a static group. Membership will vary over time. If you want the arithmetic to be correct, you can take turns playing at who is among the big Twelve each day. Have some fun with it."

Peter raised another objection. "Women can't be your apostles. I understand that among ourselves we try to treat each other as equals, regardless of gender. But out in the real world, women are forbidden to teach and testify. Even if our women speak up, nobody will believe them."

"Other *women* will believe them," I assured him. "You don't have to go to a synagogue or stand on a mountaintop to tell your stories. Women tell lots of stories to each other when they are alone together. While they are cooking, one woman might tell another, 'The kingdom of heaven is like a pinch of yeast that makes a whole loaf of bread rise.'"

"Yeah, Peter," Mary added scornfully. "A lot of women are going to believe us before they believe a hot-tempered, long-winded, heavy-handed *man* like you. I think the Rabbi calls you his Beloved Rock because you have rocks in your head."

"Yeah, Peter!" Several of the other women shot him dirty looks.

He glared back at Mary.

I stood and began wandering among them to defuse the situation. We already had explored this group dynamic thoroughly on many previous occasions. People relied on and yet resented Peter's leadership and his hasty judgments. Peter for his part struggled with how to stay true to himself and yet hold power in God's confusing kingdom where the last are first and the first last. Now his soul burrowed further into my divine heart so it could drink more deeply from the reservoir of love there.

"It's all right for people to say what's inside them as they try to understand a new idea," I assured them. "Soon enough you'll be on your own and out of each other's way. It's all right." I repeated the phrase a few more times as I grazed my fingers over their heads, feeling for the glow of the Holy Spirit and sensing their moods. Only a few harbored serious doubts. Peter and Mary looked away from each other.

"Any other questions or comments?" I asked.

The quiet stretched long. Finally Peter and Mary let their eyes meet. They regarded each other impassively. Neither one blinked.

Judas broke the silence with the subtle, self-deprecating humor of which he was a master. "Thirty-two equals twelve and, believe it or not, it really is all right with me. It's just another mystery of faith. Why not?"

We all laughed. All resistance melted away, except for the nuggets of fear lodged in a few souls.

"I believe that each of you is ready to go out and teach," I said, "but you don't have to do it now if for any reason you'd rather not. You can stay with me longer. There's no shame in it. If you're not going to accept the role of apostle today, go rejoin the others so I can talk to the apostles alone."

A handful of people walked away. John was one of those with misgivings, but he stayed anyway. I looked at him thoughtfully until he felt my gaze and flashed a brave smile at me.

I knelt down in the center of the group that remained. They saw my serious expression and gathered closer to me. "I have given you authority over all the enemy's power. Nothing will injure you." I told them.

They exchanged glances of amazement.

"Here's how I want you to use your new powers: heal the sick, raise the dead, cast out demons."

They watched me, expecting me to conduct some kind of ceremony to give them what they already possessed. I examined the last luster of the Holy Spirit still resting on all of them as before. They had received these gifts earlier that morning when the Holy Spirit first landed on them, long before they knew it.

"You already have my blessing," I declared. "I'm sending you out in pairs, so if two of you agree that you want to travel together, that's fine. Otherwise, come to me and I'll match you up with someone."

Nobody stirred.

"I'll see you when you return," I added.

Still nobody moved.

Finally Andrew ventured a question. "You don't mean for us to go right now, do you?"

"Yes, I do."

They howled in protest. Everyone had an objection: "But where should we go?"

"How long should we stay?"

"Aren't you going to teach us how to cast out the demons first?"

They wanted time to give away their extra tunics, their staffs, their gold, their silver, and their copper. They wanted to say long goodbyes to their friends, me included. The pain of separation was so sharp that it made me realize for the first time that I was sending away all my closest friends. I was going to miss them terribly.

The last wisps of euphoria from the previous night receded. I could no longer perceive the glow of the Holy Spirit around us. I hadn't thought to ask Her any of the practical questions that they were now raising, and in this downcast state of mind I wasn't going to be able to perceive Her answers.

"All right," I conceded. "You can stay another day if you like. Talk and pray with your partner about where to go, and do whatever you need to do. I'll be available to you for discussion and prayer, too. But all of you should be gone by this time tomorrow."

I got up and stretched. I didn't want them to notice that I was in any way sorry to see them go.

Out of nowhere came a sexless voice that I recognized as Satan. "They'll run off when you drink your Father's cup, too. But I'll never leave you alone."

I shivered at the reminder that progressing in my ministry inevitably meant moving closer to my own death. My disciples began to mill around, deaf to Satan's voice.

Mary bounced right up to me, her eyes even more

luminous than usual. "Will I be able to cast out my *own* demons, too?"

"Yes."

She stepped closer and placed her palms on my upper arms and tipped her face up to mine so I could see the full measure of her gratitude. Part of me wished she would give me the kind of amorous look that Andrew got from her that morning, but she never looked at me that way.

"You really want me to grow!" she exclaimed. "After what happened yesterday, most men would be trying to exert more control over me, not less."

I smiled at hearing her confirmation of the Holy Spirit's plan. I placed my hands on her waist. Mary's soul opened at a new, deeper level, and I felt the pleasure of divine power being sucked through me as her soul gulped it down in trust.

"Today I keep having this strange feeling like I'm being kissed, but nobody is kissing me," she mused.

"Me, too." We continued to enjoy the soul intimacies in silence until she couldn't bear to be loved any more completely.

"I don't know who I should travel with," Mary said as we released each other.

I looked around to find her a partner. Andrew was watching us, half hoping and half dreading that I would do something scandalous and send him and Mary off into the world alone together. That felt wrong.

I saw that Judas had paired up with a former tax collector named Matthew. John and James were talking with vigorous gestures while their mother Salome sat beside them. Her soul twinkled at me. She was old enough to be Mary's mother, probably even her grand-mother.

I motioned to Salome to come, which she did with a big smile. Mary's eyes lit up, and they embraced.

"My daughter, let's travel together," Salome said. It was obvious that they both felt how precisely each one's abilities mirrored the other's needs.

I moved on to help some of the others find their partners. It looked like everyone had chosen a mate by the time Peter and Andrew approached me.

"Andy and I are going to travel together," Peter announced. Andrew's eyes twinkled with mischief. "Even though he is a long-winded—"

Peter wrestled him playfully to make him stop. "That's enough!"

Andrew chuckled and broke free to go dance with the rest of the apostles.

When we were alone together, Peter draped a muscular arm over my shoulder in his big brotherly manner. "Who's going to take care of you while we're gone?"

Nobody had asked me that. I searched his face, noting the furrows of concern in his forehead and the crinkles of kindness at the corners of his eyes.

"What are you going to do without your Beloved Rock and all these others?" he asked me. "You're sending away all the people you depend on the most. Andy and I are going to Judea, and so are some of the rest. Joanna and Susanna are planning to visit some wealthy women they know in Jerusalem. A lot of us could be gone for a month or more. Who's going to look after you?"

"My Father."

"I thought you'd say that," he frowned. "Don't forget you're human too. You have human needs."

I delved deep into his eyes to see how I was being reflected there. I had never intended for my faith to come across as arrogant inhumanity. "Of course, I have needs, lots of them," I acknowledged, chastened.

Peter watched my human self comprehend that the Holy Spirit's purpose in sending out the apostles was not just to foster growth in them and the new people they would meet, but also to push *me* to grow as well. In that unguarded moment, we were both just two people humbled by God's unexpected activity in our lives.

Peter squeezed my shoulders consolingly. "Never mind. Before we leave tomorrow morning, I'll organize some of the disciples who are staying with you and make sure they know how great your needs really are. You're right to send us away now."

"Yes, it's good for all of us, myself included," I said. He followed my gaze to the hilly horizon.

✛ ✛ ✛

That night John asked to join me in my bedtime prayers. We climbed to the starlit hilltop and sat among the wildflowers. Moonbeams brought out the smoky wisps running through John's black curls. His eyes glinted at me like the nearest stars, inviting exploration. I moved close enough to see his wrinkles, the evidence that he had lived and still kept smiling.

"I'd like to pray by singing a new song I'm composing about you," John proposed.

"Go ahead."

"In the beginning was the Word, and the Word was One with God because the Word was God," he chanted. His rich bass voice resonated with the passion and faith that had inspired his lyrics.

It was so sublime that I froze, hardly even breathing, so that I could absorb and savor all that the moment had to offer.

Raw emotion made his voice swell and ebb in a lullaby that rumbled like thunder.

"And the Word became flesh and lived with us, full of love and truth. And from that abundance we have all received, grace after grace."

I stayed still until every last vibration had faded away—a long time because my divine senses were attuned to the most delicate reverberations.

"You've given me so much," he said, then his mood soured. "Maybe too much."

"Too much?"

We easily slipped into our favorite position for talking about our spiritual journeys: We lay next to each other on the earth, with John nestling me under his sinewy arm while I rested my head on his shoulder. The night air was chilly with a hint of rainstorms to come and I snuggled against John's tall body for warmth.

He made his complaint more specific. "Maybe you should find someone else to be your apostle."

My compassion steadied me. "You doubt my judgment?"

"No. Well, yes, I guess I do in regard to me."

"Being an apostle is no big deal."

"I have faith struggles that I've never told you about," he admitted.

I took a moment to carefully consider his whole being and his relationship to me. Of course, there were parts of our lives that we hadn't discussed with each other yet. I had granted him privacy for his thoughts, as I did for everyone unless they invited me into that kind of intimacy. Still, there was no block between his soul and my divine heart. His soul was ablaze with holy light in royal reds and blues, while my divine love fed the flames.

"You can tell me anything, Beloved," I assured him.

My last word caught his attention and drew his dark-sparkling eyes to mine.

"You've known from the start that I like sex with men," he said. "Maybe you already figured this out, but Lazarus and I are more than just friends. We have a sexual relationship. And he's not the only one. I have a sex buddy named Bart who works for the high priest. I met him while you were teaching at the Temple. Actually I do it with guys almost everywhere we go. Samuel was my first and only long-term lover, and ever since the Romans killed him, I've been juggling multiple affairs and one-night stands."

We gazed at each other, each wondering what the other would say next.

Finally I broke the tense silence. "I know about all that. I can't help seeing who has had sex with whom. When people have sex, they leave an imprint on each other's souls in the most conspicuous way. Since you brought it up, there *is* something that I've been wondering about you and Lazarus."

"What?" John asked cautiously.

"Why don't you settle down and marry Lazarus?"

"I can't do that!" John exploded.

"Why not? I mean, the two of you seem compatible."

"Because the Law says that marriage joins a man and a woman—and Lazarus and I are both men!"

"Oh, I keep forgetting who's male and who's female," I apologized.

John seemed to find my attitude exasperating, but also somewhat endearing. "How can you forget something like that?!"

I thought for a moment, then suggested, "Why don't you get married to him anyway?"

"If I could marry a man, then I would marry *you!*" John blurted out.

A thunderbolt of joy shot through my whole being and left a pleasant tingle throughout my genitals.

John immediately started backtracking. "Forget I said that. I don't know how we got on this topic."

"Wait," I interrupted, touching his cheek just long enough to call him back to his previous thought. "I can't forget that you want to spend the rest of your life loving me. I treasure that! My Bride at this point in my life is the Holy Spirit, but after I unite with Her permanently, I'll be Bride or Bridegroom to everyone who loves me, including you. I'm trying to prepare you for it. That's one reason I'm sending you away to teach and heal people—to prepare you for our union."

I wished that John would take me in his arms and kiss me then, but suddenly his sense of vulnerability flamed into anger. "Marriage between me and you is impossible!"

I longed to convince him otherwise. "Just a tiny amount of faith no bigger than a mustard seed will give you the power to move mountains. Faith makes everything possible."

John glared at me.

"We *can* be wed."

"You mean...?" Hope made him turn toward me, poised to take me all in. He scrutinized me with his senses and his soul, then reached out a hand. He stroked the place where my neck met my shoulder, running his fingertips along a vein where he could measure my pounding pulse. The way he looked at me made my spirit soar, even as my body prepared to plunge into total encounter.

I was keenly aware that this was a fine opportunity to experience in my own body the ecstasies that explode when two human beings express their love for each other sexually. John knew that I was attracted to him, but I had hidden the intensity of my sexual desires so as not to overpower him or distract him from God. Now, for one of the only times in my life, I tried to push my divine awareness away and block it out. I didn't want to know what was happening in John's soul or influence him on that level. I just wanted him to kiss me with those full, sensuous lips of his.

All he would have to do was lean a little bit closer and our lips would meet. I made absolutely sure that I wasn't using my divine power to get my way. Of course, he already knew about my divinity. There was no escaping that. I waited in silent suspense and longing, as all humans do.

My mouth was so sensitized that I could feel the heat

of his lips right before they made contact. We kissed soft and slow, a cordial meeting of the tongues. With me no longer holding back, our kisses quickly became wet and hard. I couldn't get enough of his aroma and taste, which were wild like a thunderstorm. We were trusting and thrusting with our tongues in our most passionate embrace ever.

John lay down and pulled me on top of him. Our legs entwined. He ran his hands down my back and over the hump of my rear end. I more than cooperated as he planted one palm on each side of my butt and pressed down firmly, grinding me into him. I didn't care that he could feel, through our woolen robes, that I was as aroused as he was. I wanted to guide him and glide him into me. I wanted to let him enjoy melting into me.

He reached under my tunic and slid his gnarled fingers beneath the back edge of my loincloth. I felt like I did when I was making love with the Holy Spirit, except the physical component subtracted something from the experience, while adding the imperatives of the body. John's new, naked touch inside my loincloth made my body demand full flesh-on-flesh connection. Along with the craving, John's song came into my mind: "The Word became flesh."

When I remembered that phrase, my divine awareness came flooding back. There was really no way to proceed and engage myself sexually while blocking my divinity, anyway. When I was in touch with my divine heart, John's human fragility became all too clear to me. I stopped kissing him and propped myself on my elbows so that I could look down at him while he lay below me on his back. I looked tenderly into his dark eyes, releasing my pent-up love for him there.

"You want me as much as I want you!" he marveled. He exulted in having his suspicions confirmed.

"Yes, but it's more complicated than that. I'm still your Messiah, too. If we tried to form the kind of sacred sexual bond that I'd like to have with you, I would end up overpowering you. You wouldn't be able to say no to me."

"I don't *want* to say no to you!"

"That's why I have to be the one to say no—for now."

Naturally, John was disappointed.

He clung to me and I ached to bring his body to the peak of sexual passion, even if I couldn't go there with him. With my divine awareness I could now see exactly how and where to touch him to enhance his pleasure, including some simple caresses that I hadn't thought to do when we were kissing. I had the ability to stimulate his soul simultaneously and send him shooting into raptures that united his body and spirit in glorious ways that he never dreamed were possible. Everything that I could think to do was sure to delight my body, too. But he would get lost in these erotic soul-pleasures if I bestowed them now, before he was ready. What I loved most in John was his free will, and when I faced the fact that any sexual contact with me in the flesh would compromise his freedom, my desire began ebbing away.

I settled back to my previous position lying at John's side. "Anyway," I whispered to him, "the sacred sexual bonding is meant to occur in the context of a lifetime commitment. I can't make that kind of exclusive commitment to you. As Messiah, I belong to the world."

"Oh, Lord...." His words began as a lover's protest, but as he repeated the phrase, I came to know that he was praying. I let myself become more vulnerable to him as he surrendered his will to God.

His soul looked like a waterfall in which gorgeous gems tumbled, flickering red and blue as they worshipped my divinity. I longed to light it up with my divine love and shine through all its colors so that there was no part of it that was not subsumed and saturated by me. The yearning for union was similar to the desire that I had felt when we were kissing. At that time my divinity got in the way, but now I faced the opposite problem. I realized that I couldn't completely interpenetrate his soul while I was still in the flesh. First I myself had to carry out God's will in obedience to the point of death...and resurrection. Only that could make my wedding with John possible, and I felt new resolve to face whatever my Father's cup held for me, blood and all.

"Oh, Lord," John murmured over and over. His prayer dripped like honey into my divine heart.

I prayed, too—not for anything specific, not even with words. I let each breath align me more wholly with the One who was my Father, my Bride, and my own divine heart. I relaxed into the restorative place that exists beyond the reach of language. John's breath slowed to match mine for a while. We bonded in prayer, pledging our lives to each other. Then John stirred.

He nuzzled my ear, whispering, "Are you ready to go back to the camp?"

"I'm going to spend the night right here."

"Okay. I'll see you tomorrow. I want to go get a good night's sleep because I'm leaving tomorrow to be your apostle."

✛ ✛ ✛

When I walked downhill the next morning, I recognized John's lively flute music. I heard Peter and the women who had sneered at him all singing together: "I will pour my spirit on all people. Your sons and your daughters shall prophesy, your elderly will dream dreams, and your young people will see visions. Even the male and female slaves will be blessed." This scripture from the prophet Joel had become a particular favorite of my disciples, and they sang it often.

I reached a level, grassy place and saw that those who had paired up were beginning to dance with each other. My presence caused everyone join the dance. John put away his flute and joined the line of dancing apostles who were beginning to form a double ring around me. They did a circle dance with me swaying in the center. They were clapping and singing a song they had made up based on some of my teachings. Doves and sparrows chirped along from the trees around us.

"Blessed, blessed, blessed are...?" Then they waited for me to fill in the blank.

"The poor!" I called out. The music and the moment set my toes to tapping.

They sang back, "Blessed are the poor, for they own the kingdom of God."

"Blessed, blessed, blessed are...?"

"The hungry!" I responded.

Again they sang back my complete thought. "Blessed are the hungry, for they will be filled."

"Blessed, blessed, blessed are…?"

I decided to coin a new one for the occasion. "Blessed are you," I sang, letting my voice swell with emotion. My feelings in that moment were complicated, and I let it show in my choice of words and the intricate melody I created for them. "Blessed are you when people hate you, and when they exclude you and insult you because of the Son of Man. Rejoice in that day, for you are being richly rewarded in heaven."

Nobody could remember it on first hearing, so they just sang back, "Blessed are *you*!"

We sang it back and forth for a good, long time. We all sensed that we had reached a certain kind of pinnacle and things would not be the same when the apostles returned. Eagles circled overhead. As my apostles whirled past me, my divine heart sensed the rotation of the earth as it, too, danced in time with us.

I pushed the refrain faster and faster until we were all spun into one dizzying union with God: "Blest are you, blest are you. You, you. Blest, blest! You are blest, you are blest. Blest, blest. You, you!"

coming soon
from androgyne press:

jesus in love
at the cross

Project: Queerlit Contest semi-finalist

an excerpt

an excerpt from the upcoming sequel
to jesus in love by kittredge cherry

jesus in love
at the cross

WORD SPREAD ABOUT WHERE I WAS, and within a
few days a huge crowd had gathered around me in the
unpopulated bluffs high above the Sea of Galilee.
People were eager to hear me teach and get the healings
that just seemed to happen wherever I went. The healings were becoming more frequent and more dramatic,
too. I wandered amid the sea of people on the grassy
hillsides and studied them, trying to sense what they
really needed from me. My way of perceiving was to see
a person's energy aura first, before I noticed their body.
Seeing souls often got me in trouble because I didn't
respond to people based on their gender, age, or other
physical attributes like everyone else did.

I moved to a high place where most people could see
me and prepared to speak. I didn't exactly give speech-
es. I had conversations with enormous numbers of people all at the same time, but to me—and to them—it
felt like we were speaking one-on-one.

"God's power is like yeast. It's small and almost invisible, but it transforms everything," I began.

Some women in the crowd nodded. They knew about baking with yeast.

"But yeast is unclean!" a man objected. "That's why we use unleavened bread for offerings."

"Exactly. You're so sure that you know what's holy that you miss what God is doing. Your certainty blinds you. God's power manifests through the unexpected, the unclean and the unholy. It's not going to look like what you expect. It's like—"

Before I could say anything more, someone with a hungry soul came up and interrupted me. "The last bunch of apostles just got back, and Andrew and Mary need to talk to you," whispered one of my most trusted disciples.

"I'll be with them as soon as I'm done teaching, Judas."

"They need you now," he insisted. He fixed his cat-like, implacable eyes on me.

I looked over and sorted out the souls. Mary's was unmistakable: fluid and deep like a river with many crosscurrents. Her soul had been muddy and infested with demons when I first met her, but now it was almost clear. There was a resonance between her flowing soul and Andrew's airy one. Their on-again, off-again love affair had left their sexual imprints on each other's souls.

I was surprised to see Mary and Andrew together now because they had left in two separate pairs. To double-check, I studied them with my human senses. Mary was standing with her weight on one leg, jutting out a plump hip in a way that was unconsciously voluptuous. Beside her was Andrew, the youngest of my inner circle, a homely but well-proportioned fellow on the cusp of full adulthood. Andrew's usual puppy-dog face now wore a hang-dog expression. Their clothes were torn, indicating that they were in mourning.

Judas persisted. "It really is an emergency. They told me what it's about."

The sorrow in his eyes made me decide to cut my teaching short. "Judas will explain," I announced to the crowd. Then I whispered to him, "Right?"

His mouth dropped open in shock at the sudden new responsibility, but he affirmed, "Right. Should I tell them the one about the mustard seed?"

"Okay, but put it in your own words."

My disciples knew all my stories well—too well, really. They had gotten bored hearing me retell my stories, so I had sent them away to teach them to others, and to develop their own teaching tales.

Judas began speaking while I walked over to Mary and Andrew. They seemed exhausted and solemn, but nothing could dim the intelligence that sparkled in Mary's eyes. Not even the sexual abuse that she had suffered as a child. We had both grown through the process of healing those terrible memories.

"You're here," I smiled and gave a hug to Mary, then Andrew. Our society had strict rules about who was allowed to touch whom, but I didn't care. My divinity made it hard for me to notice who was "untouchable." I liked touching people.

"Well, what's so urgent?" I asked.

Mary spoke first. "Rabbi, have you heard?..."

about the author

PHOTO BY KATE BURROUGHS

KITTREDGE CHERRY is a lesbian Christian author whose ministry put her on the cutting edge of the international debate on sexuality and spirituality. She offers spiritual resources through JesusInLove.org., the first website devoted to the queer Christ.

Cherry was ordained by Metropolitan Community Churches and served as clergy in the lesbian, gay, bisexual, and transgender community for seven years until health issues forced her into a more contemplative life. One of her primary duties was promoting dialogue on homosexuality at the National Council of Churches (USA) and the World Council of Churches.

A native of Iowa, Cherry has degrees in journalism and art history from the University of Iowa, and a master of divinity degree from Pacific School of Religion in Berkeley, California. Her books include *Hide and Speak: A Coming Out Guide*, *Equal Rites: Lesbian and Gay Worship, Ceremonies, and Celebrations*, and *Womansword: What Japanese Words Say About Women*.

The New York Times Book Review praised her "very graceful, erudite" writing style and her poetry has won several awards. She has also written for *Newsweek* and the *Wall Street Journal*. Cherry and her partner, Audrey Lockwood, live in Los Angeles.

Printed in the United States
65223LVS00001B/10-27